WINNING HER HIGHLAND WARRIOR

Time to Love a Highlander Series
Book Three

by Maeve Greyson

ARE YOU SIGNED UP FOR DRAGONBLADE'S BLOG?

You'll get the latest news and information on exclusive giveaways, exclusive excerpts, coming releases, sales, free books, cover reveals and more.

Check out our complete list of authors, too!

No spam, no junk. That's a promise!

Sign Up Here

www.dragonbladepublishing.com

Dearest Reader;

Thank you for your support of a small press. At Dragonblade Publishing, we strive to bring you the highest quality Historical Romance from some of the best authors in the business. Without your support, there is no 'us', so we sincerely hope you adore these stories and find some new favorite authors along the way.

Happy Reading!

CEO, Dragonblade Publishing

Additional Dragonblade books by Author Maeve Greyson

Time to Love a Highlander Series
Loving Her Highland Thief
Taming Her Highland Legend
Winning Her Highland Warrior

Highland Heroes Series
The Guardian
The Warrior
The Judge
The Dreamer
The Bard
The Ghost

CHAPTER ONE

An Lochan Uaine (The Green Loch)
Cairngorms National Park, Scotland
March 2, 2021

B ACK TO SQUARE one. All because of lust.

Satia St. Clair trudged down the path from the main road, oblivious to the peaceful shushing of the wind through the Caledonian pines. *An Lochan Uaine*, more simply known as the Green Loch, lay ahead, but even its gently undulating surface failed to lift her spirits. Her beloved Highlands offered no joy this day. Instead, the ancient land mocked her like everyone else.

She leaned sideways to keep the nylon straps from the bundle of plastic collection tubes from slipping off her shoulder again and skidded across a patch of loose rocks in the process. A frustrated growl escaped her. Even the woodland trail fought her now. She clenched her teeth tighter. Pure stubbornness pulled her through before. It would pull her through again. As she sidled between a pair of leaning trees, she gave Breanna Parker, her best friend—only friend really—a determined thumbs up. "At least with less equipment, it only takes one trip from the car. Right?"

"Not a soul answered our adverts for an intern?" Breanna

struggled to weave through a tangle of low-hanging limbs without dropping any of her load. "None of them? I covered every board in the science wing and posted announcements in all the online student chat rooms." She stumbled on a tree root and cursed under her breath. "Are ye certain ye checked the new email address I set up? Not the old one, mind ye, but the new?"

"I checked them all, Bree." Satia lowered a stack of shoddy cardboard boxes to the ground. Boxes that should've been aluminum cases fitted with shock-absorbing inserts to protect delicate instruments and samples. But no, the university council had confiscated those when they accused her of fraud after Cameron "the Maggot" Stote reported her initial findings as his own during a televised press conference. The conniving worm had even published her paper in his name and uploaded his photograph in place of hers.

She shoved her hands in the pockets of her down jacket and faced the light strip of the pinkish blue sky gradually growing wider across the horizon. Dawn soon. Good thing. The council had also changed the locks on the storage unit containing all her battery-operated light stands. "No intern wants to link their name with mine. The only emails were the ones telling me what a disgusting plagiarist I am—several in languages I didn't recognize. It appears my shame hit worldwide in the scientific community."

"How do ye know they called ye a disgusting plagiarist if ye couldna read the language?" Breanna dumped her load of bulging canvas totes beside the boxes.

Satia blew out another frustrated huff and faced the chilly north wind. She raked back the wildness of her long blonde curls and secured them with a ponytail holder. "The internet knows everything. Including how to translate insults."

"I uninstalled yer old email so ye would stop reading those," Breanna said. "That's twice now. Did ye reinstall it? Again?"

Satia scanned the shadowy waters of the loch, wishing she had drowned Cameron when she had the chance instead of succumbing to his con and sleeping with him. "I have to know what they say so I can fight them and take back my power." She kept her gaze locked on the rippling surface she still found so mesmerizing even after three years of meticulous study. The beguiling turquoise green of the waters came alive as morning sunlight gave it the colorful prisms of a precious, rare jewel.

Breanna hugged an arm around her. "Ye know I love ye, pet, but ye have to let it go. All of it. He only published yer initial findings and conned everyone at the press conference with vague answers. When we expound on yer theory and validate it with solid data that Cameron doesna have, that'll show everything to be yers, just as ye told them." She tightened the hug, then gently jostled her. "Look here now, I brought along a thermos of yer favorite tea. It's colder than old Scratch's heart this morning, and yer wee loch there will be even colder. Did ye wear yer thermals like I told ye?"

Satia eased herself free of Breanna's hold and moved to the water's edge. Her dear friend didn't understand. Not this time. As foster sisters in at least four different placements and also while living on the streets, they had bonded as young children. Helped each other survive. Bree was her only kin and understood her better than anyone. At least, under normal circumstances. But even Bree didn't understand the bitter depths of this betrayal, nor the other driving force behind the research. Satia had to ensure Bree's own health and wellbeing remained solid and cancer-free for years to come.

"Here, pet. Drink yer tea." Breanna nudged her as she held out a steaming cup. "I still say it's a bit early in the year to get in that water. Can we not collect what ye need from shore? Leastwise 'til it gets warmer? I'm not liking the idea of ye perching on that ledge in just yer waders. Not with it still so nippy."

"Diving equipment, suits and all, are locked up in the unit with the lighting, remember?" Satia warmed her hands on the mug as she sipped. Black tea with lots of milk. Bree always took the best care of her. They took care of each other. "Thank ye, love." She offered her friend a reassuring smile. "I'll be fine because ye're here to watch over me." After another sip of the warming brew, she added, "Ye always stick with me. Whether in good times or bad, I know I can always count on ye."

"Always, pet." Breanna squinted at the sky while the breeze whipped her black curls into her face. "Wind's picking up." She turned and fixed a stern glare on Satia. A frustrated urgency in her voice added to the worry in her dark brown eyes. "Please wait 'til another day. I dinna have a good feeling about this." Her sleek brows quirked higher. "Ye know how I am. I've got one of my feelings. Please listen this time, a'right?"

Satia refused to comment. They had debated Bree's belief in an eerie sixth sense over many a bottle of wine and concluded they would never see eye to eye on this topic. They had finally agreed to disagree.

"I know ye dinna believe in it, but I'm telling ye—I am always right about these things. Well, mostly." Breanna refilled Satia's cup. "And I feel downright iffy about today." With a coaxing grin, she leaned in and bumped her shoulder against Satia's. "Come on, now. See sense. How 'bout the library? I'm sure there's more to be found downstairs amongst yer favorite chronicles. It's a mite dusty, but at least it's dry and warm. Ye can collect samples in a month or two."

No use arguing. Satia had learned long ago the only way to get around Bree was to keep moving forward. She balanced her tea on top of a rock, popped open the flaps of a box, and pulled out her waders. "Be a love, will ye? Get one of the longer sample tubes ready with the longest cording we've got. I'll not get new data if I dinna hit deeper water."

"I hate it when ye ignore me. Ye know that." But rather than pout and refuse to help, Bree did as asked, just like always.

Satia stepped into the waders and cinched the suspenders as short as they would go. The oversized waterproof overalls were about three times too big and gave off the pungent aroma of dead fish and oily rubber, but she'd gotten them free from a kindly fisherman she'd befriended at the corner pub. After losing her funding, free was essential.

"We could fit in these together, Bree." She practiced shuffling around in the large rubber boots. Even wearing three pairs of her thickest wool socks, the things still swallowed her.

"Ye're going to fall face first, fill them with water, and drown." Breanna held up a neatly wound nylon strap with heavy-duty carabiners attached to each end. "Hook this around ye, so I can haul ye to shore when ye go under."

"I will not fall." Satia waved her away. Bree worried too much. The small loch was not treacherous. A favorite swimming hole with holiday travelers in the summer, it was cold from snowmelt but still docile enough in most spots. The depth of the water on the ledge only reached a little above her waist, and the blue-green depths beyond would only get a taste of her collection tubes, not her.

"Please, Satia." Bree looked ready to cry.

"Fine." She took the strapping, wove it through the suspenders, and secured it with the clip. "There. Are ye happy now?"

"I'll not be happy 'til ye're out of that water and back in the car." Bree unwound the black strapping and anchored it to a tree. "My gut isna happy with this. I'm telling ye, something bad is going to happen."

"Yer gut isna happy because ye ate that chili from a week ago that I shouldha thrown out." Satia picked up the pole and tested the plunger in the tubing. When Bree didn't offer a comeback, she turned to see why. Even in the soft light of dawn, she spotted tears shining on her sweet friend's face. "Bree?"

With an embarrassed sniff, Breanna swiped at the wetness. "This is wrong, Satia Nicole. Dangerously wrong. I feel it."

Bree only called her Satia Nicole when sorely distressed. If angry, she would have used Satia Nicole Josephine St. Clair. Satia clomped across the rocky shoreline until they stood toe to toe. She took hold of Breanna's shoulders and squeezed. "I have to do this. I canna rest until I've convinced everyone that I'm not a fraud, a thief, or a joke." She resettled her grip and gave Bree a soft shake as she leaned in closer. "And think of all the people this can help if I get the data I need. That elusive strand I need to confirm can bolster so many treatments. Might even turn them into cures." She squeezed Bree's shoulders tighter. "Yer cancer? It scared the hell out of me, Bree. What if ye hadna caught it early enough? This discovery might even strengthen treatments for when it's already spread to lymph nodes." Tears almost sprang free as she vocalized the fear neither of them ever spoke aloud. "What if yer cancer comes back? I want to help ye." She shook her head. "I canna bear losing ye, sweet sister."

Bree refused to look her in the eyes. "I'm not worried about all those people. Or me. I am worried about ye." She fidgeted with the nylon strapping between her fingers. "I canna lose ye either, Satia. Please wait 'til another day."

Satia released her. "Ye willna lose me. If it'll make ye feel any better, feed out the line as I walk."

Too many emotions spoiled a day of research. Emotions spoiled everything, in fact. She loved Bree dearly, but this had to stop in order for her to accomplish what needed to be done. Once she got the samples collected, Bree would see her worried gut was just a reaction to eight-day-old chili.

As she waded out into the water, she held a hand high and forced a lighter tone. "And dinna be yanking me onto me arse just to prove me wrong. Understand?"

"If it was later in the year, I would." Bree flipped a potential tangle out of the line. "But I dinna want to be the one stuck looking after ye when ye get a wicked head cold from hypothermia."

"Ye lie." Satia edged farther out onto the ledge. "Ye love taking care of me. Just like I love taking care of ye." She pulled off her gloves and held them between her teeth as she slipped her wrist through the loop in the specimen tube line and snugged it tight.

She should've done it onshore, but Breanna's uneasiness had

distracted her. That gave her pause, making her worry about what else she might have overlooked while trying to appease her friend. With a roll of her shoulders to shake off the eerie feeling, she slid her feet closer to the edge of the drop off then waited for the cloud of silt to settle. At least now, if the weighty collection tube slipped out of her hands, she could easily reel it back.

When the frigid water lapped higher than her waist, she gulped in a deep breath. By jings, Bree had called one thing right. The Green Loch in early March was colder than Satan's heart. The iciness of the water surged through every layer of rubberized waders, jeans, and thermals. She might as well be naked. If she had nicked her wetsuit and worn it, she could've peed in it to keep warm for a little while. As it was, she nearly peed from the cold.

She braced against another muscle-cramping shiver. No sense dwelling on it. After yanking on her gloves, she pulled another weight from her pocket and screwed it onto the end of the tubing. Bree never added enough weights.

Satia swung it out beyond the ledge and watched the white plastic cap disappear into the darkness. As the tube sank, she fed out both lines, one for the plunger and one for the casing, reassured by the colors that Bree had used the longest recovery rope they owned. The fluorescent yellow, a little over a hundred meters, would get her to depths she hadn't sampled before.

As she came to the end of the line, she gave it a gentle tug and bobbed it. Even with all the rope let out, the tube still floated free, not even brushing against the bottom. That realization made her frown. How could *An Lochan Uaine*, one of the tinier Highland lochs, have such a massive drop-off? She'd never encountered that in the past three years.

A firm jerk on the strap attached to her waders made her turn. Bree's terrified expression startled her.

"What's wrong?"

"Are ye all right, Satia?"

God bless poor Bree and her silly premonitions. Satia indulged her with a smile and a wave. "I am finer than fine. Stop worrying."

Then the ledge crumbled out from under her and pitched her forward. The weighted pole tied to her wrist tugged to the right as the icy water swallowed her. Her waders filled and dragged her downward with the sample tube line running alongside her. The more she struggled to kick back to the surface, the more water the overalls gulped in, and the faster she sank.

Pull me up, Bree, pull! She flailed to the side, spiraling downward as she groped for the nylon rescue strap. If Bree pulled, she could help by pulling herself upward—if she could find it. The darkness and numbing cold slowed everything. Her lungs burned for air. The feeling left her fingers bit by bit; she couldn't find the rescue strap. She had to shed the waders and get that rope off her wrist while she still had some sense of touch left. It was her only hope of getting to the surface.

Something bumped against her leg. Or maybe not. Unbearable cold. Inky blackness. Lack of oxygen. God help her. She should've listened to Breanna this time. She managed to scoot off her gloves by rubbing her wrists together and freed herself from the tubing rope. Erratic flashes of light exploded against the blackness of her closed eyelids. She forced them open, but the murky depths revealed nothing. Saints help her; she needed air. Fingers almost useless, she fumbled with the shoulder strap clasps of the waders one last time. She couldn't die like this. She would not die before finding a cure for Bree and everyone who needed it.

The clasps released, and the waders fell away, sliding off her body. She tried to kick and push upward. Tried so hard. No use. Too late. Not enough air and so very cold. She gave in and relaxed, wishing she had told Breanna two things. One, that she loved and appreciated her, and two, if she ever drowned, just leave her body buried in the loch. The icy darkness held a peacefulness she had never known on dry land.

CONSCIOUSNESS HIT SATIA with a vengeance. She convulsed violently and spewed what felt like gallons of water. Breanna hit her between the shoulder blades over and over. Rocks dug into her as she clutched at the ground, coughing, and choking more water out.

Breanna kept hitting her. Harder with each thump.

"Enough!" she wheezed after another vomiting spasm. "I know ye're mad, but ye can beat me later."

"I would never beat ye," said a voice that rumbled deep as thunder. "Forgive me, m'lady—but I feared ye slipping away. I had to convince yer spirit to fight."

Satia rolled and tried to push herself up but collapsed face-first on the muddy rocks. "Who are ye?" She tried to rise again but face-planted a second time. "Damn this bloody weakness! Breanna! Help me!"

Strong hands took a firm hold of her upper arms, lifted her, and settled her on an impressive lap. The owner of the lap held her in place with an equally impressive arm sporting a bicep the size of a massive log. Dark eyes, devilish and striking, peered deep into hers. "Kane Macpherson at yer service, m'lady."

"Kane Macpherson," she repeated, trying to buy herself some time to gather her wits. The man's hair was black as his eyes, even blacker since water dripped from the long strands framing his handsome features. Features that would make a sculptor drool. A dusting of day-old beard shadowed his squared jaw and added a dangerous sexiness to the cleft in his chin.

She leaned away and gave him a quick up and down glance. Holy hell. The translucent clinginess of his wet shirt enhanced every ripple, every hard ridge of his chest. She had never seen such. Well, at least, not in person. Maybe in the movies, and that was a big maybe. This dark god outdid them all. Perhaps she had drowned, and he was here to escort her to Heaven or Hell.

Considering her past, Hell was the more likely destination.

"Who are ye?" she asked again. "And where is Breanna?"

"Kane Macpherson," he said, repeating his name louder and enunciating every syllable. "And I dinna ken who Breanna is, m'lady. The only others here are my men."

Still struggling to stabilize her frustrating shakiness, Satia pressed the heels of her hands against her temples. She had to be dead. No way would Breanna leave her alone at the loch unless she had drowned. But everything felt so real. Heat emanated from this strange man. Even with him as soaked as she was, blessed warmth radiated from him. She lifted her gaze to his and braced herself for the answer she feared. "Am I dead?"

His eyes flared wider. "Nay, m'lady. Thankfully, not." He tipped his head toward the loch. "I feared so when ye shot up from the depths then went still when ye fell back to the water. But when I reached ye, ye warmed to my touch and stirred."

Shot up from the depths? She had struggled to reach the surface. By no means had she *shot*. Movement to the left made her turn. Four men stepped closer. None as big as her rescuer, but all larger than most men she knew. Of course, in her wee corner of the world, most men exercised their minds and not their bodies.

Their unusual dress made her wonder if the lack of oxygen had damaged her brain cells. They had to be a hallucination. She eyed them as they approached. Each of them wore tight, legging-like pants tucked into tall boots. Their shirts were more like tunics from a renaissance fair or something. Full billowy sleeves. Open ties at the throat. The length hit them at about mid-thigh. Two of the men wore long vests over the tunics. One sported a tattered coat. It was long, too, reaching to just above his knees. Leather belts and straps crisscrossed their bodies, loaded with weapons. Antique weapons. Two-handed swords, axes, daggers, and maces. Some of the men had visible scars. Nothing severe, but proof of past battles just the same.

Actors? She didn't remember hearing about another movie being made in the area. Of course, she kept her head buried in her research, but still.

And she had yet to see Breanna.

Satia pushed to her feet, even though she hated leaving the dark god's warmth behind. Bloody hell. The wind cut through her, honed to an even icier bite by her wet clothing. She needed to get to the car and crank up the heat.

"Thank ye for pulling me out," she said, her teeth chattering. "I'll just be going to my car now." That's where Breanna had to be. Up at the car. Probably radioing for help since cell service was patchy here.

"Car?" Kane rose and stretched out a hand to steady her. The man was a solid head and a half taller than her five foot seven. Concern, leeriness, and something Satia couldn't quite put a finger on settled across his striking features. "What is a *car*, m'lady? A cart, perhaps?" He eased closer as if fearing she might do herself harm. "Are ye a victim of thieves? Did someone accost ye and throw ye into the loch?"

"Uhm…no." Satia stalled, still wrestling with the aftereffects of her watery ordeal and a touch of hypothermia. Was this a joke to him? Was he trying to confuse her even more? Balance returned but still sketchy; she swayed in a shuffling half-circle, scanning the area. Everything she saw only befuddled her worse.

More pines than usual. A lot more. No path coming down from the road. And where were the stone steps? The platform with the carved bench? The six old cairns? She veered off balance and stumbled sideways. "Bloody hell!" The rocky beach showed no mercy on her poor feet, protected by nothing but her wet socks.

The dark Highlander surged forward and swept her up into his arms before she hit the ground. He shot a fierce look at the nearest man. "Get a fire going and fetch my flask. She needs warming."

Satia curled inward, rubbing her temples as she leaned into the warmth of his damp chest. Something was very not right here. She had to be dead. They all were, and these guys just didn't know it.

"Dinna fash yerself, m'lady. All will be well." He spoke to her as if she were a frightened child. "Toff will have us a roaring fire in no time, and Rob's fetching whisky to chase the chill away."

"Where are we?" Weariness pushed her against him. Coaxed her to soak in more of his heat. If she was already dead, he couldn't hurt her—right? No harm in getting warmth and comfort where she could.

"*An Lochan Uaine.*" He peered down at her, and his voice fell as if speaking more to himself than her. "Yer eyes mirror those enchanted waters. Nay…they're even more brilliant."

She ignored the compliment. If that's what it was. He had to be wrong about where they were. This couldn't be *her* loch. It was similar—but different. Sort of. More untouched by humanity, which wasn't necessarily a bad thing, but this still wasn't her loch. She stole another look, its circumference so small, she easily ran her gaze around the entire shoreline.

An American student, one of her interns, had insulted the Green Loch by saying it was nothing more than an oversized pond. She had fired that one and sent her packing. Aye, her precious loch might be small, but it was as alluring and mysterious as the myths and legends it spawned over the centuries.

One of the men, the one Macpherson had called Toff, knelt where the stone steps should have been and arranged sticks and dried tinder. He took out an ancient-looking flint, struck it once, then bent and blew where the spark landed.

Two of the others reappeared, leading five enormous horses to a rope they had strung between two pines. The shortest of the four, presumably Rob, headed toward them, holding up a dark brown leather flask in each hand.

With a bob of his head, he gave her a lop-sided smile. "Brought mine for ye, too, m'lady." He pulled out the stopper with his teeth and offered it. "Them faery waters be wicked cold this time of year." With a half-bow, he added, "I be Rob McBride. Anything ye need, ye just ask, and I'll fetch it."

"Thank ye." She accepted the flask and held it under her nose. Dead, lost, or whatever this was, she would not make the mistake of blind trust no matter how helpful and kind these men appeared to be. Familiar fumes tickled her nostrils, promising a drink that would burn all the way down. She took a healthy swig, closed her eyes, and savored the liquid fire settling in a warm pool in her middle. "Much better," she said, then took another sip before handing it back. "Thank ye, Mr. McBride. I appreciate it."

"Just plain ole *Rob*, m'lady." Blue eyes twinkling, he bobbed another polite bow that set his light brown braid swinging.

Satia became increasingly aware that the muscular leader of the group still cradled her like a babe. "Ye can put me down now, Mr. Macpherson. I'm sure my balance has returned by now."

"Kane, m'lady." He eased her to her feet as if she were made of porcelain. With a teasing tilt of his head, he arched a sleek brow. "Might we know yer name?"

"Oh...uhm." She had never excelled at social graces. She often forgot *please* and *thank you.* Any manners beyond that were a rare bonus. "I'm Satia. Satia St. Clair."

Kane's eyes went wide again, and he shifted a step back. "Satia, ye say?"

"Aye." What was wrong with her name? Then it came to her. Dead, lost, or wherever this was, this bunch knew about Cameron's bogus claims and thought her a fraud, too. She stood taller. "Cameron Stote is a lying maggot." She thumped a fist against her chest. "That research was mine. He stole it."

"Mayhap she hit her head and doesna ken who she is?" said the red-haired hulk of the bunch in a hushed voice.

She hit her chest again. "I am Satia St. Clair, and I know exactly who I am."

"Beg pardon, m'lady." The brute fell to one knee and bowed his head. "I meant no insult." He glanced up for a half-second, then dropped his gaze again. "Jac Innes. Proud to serve ye, mighty queen."

"Mighty queen?" When no one answered, she turned back to

Kane since he appeared to be in charge. She edged a step closer. "Queen?" she repeated.

"He thinks ye Nicnevin, Queen of the Fae." He glanced aside as if unable to look her in the eyes. "To be fair, we all have thoughts on that matter." He twitched a sheepish shrug. "'Twas the way ye appeared out of nowhere. Like the depths of the loch spit ye right out."

The yellow-haired brute poking the fire tossed a glance her way. "Toff Sweeney, m'lady, and no, I dinna think ye queen of the Fae. If ye were, why would yer own loch toss ye up like a poorly digested meal?" He wagged his head back and forth, making a face as he stood. "'Course, ye did show up out of nowhere."

"And yer opinion?" she asked, turning back to Kane.

He grinned and lifted his chin in the barest show of defiance. "I think ye are of royal blood. A rare beauty in need of our help." With a gallant nod, he placed his hand over his heart. "And I am happy to be of service." He held out his hand. "Come, m'lady. To the fire. Ye're teeth are still clacking from the icy water."

She didn't take his hand, even though she wanted to. Better not. With her strength returning, time to maintain a safe distance from this fine specimen of masculinity. As Breanna would say, the man had a *pull* to him. Something that drew her closer. Like he was a natural lodestone and she, the iron.

Once she reached the fire, she knelt beside it and leaned as close as she could without getting singed. The flames crackled and popped, welcoming her deeper into this madness of faery queens, magical lochs, and men who looked out of place. And Breanna. Where was she?

The fourth man, bald as could be and looking older than the others, waved a small black pot as he walked to the water's edge. "I'll be making ye a fine broth, m'lady. That'll cure what ails ye and help ye remember what's right or not."

Kane settled down beside her. "Albie Foster's the best cook there is. Ye'll feel better once ye've eaten."

"I dinna feel bad." She scrubbed her arms, then held her hands closer to the flames. "I'm just cold."

"And confused," he added quietly.

"Ye have no idea," she admitted, finding it mildly disturbing that he read her with such precision.

Chapter Two

EVEN THOUGH COMMON sense told him to see the myths and legends for nothing more than the entertaining tales they were, Kane couldn't fully set aside the notion that this woman was none other than Queen Nicnevin, powerful ruler of the Fae. She had to be. Never had he encountered such an unusual lass.

Lit from within by a fire he couldn't describe, her eyes were a more brilliant green than the very waters that spat her out. Her hair was as white and glistening as gossamer threads of dewy web dancing in sunlight. Tall and lithe, the strange clothes she wore hugged her every curve. Not the voluptuous offerings of a full-bodied woman. Nay, this lass appeared delicate yet muscular. Temptation incarnate. Sleek as a siren of the sea. Any man would gladly follow her to the unknown depths of any waters. She had even given her name as *Satia*. All of them knew that to be yet another form of Nicnevin. He saw his own wonderings in his men's faces and knew they believed it, too.

Huddled in his plaid, she sat cross-legged in front of the fire, cupping an offering of Albie's best broth between her hands. "Stop staring at me," she said without looking up from the dented bowl.

"Forgive me, m'lady." But he didn't look away. He couldn't.

As he watched her eat and stare at the fire, he replayed the memory of how she had shot up out of the water, a graceful creature of the loch with her back arched as she reached for the sun. The sight had stolen his ability to breathe. But when she crashed back down, he had seen her distress for what it was and charged in to save her. He had met many a lass in his day, but never had he experienced an introduction such as this. It meant something. His dearly departed mother always believed everything happened for a reason.

She sat aside the empty bowl and turned a narrow-eyed scowl on him. "Where are we?"

He wouldn't draw out the name of the place again. That would only incense her more. "I have told ye, m'lady. Several times now, and my answer is still the same. I dinna ken what else ye wish me to say."

She huddled deeper into the woolen blanket and rubbed her forehead as if her head ached.

"Albie, some willow bark brew for her ladyship," he ordered without taking his gaze from her.

"Stop with the m'lady and her ladyship stuff. It's not funny anymore." She combed her fingers through her long hair, wincing as she came across tangles and picked out sticks and debris. "This canna be *An Lochan Uaine* because all my equipment is gone. And Breanna. She's gone, too." With a flip of a hand toward the woods behind them, she jerked another irritated glance in that direction. "And all the things that have been here for years and years are gone." Her mounting frustration creased her brow as she twisted and stared up through the trees. "And I have seen no tourists. Or heard any cars." She pointed up the hill. "The road should be that way. I know fog's coming in, but there should still be someone out and about." Her voice quaked with the disbelief and fear overtaking her.

"I dinna ken what a car is, m'l... lass." He scrubbed a hand across his mouth, struggling to cede to her wishes and forgo the title she deserved. "And there is no road anywhere near here."

"There be roads in Inverness," Rob said, perking up on the other side of the fire like a pup trying to please its master.

"I feel sure she knows Inverness has roads." Kane willed the man to quiet himself. The lady's condition needed careful handling—not incessant babble.

Toff stood, latched hold of Rob's collar, and pulled him up. "Come. We should check around again to ensure we have no company."

Albie rose and scooped up her empty bowl. "I shall fetch water for the willow bark." He cleared his throat with a loud *harrumph* and glared at Jac. "And ye will come, too, aye?"

Jac startled out of his daze as though someone poked him. "Aye. I need to see to the horses."

"How did ye manage that?" She eyed Kane as though he'd made the men disappear with a snap of his fingers.

"Manage what?"

"Make them leave." She leaned to one side, stretched out her left leg, and rubbed her shin.

"We have been together a long time," he said. "Over the years, we've come to understand one another." He nodded toward her leg. "Are ye injured?"

She yanked up the leg of her trews and rolled down her stocking, baring herself from knee to ankle. "I must've hit some rocks when the ledge gave way."

Kane swallowed hard, unable to take his gaze from the pale, smooth skin of her naked leg. "Are…are ye all right?" He resettled himself, plucking at his clothing to lessen the tightness of the seam cutting across his stiffening cock.

"Just a bit sore. Nothing unbearable." She covered her leg and blew out a heavy sigh. "One minute I'm drowning, the next, I've dropped down a rabbit hole."

"Ye speak strangely, lass."

"Aye, well…even though I was born north of Gretna Green, as a child, I ping-ponged back and forth across Hadrian's Wall too many times to count." Her expression hardened as though the memories of her childhood still tasked her. "I guess ye could say I'm a hodgepodge of Scot and Brit." With a faint smile, she barely twitched a shoulder. "Always considered myself a Scot, though." The smile disappeared completely. "The fosters in Scotland always tolerated me better than the Brits."

That confused him even more. He recognized some of what she said, but not all. "Ye said ye were drowning, then ye fell down a rabbit hole? In the water?"

Her intense gaze sidled away from the fire and settled on him. "Ye really do not know what I'm talking about, do ye?"

As much as it pained him to admit it, he relented and shook his head. "Nay, lass. Forgive me."

Her focus shifted to the misty waters of the loch. Thoughtfulness, confusion, and irritation battled for control over her fine-boned features. Irritation appeared to win out. "I am a research scientist, specializing in microorganisms. I've also recently become quite active in cancer studies." She tore her attention away from the loch and looked at him. "I guess that pretty much sums me up."

He blinked. The lass might as well have not spoken. Her words told him nothing. "Micro…" He didn't attempt to finish.

"Environmental biology? Microbiologist?" she said. "Cancer studies?"

"Aye." He feigned an expression of understanding. 'Twas all he could think to do to keep her talking.

It didn't fool her. With a perturbed huff, she shook her head. "Anyway, I was on a ledge in the middle of the loch." She paused and shot him a stern glare. "*My* loch—*An Lochan Uaine*—and the ledge I stood on gave way." A shiver stole across her. "Sank like a rock when my waders filled. Then the next thing I know, I'm on some strange shore, chundering out gallons of water, and everything I left at the loch, including my best friend, is gone." She flipped a hand in his direction, then drew up her knees and propped her arms atop them. "And then there's yerself and yer lot, dressed like ye're ready to film some sort of battle scene from ancient Scotland and insisting on acting the part even when ye're not shooting."

"Ye think me ancient?" He might be a year or two past a score and ten, but he was not ancient.

"Not yerself. Yer clothes. Weapons." She made an impatient twitch of an arm. "Even the gear on yer horses looks like it comes from the 1500s or something." She recovered the blanket that had slipped down and snugged it back around her shoulders. "I always liked history but enjoyed science more, so I'm afraid I might not get the dates right every time." She graced him with a sardonic grin. "My apologies to yer costumer if the 1500s isna the century for yer project. But ye have to admit, I got the ancient part right."

A gut-clenching eeriness stung him, prickling the hairs on his arms and his nape. "1500 isna ancient, lass. It is the future. One hundred and eighty-six years in the future, to be exact."

She turned and scowled at him, then tilted her head as if to improve her hearing. "What?"

"This is the year 1314. Second of March, in fact."

"1314," she repeated, the color draining from her cheeks. She sat straighter. "Ye lie."

"I do not." He ignored the insult and edged closer in case he needed to catch her before she collapsed headlong into the fire. She didn't seem well at all. "What date did ye think it, lass?"

"March 2, 2021." She pushed herself to her feet and scrambled backward. Her knuckles whitened as she clutched the blanket tighter. She jabbed a corner of it at him, accusing, pointing. "Why would ye talk such rubbish after being so kind? What's yer game? Do ye think me some daft eedjit?"

"Calm yerself, lass."

"Calm myself? Ye really think telling me to calm myself will flip a switch that'll make me shite rainbows, even though none of this makes sense?"

Although colorful and mildly insulting, the lass made a fair point. "At least come back to the fire. Surely, ye're just a mite confused." He hoped so because he agreed—none of what she made sense. Or rather, what she said was impossible.

Chest heaving as if starved for air, she didn't move. Just stared at him long and hard. Without warning, she threw off the blanket and ran, bolting into the trees, fast and nimble as a deer startled by hunters.

Kane charged after her. She wouldn't get far. Not in sock feet and still shaken from whatever she had endured. But he had to reach her before she did herself harm.

At the top of the rise, she halted, frantically turning in every direction as though hopelessly lost. As he came up behind her, she whirled to face him and stabbed an accusing finger at him. "Where is the road?"

"There is no road, lass." He eased within reach of her.

"There has to be a road." Eyes wide, she gulped in every breath. Her voice crackled with panic. "There has to be."

As gentle as mist on the down of a thistle, he pulled her close, gathering her to his chest. "There is no road," he whispered. "Never has been."

She tucked her arms in tight, curling into herself. "There will be. Someday," she said, sounding pitiful and lost.

He had no words to comfort her, nor did he fully comprehend everything that bedeviled her. So, he stood there and held her. And they would remain so until she wished it otherwise. All four of his men stepped into view, then melted back when he gave the slightest shake of his head. Nay. Watching over this woman was his task alone, and he was proud to claim it. He would protect her as long she allowed.

Tremors overtook her, prodding him to take action. He swept her up, cradled her snug against him, and strode down the hillside. A thick pallet of blankets waiting beside the fire made him smile. Some might consider his lads hard-hearted warriors, but that couldn't be further from the truth. They would help him tend her.

He eased her down onto the pallet and covered her with the plaid she had thrown aside. "I will keep ye safe," he promised, more as an oath to any powers that might be listening than to her. "I swear it."

Satia curled onto her side, tensing into a trembling ball, her unblinking stare locked on the crackling flames.

Albie softly cleared his throat, held up a steaming cup, then tipped his bald head toward her. "Willow bark," he mouthed.

Kane took it, slid an arm under her shoulders, and eased her up for a sip. "'Tis willow bark, lass. It will help ye."

"Salicin," she mumbled.

"Aye, lass. Drink it now." Once again, he did not know what she meant, but questions now would only vex her. Thankfully, his uncanny ability at reading people worked with her, as well. He prayed the blessing held strong. With this lady, he would need it.

She drank, then patted the bowl away with shaking fingers. "Thank ye, Kane."

For the first time since he'd found her, she freely allowed her vulnerability to show. It filled her voice, went straight to his heart, and latched on tight and strong. He eased her back down on the pallet and tucked the plaid up around her shoulders. "Rest, lass. Ye're safe here."

She still didn't close her eyes, just stared at the flames. "I never studied quantum physics," she said in a bemused tone.

He didn't comment. She spoke to herself. Not him. He settled down beside her. The other men, silent as specters, gathered around the fire and quietly passed the leather flasks back and forth. All except Albie. He drank nothing stronger than that vile herbal concoction he brewed each morning when the bloody English weren't near enough to keep them from building a fire that might reveal their location.

Rob handed a flask to Kane. "Want I should find some meat for supper, or will it be oatcakes come dark?"

"Meat it shall be. We'll not be dousing the fire at nightfall." Kane downed a fiery gulp, then handed it back to Rob. He looked to Toff. "Any signs?" Of them all, the battle-scarred warrior was the canniest at sensing danger anywhere nearby.

"None so far." The man cast a narrow-eyed glance around the area and shook his head. "Unless some followed from Inverness, we're too far from any other villages or towns. As well as too far from the borders. Neither the English nor those who dinna support the Bruce have much use for this place." He grinned. "Our king would be safer here than in Dumfries or Galloway."

"Aye, well...I think the Bruce is more concerned about his country than his safety." Kane tossed another stick on the fire. "He sent us this far north because of the troubles at Inverness—not to find safe haven for him in the Highlands. We will continue south to aid him in taking back the castles between here and the border."

"Edinburgh this month. Stirling in June." Satia spoke as though in a dream. "But I hate he damages them so much. He destroys some excellent craftsmanship."

All the men perked to attention and exchanged wide-eyed glances. Kane held up a hand and gave them all a meaningful tilt of his head. He rested a gentle touch on Satia's shoulder. "What say ye, lass?"

She puckered her mouth, then frowned. "Could be I shouldn't have said that. It might change something." She pushed up on an elbow as if resting on a royal couch instead of blankets beside a loch. "Like that riddle, ye know? The one where if ye go back in time and accidentally kill yer grandfather before he meets yer grandmother, then how can ye exist to go back in time and kill him?"

Perhaps he needed a cup of that willow bark tea himself. Or more whisky. Aye, definitely more whisky. Every time the beguiling lady spoke, she knotted his mind until it ached. "What do ye know about Edinburgh and Stirling?" He eyed his men. "Just among us, ye understand. Surely no harm could come from sharing a tale beside the fire?"

She pulled in a deep breath and blew it out, studying the flames as she took a stick and stirred the coals. "I did a DNA test once. Robert the Bruce is supposedly one of my ancestors." As the stick caught fire, she lifted it closer to her face, staring at the burning tip as though entranced. "That's the only reason I remember his history. I studied him for a while."

"Aye," Kane said to keep her going. Anxiousness rippled like lightning through him, and he knew the same held true of his men. Each of them had fought at the Bruce's side since the beginning. Any visions she could give would be a wondrous boon.

Still staring at the flaming brand, she waved it back and forth as if writing words only she could see. "Some three hundred men will find a secret route on the slopes of Castle Rock and surprise the guards at Edinburgh and seize it. Then the Bruce orders the defenses destroyed to prevent reoccupation by other enemies. He does that with most, if not all, the castles he reclaims." She tossed the bit of wood into the fire and tipped her head from side to side as if continuing the conversation with the embers. "He had many enemies in his own land but didn't let that stop him." A thoughtfulness came across her, tugging the hint of a smile to her lovely mouth. "We have that in common, he and I. Maybe that DNA test was legit, after all. Perhaps he really is my ancestor."

"And Stirling?" Toff asked. "What of Stirling?"

A jealous protectiveness engulfed Kane, making him hover closer to her. But he had to admit, the same question burned in his mind. As long as she didn't have issue with the others asking her these things, he would allow it.

She squinted one eye shut as if struggling to remember. "I canna remember the exact date, but I think it's the latter part of June. Twenty-third, perhaps?" She sat up, hugged her knees, and rocked back and forth with her chin propped on her arms. "The battle of..." With a snap of her fingers, she nodded. "Bannockburn! That's it. And it's June 23 and 24." Proudly, she sat taller. "The Bruce defeats Edward II of England at the Battle of Bannockburn, effectively re-establishing Scotland's independence, and also regains Stirling Castle."

"And then what, m'lady?" Jac asked in a breathless whisper. Caught up in the prophecies, he leaned forward to see around Albie. His shoulder-length hair swung too close to the flames, sizzling and popping as the ends caught fire.

"Mind yerself, Jac!" Rob yanked the man back and slapped at the sparks. "Ye'll burn yerself bald as Albie."

"Shew." Satia wrinkled her nose and fanned the air. "Nothing like the smell of burnt hair."

Jac ducked his head, then gave her a shy smile. "Sorry, m'lady. Got too excited, I reckon. But what happens next?"

Satia frowned, then shook her head. "I'm not sure. Afraid I only remember the high points. There's still some fighting for a few years, I think. A declaration that I don't remember the name of. Truce for a little while. He fathers a son. Then a treaty." With an almost imperceptible shrug, she added, "Then he dies."

"Dies?" Kane repeated as the other men gasped.

She looked at them as if she thought them all addled. "Well, of course, he dies. Everybody dies."

"In battle?" Rob asked.

A sudden leeriness came across her, breaking their fragile, companionable trust. "I dinna think so." She tightened her hold on her knees and curled inward, shutting them out. "I also think I've said enough. Too much, in fact." Blanket held tight, she jumped to her feet and hurried to the water's edge.

As Kane rose to follow, he motioned for the men to stay put. He joined her but didn't draw too close. While her chest might not be heaving with gulping breaths as before, her panic had returned. She flicked rapid-fire glances at different points across the loch, searching for the elusive answer to the same question they possessed. Where had she come from and why?

"Satia?"

"I have to get uhm…I have to find a way back," she said. Her eyes narrowed as she stared at the water. "I dinna belong here." With a bitter huff, she offered a smile that didn't reach her eyes. "I've survived in a lot of places, but I think I've met my match with this one."

"Get back?"

"To my time. 2021."

What she hinted at could not possibly be true. But what about all the things she had said? Perhaps she possessed the gift of sight, and it affected her thinking. Or maybe she had suffered some sort of attack, and her strange tales helped her keep the painful memory at bay. He'd heard tell of folks doing such before. Making up stories to survive. His own mother had done it.

Gut instinct nudged him. What about those odd clothes? Still wet as could be, since he'd not felt her calm enough to accept any alternatives. How to explain them? Their strange shiny fastenings reflected the sunlight as if taunting and arguing her defense. He refused to waver. She could've fashioned those things. Somehow. He had sworn to protect her, even if it meant protecting her from herself.

But most of all, even though he'd known her for naught but a few hours, the thought of never seeing her again bothered him. She was so—different. The wonder and enticement of her tempted him like the urge to soak in the warmth of a fire on a cold winter's day. He wanted her to stay.

"Ye canna go back in that water. Ye were half dead when I carried you to the dry land the first time. Is drowning yer wish?"

Waves quietly lapped against the shore as if echoing his question.

She shuddered and flexed her sock feet in the mud. "What I wish is that I had worn my shoes inside those waders. Big as they were, I could have and still had plenty of room."

"Jac's handy with working leather." Relief that she seemed more inclined to go along with common sense filled him. "I'm sure he can sew ye a wee pair of slippers in no time. Maybe even by morning."

"Good to know." She adjusted her stance. Her chin ticked up to a defiant angle, warning him she was about to run again. This time, straight into the water.

He grabbed hold of her arm. "I said, *no*. Ye're nay going back in there, ye ken?"

"Just because ye've been nice so far, dinna think ye can tell me what to do." She twisted, trying to free herself. When he didn't release her, she set her feet and lifted a fist, looking ready to brawl rather than run. "Ye better let me go."

"I will release ye, but if ye run in that water, ye willna like it."

She snorted. "And what does that mean?"

"Ye go in that water, and it'll win ye a smack on the arse." He shouldn't speak that way to a lady, but she gave him no choice. With a gentle tug, he turned her back toward camp, but she planted both feet and locked her legs. He pulled again, harder this time, making her stumble and plant her feet again. "Come, m'lady. Ye're still not dry from yer last swim since ye havena even shed yer stockings to hang by the fire."

"What am I supposed to do? Strip naked?" She tossed her head toward the men seated in the distance. "I'm sure the lot of ye would like that, wouldn't ye?"

"I thought to offer ye my best léine when ye calmed down. Ye will be plenty covered along with my plaid to keep ye warm. Leastwise, 'til yer things dry." Not that he wouldn't enjoy seeing her naked, but only if she wished it. Otherwise, he would treat her with the respect and mannerliness a fine lady such as she deserved. "Now, are ye coming, or do I toss ye over my shoulder and tote ye?"

She cast another longing glance at the far side of the shimmering green pool. Another subtle shiver stole across her, sending her fears and uncertainties into his touch even though she would never willingly share them. Eyes narrowing to frustrated slits, her jaw tightened as she considered his ultimatum.

He would give her time. For her alone, he could manage endless patience. Something deep inside assured him she was worth it.

Finally, she tried to yank away one last time, then glared at him. "Fine. I will wait. For now. But not because of yer threat."

She bared her teeth like a wee cornered beastie. "I'm not afraid of ye. I just need time to think. Plan." With a hearty intake of breath, she assumed an unmistakably regal demeanor. "Successful research is never achieved if the study is half-assed."

He tried not to smile but couldn't stop it, so he bowed his head and turned aside. Once he regained control, he offered his arm. "Wise choice, m'lady. Allow me to escort ye back to the fire." He raised his voice so his men couldn't help but hear. "I assure ye we shall arrange a changing of yer clothes with ample privacy and then leave ye in peace. Ye dinna have to talk of anything ye dinna wish to speak of, ye ken?"

With a roll of her eyes, she took his arm. Back on her pallet, she yanked off her knee-high stockings, all three sets of them. Rob jumped up and fixed her a proper drying rack with two forked sticks stuck into the ground and another resting across them in their crooks.

"Thank ye," she said before turning back to Kane. "Well? Where is this léine of yers, so I can shed the rest of these wet things and spread them to dry?"

In unison, his men jumped to their feet and scattered.

"I'll be fetching more wood," Albie called out.

"I'll help," Toff said, his long stride outdistancing Albie.

"Me and Rob'll check the snares," Jac shouted over the loud crunch of their boots as they galloped across the terrain. "Surely, we've caught some fine conies by now."

"Do they fear ye that much?" Satia asked. One of her fair brows hiked to an amused slant.

He liked that look. It suited her. "Respect, lass. Not fear. There is a difference." He offered her the léine he'd fetched from the bag tied to his saddle and turned his back. "Change by the fire where it's warm. I give ye my word they willna return until I call out."

"And what about yerself?" she asked. "How do I know ye willna peek?"

A sly grin tickled his mouth as he folded his arms across his chest and tossed a glance back at her. "Ye have my word. I willna peek—unless ye wish it, of course."

Her huffing snort made him chuckle. She sounded like a wee doe of the forest, blowing air to get a hunter to move and reveal himself. Again, he turned and gave her his back.

A garment hit the stones with a soggy splat. Then another. And another. Curiosity peppered his confusion, making him frown. She had not looked to be dressed in so many layers. He wondered if there would be anything left of her when he finally turned around. Movement out of the corner of his eye tempted him to steal a peek, but he didn't. He held true to his word. "Are ye covered, lass?"

"Oh, yes. Sorry."

He turned and found her draping her things across the knobby, low-hanging limbs of a dying pine. A blue surcoat that matched the trews that revealed the cleft of her arse. The plaid shirt whose clan colors he couldn't place along with a short, flimsy white chemise with long narrow sleeves that she must've worn under it. Another pair of trews made of the same flimsy white material. He frowned at the final two pieces. Lacy satin things so tiny and teasing, his mouth watered as he imagined her in them, even though he wasn't quite certain how she would go about putting them on. God's beard. He wished he had turned around and stolen a wee look.

CHAPTER THREE

THE FOURTEENTH CENTURY. Impossible. And yet, here she was.

Satia rolled over and stared at the fickle loch that had caused this unbelievable problem. The misty fog from earlier had dissipated, unveiling the deceptively peaceful waters set aglow by the light of the waning moon. How many times had she been in those depths over the last three years? Countless. Both with and without diving gear. She thought she knew the Green Loch's every nuance. Obviously, she'd thought wrong.

A pine marten scampered out of the woods and down to the water's edge. The wee furry beastie paused and stole furtive glances toward the camp, but thirst won out over fear, and it finally settled down and drank. Satia became aware of an affinity with the sleek little creature. Helplessness and epic confusion had trumped her leeriness of the strange group of men who had nominated themselves her guardians.

Scientist that she was, she had already sub-categorized the tightly knit crew.

Toff Sweeney. Old, yellow hair. Not old, really, but he acted that way. More scarred than any of the others. His face and arms attested to his many battles and the bitterness in his eyes.

Definitely Viking DNA in that one.

Rob McBride. The intern of the group. Young. Inexperienced. Devoted. She couldn't refrain from smiling. Rob had undoubtedly been a dog in a past life, and all the unconditional loyalty and exuberance of an oversized puppy had carried forward to this incarnation.

Jac Innes. Red-haired, and now slightly singed, gentle giant. Superstitious to a fault. He still feared her. Probably thought she would turn him into a toad or something. His eyes revealed his worries.

Albie Foster. Patriarch of the group—or maybe the matriarch since not only did he cook and sew, but all the men looked to him whenever they had an ailment. Questionable herbalist. Probably knew just enough to be dangerous.

And then there was Kane. Her breath caught in her throat and made her gulp with a quick swallow. There was no sub-categorizing Kane Macpherson because the man confused her. Worried her like an itch she couldn't scratch, but not in a bad way. Well, it could be bad. As she concluded earlier, the protective Scot had a dangerous pull to him. A magnetism that could be a real problem if she didn't resist.

She shifted and snuggled deeper under the double layer of plaids he had insisted on piling across her. She'd never had a man mother hen her before. The wool blankets smelled of him. That bothered her, too. She'd known the man barely a full day, and yet his scent, a not unpleasant manly musk blended with a comfort-ing note of wood smoke and the clean acidity of pine, had already imprinted itself on her senses. She could find him if struck blind.

A twitching uneasiness, the need to move and walk off this craziness, pushed her to her feet. True to Kane's word, Jac had fashioned a pair of soft leather slippers for her with astonishing speed and accuracy. Their pliable nature silenced her steps as she wandered back to the water's edge and seated herself on the weathered remains of what once had been a mighty pine. A blanket wrapped around her shoulders protected her from the chilly night. She still wore Kane's léine. With the cool dampness in the night air, her clothes would need 'til late morning to have a chance of drying.

"What is it, lass?" That deep voice should've startled her, but it didn't. Somehow, she had known he would join her. He possessed an unsettling awareness of her every move. "What troubles ye?"

"Everything and nothing," she said, unable to explain it even to herself.

He settled down beside her, not touching, but close enough, so his heat reached out and greeted her. "Ye're not unwell, are ye?"

"Only in my head and my heart."

The moonlight lit his face, its blue-white light intensifying the displeasure tightening his jaw. "Perhaps, he will come for ye."

She appreciated the compliment of his jealous tone but chose not to exploit it. Not only was she too weary, but what was the point? "There is no *he*. My heart hurts for my sister and my work." A heavy sigh escaped her. "I have to find a way back to both of them—to save her."

Arms folded across his massive chest and legs crossed at the ankles, Kane frowned at the moonlit waters. "Ye still believe ye must drown yerself to do so?"

He had voiced what she'd been too afraid to face ever since he'd made her calm enough to think this dilemma out. The trauma of what she experienced getting here made her short of breath every time she thought about it. Yet, what else could she do? That had to be the only way back.

"Satia?"

"I dinna ken what to think," she said with a sad shake of her head. "I wish I had that answer." She pulled the wrap closer. "Along with the courage to look it in the eyes."

"Ye're the most courageous woman I know." His voice softened as he bowed his head and leaned the slightest bit closer. "And I dinna wish ye to leave here. Ever."

"I have no money, no job, and nowhere to live." She shifted on the trunk, the roughness of its bark reminding her that nothing padded her arse but a thin bit of linen and blanket. "And if I get around anyone other than yerself or yer men, they'll probably burn me at the stake when I slip up and say the wrong thing." She had a habit of that. If it popped into her head, it shot out of her mouth. She had no filters. Few people other than Breanna tolerated her bluntness. "Surviving here? In this time?" She shook her head again. "I think drowning would be easier."

He rose and stood in front of her, latching hold of her shoulders and blocking her view of anything other than him. "Dinna say that. Not ever. Ye understand?" He drew closer, his face in shadow, but his intensity as clear as the light of day. "I will take care of ye. Keep ye safe. Fed. Sheltered. No one will ever hurt ye long as I live and breathe."

"I am not a lost pet for ye to adopt."

"Neither are ye a woman to be abandoned and set adrift." His tone rang with more than mere concern. "Ye will stay with me, aye? Is that such a terrible prospect?"

"Satia St. Clair and her five dwarves?" She snorted a bitter laugh. Heaven help her; weariness and confusion had pushed her to ridiculous mode. "What will I be? Team mascot or cheerleader?"

"I dinna ken what any of that means, but I know I dinna like it." Hands still tight on her shoulders, he dropped to one knee and put them face to face. "I dinna speak in jest about this." With a touch so gentle it made her shiver, he slid his fingers along her jaw and cradled her face in his palm. "Ye will stay with me, aye? Say yes, m'lady." His thumb tickled the side of her cheek, filling her with an aching weakness she could not allow. "What other choice have ye?"

"Define *stay with ye*," she said, determined to shore up her defenses. The man's voice paired with his touch was lethal. He mesmerized her, tempted her to fall forward into his arms, and toss her recently reinforced golden rule of not trusting to the wind. She would not go down that road again. Lust led to trust. Trust meant vulnerability. Never again. Besides, she wasn't staying here any longer than necessary.

She cleared her throat and hardened herself to his wiles. "Ye understand my hesitance, I'm sure. After all, while ye've been verra kind so far, I've known ye less than a day." She eased away from his touch. "It could all be an act."

The line of his jaw hardened again. Even with his face half-hidden in shadow, defensiveness radiated from him, which she found very odd. Not about his wounded pride, but that she read him with such ease. That wasn't like her. She never sensed others' moods or feelings. That's what made her such a loner. Isolated her. But with Kane, she *read* him as easily as a page with extra-large letters. "What do ye mean when ye say *stay with ye?*" she asked again.

"Ye know what I mean, lass. I see it in yer eyes." He leaned in so close she could almost taste the sweet oblivion his mouth offered. "I am nay a fool, mistress. I know ye see into my soul as easy as I see into yers."

She wanted that kiss. Hungered for it. It took every ounce of self-control she possessed to place her fingers across his mouth and firmly push him back. She almost groaned aloud at the lost opportunity. Instead, she stiffened her spine and sat taller. "I would hear yer definition in *words*, please. Ye will have to forgive me, but I have had my fill of lying, backstabbing bastards of late."

Both his brows ratcheted higher. "Lead me to them, and I shall exact proper vengeance in yer name."

She almost wished she could. Cameron would wet himself if a man like Kane demanded the truth from him. She gifted him with an appreciative smile. "That would require us both drowning in the loch, I'm afraid."

He stood and turned away, staring into the night as if turned to a sculpture of marble. Her palms itched to slide across the hard-cut lines of his body.

"Stay with me," he said again, but this time it sounded cold.

She had hurt him. Fists clenched in her blanket, she pushed back against the immediate remorse pushing her heart downward. No. It had to be this way.

"Ye will have my protection," he continued as if reading off a contract. "The respect of my men, food in yer belly, and a place to rest yer head." He tossed a glance back at her. "Anything further will be up to ye, m'lady. I place no conditions on the offer, nor do I ever go where I am not wanted. Ye have my word."

In that one glance, she saw far too much. More than she should from a man she had only just met. It shook her to her core. "Good enough," she said. "I will stay with ye until I figure out my best course of action." That's all she dare say for now.

He gave a curt nod, then held out a hand. "Come, m'lady. Ye should try to sleep now. Tomorrow we continue south."

"I need to sit here a while." Even though weariness plagued her, she couldn't sleep. Not yet. She had gone days without sleep before and done well enough. Time to do it again. Figure this mess out. She tipped her head toward the shadowy lumps of snoring men sprawled around the dwindling fire. "Go ahead with ye. I'll be along, eventually."

Without a word, he returned to his seat beside her and stared straight ahead.

"I didna mean to hurt yer feelings," she said, proud of herself for not pointing out that he pouted like a child. He'd been kind and could be so much more if she weakened and allowed it. She didn't need to be a heartless cow and torture him. "Ye're a good man, Kane, and I do appreciate all ye have done for me."

His tensed posture softened a bit, much to her relief. He turned and looked at her. "I will always do for ye, m'lady. Anything ye wish."

"Why?" Her inner demons commandeered her tongue, and weariness kept her from stopping them. "I am not a lady, Kane. Far from it. I have one friend in all the world. I'm opinionated, rude, and focus on nothing but my work, and all else can be damned. The one time I attempted socializing and playing nice with others, I got screwed both literally and figuratively—and while one was disappointingly mediocre, the other ripped out my heart." She bowed her head, closed her eyes, and massaged her temples. That should send the chivalrous warrior running.

"Tell me what happened, lass, so I might understand yer pain." He brushed her hair back from her face and tucked it behind her ear.

"I fell in lust with my research assistant, and he used my weakness to steal my work and make me look like a fool to the world."

"What is a research assistant?"

"We studied together to find ways to improve everyone's quality of life." She didn't know any other way to put it in the fourteenth century.

"Ye took him as a lover?" His tone and eyes echoed with a jealousy he didn't attempt to hide.

"Yes." She sidled a guilty glance at him, the admission soured in her gut. She had been such a damned fool. "I was an idiot. Trust me. It wasna worth it."

He gave a forced shrug. "Ye misjudged a man's character. It happens, m'lady."

"He ruined me, Kane." She had to make him see. For some inane reason, she needed his understanding. Or at least his acceptance. It had to be the weariness making her so irrational. Driven to gain his approval, an applicable comparison came to her. "If ye seized a castle for the Bruce…let's say ye saved the day, but then Toff convinced everyone he had done it while ye were off getting drunk in a brothel, how would that make ye feel?"

"I would make the man regret the day he was born."

"Right—I get that. But how would it make ye feel when everyone looked at ye like ye were a lying fool? Even called ye that to yer face?"

Comprehension lit his face as if she'd flipped a switch. But then his expression shifted, and he tilted his head to study her. "If yer world treats ye so badly, why do ye wish to return to it?"

"To clear my name." She looked down at her hands knotted in the corners of the plaid. "When it's all said and done, my name, my reputation, that's all I've got." Her eyes burned dangerously close to releasing rare tears. "That and Breanna." She sniffed and resorted to rapid-fire blinking in a fight for control. "I miss her and need to make sure she's all right."

His arm slid around her shoulders and pulled her to rest against him. "Forget the fools," he whispered. "Tell me about yer Breanna."

Unable to resist his warm, comforting strength, she nestled her cheek against his chest and melted into him. "She's canny, caring, and possesses the patience of Job to put up with likes of me." Breanna's smiling face filled her mind as she closed her eyes. "Takes care of me better than any mother. Listens to my nattering. Makes sure I eat. Even postpones her dates if she thinks I've had a bad day." A sad little laugh escaped her. "Always ready with my favorite wine and an old movie to chase away the ugly world."

"A movie," he repeated slowly.

"Never mind." She never bared her soul. Why start now with a man who couldn't comprehend half of what she said? "It doesna matter."

He curled her tighter against him. "Everything about ye matters. Never think otherwise."

"Why does it feel like we've known each other a lifetime, even though we've just met?" Her bluntness always got the better of her, and it was worse when she was exhausted. When he didn't answer, she smiled to herself. Maybe her inability to understand people held true, and she hadn't read him as accurately as she thought.

"Those who believe in the old ways would say the land heard our souls crying out for each other." The deep rumble of his voice vibrating against her cheek lulled her, cocooning her with the familiar warmth of a favorite security blanket. "The ancient ones believe that long ago we were born a mystical whole. One soul. One heart. Never needing another for comfort or companionship. But when we became too powerful, the gods split us in two and scattered our halves to keep them from rejoining. But blessed Danu hears our cries and guides us back to each other if we will but listen and follow."

"Ye make an awesome storyteller." Self-control watered down by the late hour and traumatic day, she looped an arm around him and hugged closer. "Tell me more."

"Everything happens for a reason, lass," he said so softly she would've missed it had she not had her cheek resting on his chest. "Everything."

"Everything," she repeated in a sleepy mumble, then floated off into the darkness.

KANE SAT THERE, holding Satia, his gaze following the moonlight as it danced across the rippling water. A solid sense of contentment, a subtle knowing that all was as it should be, filled him. The breeze swayed through the pine boughs, gently shushing as if demanding quiet so the lady might sleep. He counted her slow, peaceful breaths. When a soft snore escaped her, he swept her up into his arms, then held his breath until he was certain she hadn't awakened. Her head rolled against his shoulder as he eased back close to the fire. Slumber had finally claimed her fully, sending her well into her dreams.

As he lowered her to the pallet, she latched hold of his shirt, knotting both fists in the folds of its neckline. Poor lass probably thought herself falling. He leaned close and attempted to pry her fingers open without waking her.

"No," she murmured with a sleepy shake of her head. "Dinna drop me."

"I willna let ye fall," he whispered, hoping to reach into her dreams and calm her. "Rest easy, m'lady. Ye're safe now."

Her clenching hold tightened, and she yanked. "Dinna drop me!" she shouted without opening her eyes. "Stop!"

Jac, Rob, and Albie rolled to crouching readiness, all with their daggers drawn. Toff launched to a standing position, a blade in each hand. He swept the area with a quick look, then turned and scowled at Kane. "What the hell are ye doin'?" he demanded in a loud whisper.

"I canna get her loose." Kane pointed to her hold on his shirt.

"Then, for God's sake, lay with the woman so we can all get some sleep." Toff flopped back down, grumbling like an old dog disturbed in the middle of its nap. The other three did the same.

Sweat peppered across Kane's forehead and upper lip. He had promised Satia he never went where he wasn't invited. She'd made it more than a little clear that she intended to remain alone in her bed. After another glance at his men, he attempted to open her fists one last time.

"No!" She kicked, then jutted her knee in an upward thrust to unman the opponent only she could see.

"Lay with her," Toff growled.

"Do it, man!" Albie ordered in a low growl of his own.

Shielding his manparts with one hand, Kane eased down beside her, tensed and ready in case she continued her battle. Much to his surprise, and to his pleasure, she scooted close and pillowed her head on his shoulder. Her delectable scent flooded his senses. The dangerously tempting fragrance of a vibrant woman. A teasing breeze caught hold of her silky hair and tossed it across his face. The tickling strands caught in the stubble of his beard and teased across his mouth and nose. What he wouldn't give to bury his face in those tresses as she lay beneath him, crying out his name in the throes of passion.

She snuggled tighter against him, making him clench his teeth so hard his jaws ached. With her hands still tangled in his shirt, she nuzzled her face into his chest. "Cold," she murmured as a shiver rippled through her. The tip of her nose, icy as loch water in the dead of winter, pressed against his flesh through the open neck of his léine.

He wasn't cold. He was hotter than Hell's deepest fire. All because of her. Yet he reached down and snagged a blanket bunched at their feet and pulled it up over her. Sweat trickling down his back was a small price to pay for her contented sigh and the way she cuddled closer still. Shame she didn't behave this way when awake.

A LOUD SNORT yanked her to that level of fuzzy consciousness between deep sleep and almost awake, but she didn't bother opening her eyes. Instead, she closed them tighter. But the snort wedged itself crossways in her awareness. So, she vaguely studied it to make it go away and leave her alone and let her sleep in for once.

Breanna didn't snore. Satia tugged the blankets closer around her neck and tried to slip back into oblivion. Breanna must've had a guest stay over last night. Good for her. He better be a good bloke and treat her sister right, or he'd have her to deal with. A jaw-cracking yawn made her hitch in a deeper breath. The sharp tang of wood smoke sent an alarm across her sleepy senses. What the hell was on fire?

Her eyes popped open, and it all came flooding back. "Shite! Shite! Shite!" She pushed herself up with one hand while clamping the other over her eyes. Reality by the raw light of day was an ugly, wicked beast.

"Willow bark, m'lady?" Albie held a steaming cup in one hand and a pale hockey puck in the other. "And an oatcake to break yer fast, so it doesna pain ye in yer wame."

She eyed the camp as she accepted the brew and questionable breakfast. "How can I be the last one up? Snoring woke me."

From across the way, Toff barked out a laugh, then shot her a wicked grin. "Forgive me, m'lady. Ye woke yerself with that braw snort that would do any man proud."

"I do not snore."

"Whatever ye say, m'lady." Toff tapped his forehead in mock salute, then sauntered off, still chuckling with his rolled blanket tucked under his arm.

"Ass," she muttered. After confirming the contents of the cup with a hearty sniff, she downed the acrid swill in as few gulps as possible. A hard shudder followed. The hairs rose on the back of her neck. She knew who stood behind her without looking around. "Why did ye not wake me?" she scolded.

"Ye were weary, lass. It didna hurt to let ye sleep whilst we readied to move on." Kane stepped in front of her and crouched to her level. "How fare ye this morn?"

After snapping off a chunk of the gloppiest oatcake she had ever seen, Satia popped it into her mouth and chewed for a long while before answering. She'd had the strangest dream about him that seemed a little too real. Especially since she never dreamed. Well, she did. But they were always nightmares revisiting darker moments from her childhood, so she refused to acknowledge them and give them any toehold during her waking hours. But last night's dream differed. Kane showed up to save her—like the proverbial knight in shining armor. His touch, his voice, the warmth and strength of his hard, muscular chest had felt real. "I dreamt about ye last night."

One of his dark brows quirked higher. "Did ye now?"

Her chewing slowed as she replayed the not unpleasant memory. "Or perhaps it wasna a dream. Is there something ye would like to tell me?"

An uneasy sheepishness transformed the mighty warrior into a child caught stealing sweets. He even rolled his shoulders as if trying to slough away a guilty conscience. "Tell ye something?"

She almost laughed at loud. "Last I remember, I was sitting on that log over there." She cast her gaze down to the pallet, then swept it up to him. "How'd I get back here?"

"I carried ye." He jutted his handsome cleft chin upward,

knowing exactly how to use his arsenal of charm to its fullest. Then he jerked a curt nod. "And when I couldna pry my shirt from yer hands, I lay beside ye."

So, his part of her dream had been real. And he admitted it. Honest to a fault. She found that trait equally impressive and worrisome. Her heart twitched as if trying to wiggle free of her lockdown before it was too late.

"Thank ye for keeping me warm," she said in a detached tone as if he'd been polite enough to adjust the air conditioning in a pub. "I remember being verra cold until ye blocked the wind, so I'd get the full effect of the fire." She'd give him an out. It was the least she could do. After all, he had treated her with kindness and consideration. So much so, he even rivaled Bree's motherly coddling, and Breanna was a tough act to follow.

His eyes narrowed with the slightest flexing, and a corner of his mouth tugged upward. He stood and looked down at her with a sly knowing. "I kept my word, lass. I dinna go anywhere I'm nay invited. But ye refused to let me leave yer bed."

The way he inflected his comment gave her a shiver of the hottest kind. No chance of her growing cold this morning. She rose to her feet, never relishing having to look up at anyone. "As I said, thank ye for keeping me warm."

"Ye are most welcome, m'lady."

"I'll get changed back into my clothes now. I'm sure they're dryer than yesterday." With a shooing motion, she fixed him with the glare that always struck fear into her interns. "Ye will make sure no one peeks, yes?"

He caught her hand in mid-shooing, brushed a gallant kiss across her knuckles, then bowed over it. "Absolutely, m'lady. Never ye fear." His devilish air as he straightened, then strode away, made her realize he had just declared a battle of wills. Hers to return to her time. His to get her to stay.

She tried not to think about that as she took refuge in the sheltered curve of the downed tree where she'd hung her clothes. After she stripped the soft léine off over her head, she buried her face in it and inhaled. It still smelled of him, mixed with a little of her. She hugged it close for a moment. A gust of cool wind across her naked flesh shook her free of the silly spell. What the devil was wrong with her? She folded the tunic and the plaid and stacked them on the trunk of the weathered tree.

While pulling on her clothes, she stared at the loch. By jings, the thought of diving back into those depths made her cringe. But remain in the fourteenth century? That revved up the urge to cringe even tighter. She was no history buff, but she knew the dangers and miseries of this time well enough from what she'd studied while sorting through the archives in the library. As she buttoned her faded blue and gray plaid flannel shirt, she paused and assessed her clothing. Jeans? Bright blue down jacket with patches on the elbows? Snug thermals under all of that? If anyone besides Kane's men saw her, what would they think? A definite problem while she worked on bolstering her courage into taking that dive or finding another way home. After all, she'd made that vague promise to stay with Kane until she figured out her best course of action.

"I'm decent," she called out as she scooped up the borrowed apparel and emerged from her wilderness dressing room. The camp was deserted, nothing more than a black spot of wetness where they'd doused the fire. She turned and scanned the hillside as far as she could see into the trees. No one there either. Cocking an ear, she listened, concentrating on identifying the faintest sound. Nothing but birdsong and the rustling crunch of wee beasties in the woods, probably squirrels in search of breakfast. "Hello?"

No answer.

Maybe they'd decided she was more trouble than what she was worth. Wouldn't be the first time someone thought that about her. "Fine, then. I needed to stay here and study the loch, anyway." She'd not been all that keen on leaving the area but figured she'd find her way back easily enough. After all, she knew this part of Scotland better than the back of her hand.

But faintly bruised feelings twisted a painful knot in the middle of her chest. After all his talk and acts of chivalry, Kane had left without her. And without a proper goodbye, even. She hated to admit it, but all his m'ladying and alpha protectiveness had been kind of nice. Apparently, she misjudged him—read him all wrong. She blew out a bitter huff. History repeating itself, that was. At least she'd had no research for him to steal.

She placed his shirt and blanket on top of a boulder and strolled to the water's edge. Research. She needed to concentrate on research. Forget about Kane and his *pull*, as Bree would say. Work never failed her. Not like people did. She raked her hair back out of her face and secured it into a messy braid. Time to think and examine every variable about how she had gotten here. As she stared at the water, all else fell away other than her silent calculations. A vague commotion up in the woods distracted her for a moment, but she shoved it aside. "Concentrate. It's just deer or something." She closed her eyes and returned to reliving every second in the water.

"Well, lookie here," said a strange voice behind her.

"We should take her," wheezed another. "She's prolly their whore."

Satia opened her eyes and turned, half afraid of what she would find. She was right to be afraid. So right, in fact, that she forgot to breathe.

Six grubby men. Some partially bent and trying to catch their breath. All sporting wicked daggers and dangerous leers.

CHAPTER FOUR

"THERE THEY ARE." Stoked with rage, blades ready, Kane led the charge down the hillside. He and his men barreled through the trees, their blood-curdling roars splitting the air. Five of the six traitors on the shoreline turned to meet them. The sixth lunged toward Satia. Kane pounded faster. No one threatened the lady!

She evaded the cur and took off around the loch, skipping across the rocky ground with the graceful agility of a Highland deer. The man gave chase, but Kane halted him, throwing a dagger with such force that it buried deep in the fool's lower back. The devil pawed it out but crashed to his knees and sagged to the side as one of Toff's arrows found purchase in his neck.

Kane finished the man by slitting his throat. He turned to engage the rest only to find the battle ended before it started. His men had swiftly dispatched the others, sending them to meet their final judgment. He sheathed his sword, recovered his dagger, and wiped it on his thigh. As he returned it to the scabbard under his arm, he turned and scanned the rise beyond the opposite shore, searching the landscape for Satia.

"Any others?" he shouted to his men without ceasing his search for the lass.

"None," Toff assured, coming to a halt beside him and scowling at the same area. "I feel sure that be all of them." The intensity of his expression relaxed into a grin, and he pointed. "There. In that tree. See her?"

Relief flooded Kane, enabling him to breathe easy once more. He loped around the loch and up the hillside to a sprawling pine where the agile minx hid high among its branches. "'Tis safe, m'lady," he called up, unable to keep from smiling when she peeped down through the lush green boughs like a wee frightened squirrel.

"How safe?" she called down, still hugging the trunk while astraddle a limb.

"They're all dead," he said. "So, I reckon it canna get any safer."

"Ye killed six men?"

He found her shocked tone curious. Did she not realize they would have killed her? And they would have done much worse things to her first. He resettled his stance and gave an indifferent shrug. "Actually, we killed ten in total. Four atop the ridge. The six who threatened ye escaped us and made their way here afore we caught them. These traitors were among those we ousted in Inverness. Loyal to Edward and intent on causing turmoil." He waved her down again. "Come, m'lady." But then it occurred to him she might not wish to witness the carnage. "Or, if ye wish, ye can stay up there 'til we get them buried."

She closed her eyes and bowed her head against the tree, either praying or deep in thought. Kane couldn't decide which. Surely, she would be more comfortable on the ground. "Ye can say yer prayers here at the base of the tree." He glanced back to where the fighting had occurred. "Ye canna see all that much from here."

She still didn't answer.

"M'lady?"

"Stop *m'ladying* me. I dinna mind it from the others, but it rubs my fur the wrong way when ye do it. Call me by name.

Please?"

Her order not only made him smile but sparked a warmness in the center of his chest. He quietened his tone. "Come down, Satia, and wait here while the lads and I finish this."

Loose bark and debris showered all around as she worked her way downward. She had achieved an impressive height.

"Coming down is a lot harder than going up," she said with a strained grunt as she clambered from branch to branch. When she reached the limb closest to the ground, she swung down, released, and rolled when she hit the ground.

Concerned at what looked to be a hard landing, he hurried to help her up. "Are ye all right?"

Her shaky smile eased his concerns, but a scrape on her cheek made him look closer. "Ye bleed." He gently took hold of her chin and turned her face to peer closer at the minor injury. "Are ye hurt anywhere else?"

"I'm fine," she said. "Just haven't scaled any trees since I was a wee bratling." Her shaky smile puckered into a troubled pout as her cheeks flared to a deep red. A shadow of fear—not fear exactly, but something—flickered in her eyes. "I thought ye had left me," she softly accused. "No one answered when I called out."

"I swore to protect ye, lass." Still cradling her face in his palm, he was reluctant to let his hand drop away from the velvet of her cheek. "We merely meant to give ye yer privacy." Her silence bade him release the words he had hesitated to speak before. "I would never leave ye, Satia. Ye are the one who wishes to leave me—remember?"

Then he claimed the kiss he had wanted since first setting eyes on her. He would sample her sweetness if she allowed it. And she did. The tasting proved as exquisite as he had known it would. She opened to him, welcoming the hesitant flicks of his tongue. Her hands slid up his chest, and she leaned in, stretching to encircle his neck with her arms and draw closer. He tightened his embrace. Aye, this was well worth the wait.

Then she pushed free and stepped back with her fingers pressed across her lips. "Sorry." With a fluttering wave, she turned away. "Caught up in gratitude, I guess." She paused and bowed her head. "Anyway, thank ye for stopping that bunch. Wish the killing hadn't been necessary, though."

"It had to be done, lass," he said, not quite certain what had just driven a wedge between them. "We showed them mercy in Inverness and let them go. Their choice to follow and seek revenge was a poor one."

Still not facing him, she nodded. "I can see that." After a long moment of strained silence, she hugged herself and turned back to him. "So, I should be safe enough here now—right? What with them gone and all?"

"A woman alone is never safe in the Highlands." Was she afraid of him now? Did she think he meant to force himself on her? "If this is about the kiss—"

"It is, and it isn't," she said before he could finish. Still hugging herself, she tipped her head toward the water. "I should stay here at the loch. It shouldna take me that long to sort things out."

"Ye said ye would stay with me."

"I said I would stay until I worked out my best course of action." Her chin lifted to the angle it always hit when she was about to say something he wouldn't like. He'd already learned that about her. "How can I figure my best course of action if I leave here?"

"Sometimes stepping away and clearing yer head opens yer eyes." Even though all he wished to do was pull her back into his arms, he spoke the words she needed to hear. "And dinna fear, lass. I willna force myself upon ye. Not ever."

"I didna say ye forced the kiss." Her defensive tone revealed all the uncertainties she struggled to hide and how much she hated he might see it. 'Twas more than a little clear that Satia hated appearing vulnerable.

"Come. We are packed and ready." He held out a hand. "I'll take ye round the far end of the loch, so ye dinna have to go where they're piling the cairns." He motioned toward her strange jacket with the odd puffiness beneath its bright blue sheen. "We shall stay at Rob's home a night or two before we continue on to Edinburgh. I'm sure one of his sisters can help ye with proper clothes. That will make ye safer still." When she didn't take his hand, he cast a pointed look at the shimmering waters, then shifted his attention back to her. "Ye said ye would stay and travel with us a while. I would never have taken ye for a liar."

"I am not a liar. I said I would stay with ye until I figured things out, remember?"

"Have ye figured things out then?" He nearly had this argument won. Her wavering uncertainty filled the air.

"No, damn ye." She shoved past him and stared down at the shore. "All I know to do is dive back in that water and swim deep as I can."

"But ye fear it."

"Well, of course, I fear it." With both hands pressed to her cheeks, she shook her head. After pulling in a deep breath and hissing it out, she let them drop. "I dinna ken which I fear more. Dive deep until I pass out or stay here."

He stepped up beside her. "Appears to me that facing the fear of staying with me gives ye better odds than drowning and hoping to get back to wherever ye came from."

"Ye make a convincing argument." Her eyes narrowed. "But I have always faced my fears and, somehow, going with ye makes me feel like I'm cheating and running away."

She needed an assurance. An out. This woman was harder on herself than anyone else ever could be. Whatever demons haunted her, they were fierce. "I will bring ye back here, Satia. Whenever ye are ready. All ye need do is ask."

Her side-eyed glare said she didn't believe him. "Ye're telling me, ye'll drop whatever ye're doing, whether it be storming castles, hunting down traitors, or shining the Bruce's boots just to bring me back here. Whenever I ask."

"Aye." He ignored the insult, knowing she lashed out to keep herself isolated. While he wouldn't like returning to the loch, if that's what it took to put her at ease and keep her from drowning herself this day, he would gladly give her that oath. "What say ye?"

After another glance at the water, she blew out a frustrated sigh. "Agreed."

He offered his hand again. "To the horses then, aye?"

"To the horses." She pondered his outstretched hand. "I can walk just fine without help, ye ken that, right?"

"I am sure ye can, but ye are a lady, and I would steady ye as we make our way down the hillside." It also gave him another chance to touch her, but he didn't add that. Nay. For now, he would use the excuse of proper behavior toward the gentler sex.

"Yet another reason I will never make it in this century." She grudgingly took hold of his hand.

"How so?" he asked. She had confused him again.

"First, as I told ye before, I am no lady." She lifted their clasped hands and shook them. "And second, I never learned all the social niceties of my time, much less what's expected of me now."

"Ye underestimate yerself, lass." He tucked her hand in the crook of his elbow with a reassuring pat. "Just because ye speak yer mind and dinna tolerate any havering or sass, doesna mean ye are not a lady." He tossed her a wink and a smile. "It merely means ye ken yer own mind."

She laughed. "I know many who would disagree."

She came to an abrupt stop and stared through the trees at the men piling stones atop the bodies. The echoing clack of rock hitting rock sang out a last mournful song for the dead. Six cairns all in a row. The bodies protected from scavengers and time by rocks and boulders gathered from the shore. Most wouldn't bother to treat their enemy with such respect, but Kane and his men weren't *most*. They would bury the other four men they had killed where they'd dropped them in the woods.

Locked in place with her fingertips pressed across her mouth, her delicate features paled to the shade of fresh cream.

"Satia?"

She didn't speak, but a slow trembling took hold of her body and gradually increased until shaking her so violently, she leaned against him.

He started to scoop her up into his arms, but she stopped him. "No—I'll be all right. Just give me a minute."

"Forgive me, lass." He felt like a complete and utter fool for rushing her. "I shouldha waited with ye on the other shore to keep ye from witnessing such."

"It's…it's not that." She pinched the bridge of her nose, rubbing the inner corners of her eyes as though ridding them of grit. "I have seen those six mounds of stone before. In my time." Her voice softened, took on a quivering, reverent tone. "Ye will be proud to know yer men's cairn work lasts over seven hundred years." With a nod toward the mounds, she looked almost ready to cry. "They're a mite smaller and quite weathered, but they still faithfully mark those remains." She softly huffed a bitter laugh. "I believed ye before, but seeing those again and discovering their true origins gobsmacked me, I guess."

"What is *gobsmacked?*" It sounded horrible. As if someone slapped her across the mouth. He stared at the graves, trying to visualize the place through her eyes. "Is *gobsmacked* demons?"

"No." She shook her head. "It's shocked. Surprised. Shaken." Still staring at the rocks, she gave a weak shrug. "Kind of like seeing the ghost of a person ye once knew." She turned and trudged onward toward the horses as if determined to plow through anything that tried stopping her. With an impatient flip of a hand, she continued, "I canna say why it hit me so hard. Guess it just drove everything home when I saw the beginning of something I had stared at for years and never really known its origin." She flinched as though in pain. "Or that I would be here when it happened."

He couldn't comprehend how any of what she said could be true but decided, without a doubt, that it must be. Sincerity, passion, fear, and determination surrounded her whenever she spoke of her home. She didn't speak as one tetched in the head or confused. Satia was quite sane. She had somehow come to them from the future. Perhaps the old legends were more than just stories. This new understanding strengthened the strange bond he felt forming. She had been sent back here for a reason. The gods, or the Fae, or whatever power sent her back here for him. But he wouldn't tell her that. Not yet.

When they reached the horses tethered on the line, she skittered to one side, eyeing them as though she feared they would eat her. "Uhm…I have never ridden a horse." She caught the corner of her lip between her teeth. One beast turned to eye her, and she jumped back. "Do they bite strangers?"

"Not usually." He didn't add that they might if they took a mind to. Instinct told him he'd never get her on a horse if he told her that. "How do ye get from place to place in yer time? Carriages?"

"Cars. Trains. Planes." She sidled another step back, her focus still locked on the animals. As if suddenly aware that she had confused him again, she briefly glanced his way. "Inventions that dinna require animals. Cars either run on petrol or electricity. Like carriages without horses. Trains have their tracks. I'm not sure what powers them. And planes fly. They run on their own sort of petrol, too."

He couldn't imagine such and wasn't too sure he wished to if he could. "Fly like a bird?" Of all she had described, that sounded the most amazing, as well as the most frightening.

She continued chewing on the corner of her lip while eyeing the horses. "I'm not too sure I should tell you much more about the future. It might change something we dinna want to change."

"I promise ye, lass, I shall repeat yer words to no one." And he wouldn't either. If he did, they would surely lock him up, thinking he had lost his mind, which set him to thinking. "But take care with what ye say to anyone else, ye ken?"

Still staring at the horses, she agreed with a quick nod.

Toff, Rob, Jac, and Albie joined them. "To Edinburgh, then?" Toff asked.

"To Rob's homestead first," Kane said with a tip of his head toward the lad. "Think ye one of yer sisters might spare some clothes for our lady?"

Rob grinned as he untethered Kane's horse and handed him the reins. "Most certainly." After a friendly up and down glance at Satia, he continued, "Ye're about the same size as Anne, if ye dinna mind me saying. And if nothing of hers suits ye, Laoiri's almost tall as yerself, so her kirtles wouldna be too short." His brow puckered. "Mairi's might do, but she's wide in the arse from having both her bairns." He cast a panicked stare at all of them and held up a warning hand. "But dinna any of ye tell her I said that. She'll box my ears."

Satia smiled. "Yer secret's safe with me."

"And then there's Jennet," he hurried to add as though he had forgotten. "But her kirtles are drab, dreary things." He bowed his head and gave reverent sigh. "Widowed, ye understand."

"How many sisters do ye have?" Satia quick-stepped around Kane, placing him between herself and the horse that stepped toward her with a curious sniff.

Rob shrugged. "Just the four."

"I see," Satia said. "Four sisters. Nice."

It became clear she was stalling. Kane turned, caught hold of her hand, and pulled her out from behind him. "Here, let him sniff ye good and proper. *Mèirleach* willna hurt ye. He loves the ladies, and they love him. His name is the Gaelic for *thief*. I named him that because he steals their hearts."

Satia extended her hand, knuckles up, while leaning away as though ready to run at the first sign of teeth. "Good to meet ye, *Mèirleach*."

The great black horse snuffled her hand, then swung his head closer and sniffed her face, rumbling out a contended grumbling the entire time.

Kane stepped behind her and blocked her from fleeing.

She pressed back, flinching, and turning aside. Tight against him and eyes shut, she dug her fingernails into his arm. "What's he doing? Trying to decide if I'll taste good?"

The other men laughed. He shot them a glare that silenced them. "He's merely getting to know ye. He'll smell my scent on ye and realize ye're a friend."

"Then rub all over me." With her eyes still closed, she pressed back tighter against him.

He bit back a suggestive retort and cut another silencing glare at his men. They immediately busied themselves with their own mounts while trying to stifle more laughter. "He willna hurt ye, lass. Open yer eyes and befriend him."

The animal rumbled another quiet greeting, gave a soft snort, and resettled its front feet.

She shifted against him with a deep inhale and stiffened her spine. "I am not a coward. I've just never been around animals all that much. Especially not ones this big." She held up a hand and displayed a small space between thumb and forefinger. "I study microorganisms. Wee things ye canna imagine." Her hand dropped, and she squared her shoulders. "I am not a coward."

"I would never think ye a coward." He took her hand and placed it on the magnificent beast's shaggy neck. "He likes if ye stroke him like this, then scratch behind his ears."

"He is verra handsome," she admitted as she slid her hand along the animal's muscular throat. "And verra big."

"Aye, he's a fine warhorse descended from a good bloodline. His sire was one of the best destriers in England."

"England?" She allowed him to lift her up into the saddle and seat himself behind her.

"Aye, England." He chuckled as he encircled her with his arms and took hold of the reins. "Cattle are not the only things that can be artfully lifted, ye ken?"

She grabbed his arm and pulled it around her waist. "Dinna let me fall. It's a long way down."

"This from the woman who scaled one of the tallest pines in

the Cairngorms."

"Aye, well, pines dinna move and jostle ye."

If he had known about her fear of riding, he would've gotten her in the saddle sooner just to enjoy her nearness. "Try to relax, lass. 'Twill be easier on ye, if ye can. We've much traveling to do once we leave Rob's home."

She maintained a tight, two-handed hold on his arm around her waist. "How far to Rob's?"

"Not far. We should get there just past midday. 'Twas where we were headed when we stopped at the loch to give the horses a rest."

They rode along in companionable silence for quite some time, until he caught sight of her worried scowl whenever her head turned to take in the landscape to the right. "We're headed east of the Cairngorms through the pass to Loch Avon. Rob's land runs along its shores."

"I'm well aware of where we are." She sounded diminished and afraid. "It's not all that different from…" She didn't finish. Instead, she twitched an uneasy shrug. "Never mind."

"I wish I could make this easier on ye, lass." He coaxed *Mèirleach* to a faster pace. "Perhaps, that's why the powers that be chose me to be the one to find ye. So I could keep ye safe and make yer journey as bearable as possible."

"I dinna believe in such things." She shifted forward as though trying to put some space between them. "Why would fate or whatever it is try to help me now after all this time and everything that's happened in my life?"

"Who's ta say?" All the tales his mother used to tell came flooding back to him. "We are but pawns on the gods' chessboard. All we can do is make the best of the moves we are given."

"Aye, well, I've never had much patience for chess. Hate the game, in fact." She tossed her head and gave another twitch of a shoulder. "With science, I always know what to do. Some even say I'm gifted. But making life choices? I'm usually a damned fool."

"Everything happens for a reason," he said, repeating Mam's favorite saying.

"Aye, and sometimes those reasons are rubbish." She bowed her head for a moment, then sat taller as if drawing up all her strength to battle her demons. "Sorry. I dinna mean to sound so ungrateful. I appreciate all ye have done for me. My arrival here couldha gone much worse." She cast a glance back at him. "Dinna think I don't realize that. Ye are a rare man, Kane Macpherson, and I wish I could see the world through yer eyes."

"Stay with me long enough, lass, and ye will. I promise." He added nothing further. She needed time and space to acclimate to everything she found so strange. With her, he would develop endless patience, hoping someday she would realize her choice to stay was not a poor one.

"I'll ride ahead and let the lasses know we're coming," Rob shouted, thundering past them with a grin and a wave.

"He's got to be the happiest individual I believe I have ever met." Satia sounded more than a little jealous.

"He never looks back." Kane selected his words with care. "The lad hasna had an easy way of it. His mother died birthing him, and his father drowned when Rob was but a youngling of seven or so. Upriver from the loch while checking baskets for the day's catch. Rob was the one who found him. His sisters raised him and kept hold of their land." He didn't add that he and his men saw to it they had what they needed because it wasn't charity to be spoken about. 'Twas merely the right thing to do.

"It's difficult to leave the past in the past." She relaxed back against him as if seeking comfort. A soft laugh shook free of her. "Many a therapist has gotten quite rich because of that. I think I paid for mine's new flat."

"What is a therapist?"

She didn't answer, just took in the scenery as if seeing it for the first time.

"Satia?" Instinct bade him keep after her. The only way they would develop a closeness was if he understood everything about her.

"A therapist is a listener," she finally said. "Ye tell them yer troubles, and they help ye work through them." She twisted around and gave him a smile. "Ye would make a grand therapist because ye listen and dinna accuse or cast blame."

Her kind words gave him hope. Warmed him. But he also found the concept of paying a person to listen to yer worries rather strange. "Are there no priests in the future?"

"There are." She shifted in the saddle as if suddenly uncomfortable with the subject. "But they're like everyone else. Ye have to be careful who ye trust."

"Ye can trust me, lass. Always."

"I know." It seemed as though the revelation surprised her. With a flip of her braid to the front, she fidgeted with it before tossing him another lopsided smile. "That's the strangest part about being here. Ye won my trust quicker than any man I have ever known." One of her pale brows arched to a cynical slant. "Congratulations."

Before he could accept the questionable praise, Albie rode up and gave the signal to stop. Alarm filled Kane, making him pull his mount to a quick halt. Albie never acted in such a way unless it was something dire.

"What's wrong?" Satia's fingers dug into his arm as she twisted in the saddle and frantically scanned the area.

"I dinna ken." He swung to the ground, then put the reins in her hands.

She lifted the strips of leather and looked at him as if she thought him sorely addled. "What am I supposed to do with these?"

"Stay ready, and if aught goes wrong, ride off as fast as ye can." He pointed south. "That way."

"Ye have lost the plot." She neatly piled the reins on the front of the saddle. "Get me down from here. I'll run if something goes wrong. I canna drive a horse."

He stepped away with a firm shake of his head. "Nay, lass. Ye have a better chance on *Mèirleach*." He would not budge on this. She had to realize and accept he knew what was best for protecting her.

Albie appeared at his side, looking grim as death. "There is no danger, but ye need speaking to before we reach Avon and get tangled in that gaggle of nattering women."

"So, I can get down now?" Satia called out. The woman possessed the keen hearing of a spoiled bairn.

"Let her down, but I must speak with ye in private." Albie tossed a disgruntled glance her way.

Unsure whether to be befuddled, angry, or both, Kane went back and helped Satia dismount. "Stay here, aye? 'Til I get this sorted. I dinna ken what's gnawing at him."

She leaned to one side and peered around him, eyeing Albie. "I dinna think he likes me," she whispered.

"Albie has little patience with any woman. Not just yerself."

"I'll stay here," she said, still talking low. "If it's about me, tell me when ye get back, aye?"

"I will," he agreed, wondering if he had just made a promise he shouldn't. He turned and strode a suitable distance away, then waited.

Albie joined him, rubbing his bald pate as if it were a wishing stone. A sure sign that something serious troubled the man. "We shall leave her with them, aye?"

"By *her*, I assume ye mean Lady Satia?" Kane would not allow even a hint of disrespect slanted toward her. Not even from Albie.

Albie's mouth tightened before he managed a curt nod. "We've warring to do. It's nay right to keep her with us." He shifted his weight back and forth and toed the ground like a rooster scratching for bugs. "It's nay right to keep her with ye. Ye are a fighting man. No land. No title. Nothing to offer a wife. Dinna let something start that ye canna finish."

"Ye assume a lot, man." His patience spent, Kane gritted his teeth. He respected Albie, but this was none of his affair.

"I see how ye are with her." The agitated warrior continued

scrubbing his knobby hand across the slickness of his head. "The way ye look at her, even though ye've known her naught but a short time. 'Tis pure folly. Just like yer mother and her mother, as well, with their ill-fated loves. None of yer bloodline have ever known when to leave well enough alone—and end up losing their souls because of it. Remember the curse."

Resentment he had carried since childhood refused to be held back any longer. Kane grabbed hold of Albie with both hands and shook him with a jerk so hard the man's head snapped back. "Mind yer words, old man. They verra well could be yer last."

"Just bear it in mind, aye?" Albie didn't flinch nor show any fear. "Afore it's too late. Leave her with the McBride sisters and be done with her." He bared his teeth. "Ye're nay the marrying kind, and ye know it as well as I. Yer ancestry willna bear it. Even yer mother said so. Ye said ye heard her say the words again right afore she died. Just like her mother did."

Before he snapped the man's neck, Kane shoved him away. "Back to yer horse afore I kill ye."

Head bowed and mouth clamped shut, Albie stomped back to his mount.

Kane eyed Toff and Jac. Both men knew exactly what the conversation had been about. He saw it in their faces. He also saw they agreed. All of them could go straight to hell, even though he knew in his heart they were right.

CHAPTER FIVE

E VEN THOUGH KANE had promised to tell her what Albie said, he didn't. Or at least he hadn't yet. He'd put her off, saying they would talk later. Once they settled in at Rob's home.

Satia stole covert glances at crotchety old Albie as they traveled in a tighter group, wondering what he had told Kane and the rest of the men. Whatever it was, it had put Kane in a foul mood. In fact, every one of them was snappish as a university student with a maxed-out credit card and no cash.

Obviously, her unconditional acceptance into their medieval club of testosterone had ended, and she had a pretty good idea why. These men were nomads fighting for a cause. Women weren't historically part of that group. At least, not yet. And not women like her. High risk. Not only a danger to herself but to those claiming to befriend her. It all came down to superstitions. She'd read enough about witch hunts to know she was a prime candidate for the fiery stake.

Kane shifted, guiding the horse more with a squeezing of his powerful legs than the reins. It pivoted her awareness back to him. Or at least brought it more to the forefront. How could she not be aware of him at all times? If only he had been born in her century. She wondered if he would be the same man. Doubtful.

Nature versus nurture. The nature of the fourteenth century had molded him into the rare find she found increasingly impossible to pry out of her thoughts. Especially after that kiss. Treacherous ground indeed since she was going back to her time. Somehow. She couldn't abandon a shot at a possible cure that would save Bree, should her cancer ever return. And then there was the matter of knocking that smug look off Cameron's lying face. That alone was worth another chilling dive. Maybe. The thought of those dark, icy depths still made her shiver.

A thatched roof came into view as they cleared the last bend in the pass. Satia couldn't imagine how anyone scratched out a living in this rugged, unforgiving part of the Highlands. Unless you were an eagle, a falcon, or a red deer, survival would be difficult. Mountains on all sides. Sparse ground cover scattered among the rocks and packed soil surrounding the body of water that sourced the River Avon. Even though she had yet to meet Rob's sisters, she already admired them. Life here would not be for the faint of heart.

A pair of wee, towheaded lassies rounded the corner of the modest stone dwelling, gleefully squealing as young Rob chased after them. Satia smiled as he grabbed them up, one under each arm, and spun in circles, making them squeal even louder.

"He loves those bairns," Kane mused. "Wish we could leave him here to watch over them."

"Ye make it sound as though he's yer prisoner."

"He is a prisoner. Pride and duty rule him, lass. That's worse than being a prisoner to any man."

Before she could comment, a pair of women came around the other side of the cottage. One short and wide. The other tall and fierce with wispy brown hair pulled back in a stern bun. Satia figured the shorter lass to be Mairi, the mother of the twins. The other, she would have to wait for proper introductions.

Suspicion and a hint of jealousy pinched her when the lanky, feral lass melted into a smiling sunbeam aimed directly at Kane. "She likes ye," she said, then regretted it. Everything that popped into her head did not need to come out of her mouth—especially in this century. She clenched her teeth, determined to do better.

"Laoiri likes everyone. She's a kind lass."

At least he seemed oblivious to his admirer. She ground her teeth tighter together. What difference did it make? He didn't belong to her, nor ever would. Just like she didn't belong in his world. That realization made her stomach knot and threatened to shove her oatcake breakfast back out. It took a hard swallow to push it back down. She shook her head. This was ridiculous. She shouldn't...no...she *would not* feel this dangerously queasy toward a man she had only met yesterday.

"What is it, lass?"

"What?"

"Ye shook yer head. Why?"

"Internal conversation," she said, then changed the subject. "Rob said Jennet's a widow, but he didn't mention Mairi's husband. Where is he?"

"She has no husband." His voice echoed with such a cold hardness it tensed her. "And dinna speak of it because the father of her bairns raped her."

"Oh...I am so sorry." Thank goodness she had asked him and not Mairi. "Was he brought to justice, I hope?"

"Aye." Kane halted, dismounted, then helped her down. "The lads and I hunted the bastard down and killed him. Slowly."

As the women approached, she stepped closer and lowered her voice. "Is there anything else I should know?"

His dark brows knotted over the bridge of his aquiline nose, adding a thoughtfulness to his frown. "Take care what ye say, ye ken? No talk of things only ye would know. Yer prophecies from yer time. Nothing about where ye are really from, aye?"

"We expected ye sooner," Laoiri scolded with an affectionate flutter of her lashes as she closed the distance between them. She didn't spare Satia the slightest glance. Her attention belonged to Kane alone.

"Laoiri!" Mairi huffed to a stop and patted a small square of yellowed linen across her sweat-peppered forehead. "Dinna be so rude." She gave Satia a smiling curtsy. "Welcome to our home, Lady Satia. Our Rob says ye had quite the terrible fright what with them curs from Inverness chasing ye clear to *An Lochan Uaine*. Thank the heavens our lads here came along and saved ye."

So, that was the story they went with? Fair enough. Satia smiled, then made a polite dip of her chin. If she tried to curtsy with her legs still shaky from her first horse ride, she'd fall square on her arse. "I am verra thankful these fine men came to my rescue."

Patting the linen to her throat, Mairi bobbed her head. "I be Mairi, and this is my rude, eldest sister, Laoiri."

"Mairi!"

"Well?"

Satia decided then and there that Mairi was her favorite. "Pleasure to meet ye, Laoiri."

Laoiri responded with an impatient smile. "Rob says ye're in need of clothes, and I can well see it with me own eyes now that ye stand in front of us. We've already pulled together a few things to replace yer stolen items."

"Stolen?"

"Aye," both women said in unison, each giving her a curious tilt of their heads.

Laoiri continued, "Rob said those devils stripped ye down, but ye escaped before they did their terrible acts upon ye." In perfect sync, the sisters crossed themselves three times. "Right canny of ye to sneak back and steal some of their things to keep yerself covered whilst ye ran away."

Apparently, young Rob wasn't as utterly guileless as he looked. In fact, the lad was a very creative liar. Satia tossed up both hands as though surrendering. "I had to do what I could. I'm sure both of ye wouldha done the same."

"Too true," Mairi agreed, then shifted her attention to Kane. "And well done again, our Kane. Coming to the lady's rescue."

Her bottom lip trembled the slightest bit, and her soft gray eyes misted over. "Special place in Heaven for ye, my fine lad. Right there amongst the angels."

"Unca Kane!" The pair of rambunctious lassies plowed into him at full speed, latching hold of his muscular legs like a duo of wee pine martins about to scale their first tree.

"Ho, there! My favorite lambs. Did ye miss yer Uncle Kane?" He scooped them up, holding one in the crook of each arm.

"Aye, we did," said the tot on his right.

"Did ye bring us cakes?" asked the wean on his left.

"First, ye must mind yer manners and say hello." Kane turned them toward Satia. "This is Lady Satia." With a nod to his right, he added, "Lady Satia, this is Gara." He tipped his head to the left. "And this is Greer."

"Him's the only one who can tell us apart," Greer said, then patted his chest. "Did ye bring us more cakes or not?"

"We're 'posed to say *welcome* to the lady," her sister scolded before turning a chubby-cheeked smile on Satia. "Welcome, Lady Satia."

"Thank ye, Gara. I appreciate ye sharing yer home."

The little one shrugged. "We hafta. Mama says so."

"Gara!" Mairi scolded.

Satia held her breath to keep from laughing.

Kane carefully lowered them to the ground and pointed them toward Albie. "Run, see Albie. He's got yer cakes."

Satia figured the grumpy man would turn tail and run, but he welcomed the children as though they were his own. They bounced around him, yipping like tiny dogs ready for their treats. With more laughter and chattering than she thought he had in him, Albie doled out some, but not all, of the special cakes that were apparently a requirement for admission to the house.

"Come, m'lady. Meet Jennet and Anne." Mairi waved her forward. "They're finishing the wash, so the things we gathered for ye would be all fresh and clean.

Satia smiled and followed but couldn't help noticing that

Laoiri stayed behind with Kane. "I hate to be so much trouble," she said to Mairi. "But I do appreciate yer generosity." Acting as if what she wore weren't her age-old favorites, she frowned down at her jacket and jeans. "Ye can imagine the dangerous stir I might cause were I to enter a village wearing these."

"Most certainly, m'lady." Mairi gave a wide-eyed nod and led the way down to the rocky shoreline where two women squatted, scrubbing and wringing out clothes. "Jennet... Anne...I present the Lady Satia."

As soon as they both looked up, Satia saw their resemblance to Rob and the other two sisters. All the McBride family had light brown hair, gray eyes, and roundish faces blighted with red patches of rosacea across their cheeks and noses. Neither woman spoke, just studied her as if comparing her to the story their baby brother had fabricated.

"Thank ye so much for yer kindness," she said, hoping to fit in at least as long as she was here. Instinct told her they were leery of her. Laoiri especially didn't like her staying. The lass wasn't openly hostile, but that tall hen wanted Kane all to herself and would not tolerate any competition. "As I told Mairi, I am sorry to have caused ye so much trouble."

Anne rose, standing stiffly while twisting a creamy white bit of clothing between her reddened hands. "We're glad to be of help, m'lady," she said. "We understand how things can be, and this is our chance to pass along blessings we ourselves have received." As she shook out what looked like a long, linen nightgown, she sidled a step closer and lowered her voice. "Jennet doesna speak. Not since her Thomas passed."

"I am so sorry." Both for Jennet's loss of her husband and her inability to speak.

Jennet looked up, made a polite dip of her chin, then turned her attention back to sousing a large dark cloth up and down in the crystal-clear water.

A familiar awkwardness settled across Satia. She glanced all around, wishing someone or something would snatch her out of this uncomfortable situation. She had no idea how to spew idle chatter. Never had. If you looked up social awkwardness, her picture would be here. And if she didn't guard every word she said, she stood the chance of giving her unbelievable truths away and causing an even bigger mess for herself and everyone concerned.

When Jennet rose with the dripping garment and started toward a rope tied between a pair of crude posts, Satia jumped in to help. "I'll hang it to dry. I can help."

The girl's dark brows rose in surprise. After a hesitant nod, she handed over the sopping length of cloth and returned to the water's edge to submerge the next item.

Satia considered that a win. Hopefully, she had found the way to be a proper guest by helping with the chores. As she straightened the heavy gown on the line, Mairi joined her.

The matron's reproachful air made it clear Satia had erred. "Ye are our guest, m'lady, and just come from a terrible time." With a gentle but firm tug on her arm, Mairi turned her toward the open door of the dwelling. "Come. I'm sure a wee cup of honeyed wine wouldna go amiss, now would it?"

"But I can help." Satia tried to return to the shoreline, but Mairi held fast and prevented it.

"I am certain ye can, but it wouldna be proper. Not for a guest." She tugged on her again. "Come. Best enjoy the quiet as it comes. Once my lassies tire of nettling the men, they'll descend on ye next."

Satia relented, unable to resist since Mairi's determined mother-henning reminded her of Breanna. The bittersweet memory saddened her, making her swallow hard and blink fast to fight the sting of rare tears. She missed her sister so.

"Och, there now, dinna weep." Mairi wrapped an arm around her and gave a reassuring squeeze. "All will be well now. Ye are safe here." With a shy dip of her head, she patted Satia's shoulder once more before letting her arm fall away. "Forgive me, m'lady. I didna mean to be so forward, but I've never been able to resist a hurting lamb."

"Call me Satia. Or lass. Or whatever ye like." She felt an unusual affinity to this kind woman. "I promise I'm no high and mighty lady."

Mairi smiled. "Good enough then." As they stepped across the threshold, she motioned toward the long worktable on the right side of the room. A pair of sturdy benches were on either side of it and a chair on each end. "Sit ye down, lass. I'll fetch a cup for ye."

Satia seated herself on the bench between the table and whitewashed wall. Old survival habits died hard. Never did she sit with her back exposed. She smoothed a hand across the table's nicked and worn surface. This solid bit of oak held years of history. A wide hearth with stone shelving and small insets filled with cookware and supplies was centered in the back wall of the long room that made up the entire main floor of the dwelling.

A sturdy ladder to the left of the fireplace led to what Satia assumed was a loft. Patchwork blankets strung along a rope separated the farthest end from the rest of the living area. She assumed the cloth walls hid either pallets or a private place to access the chamber pot. At least she thought they used chamber pots in this time. She'd not seen an outdoor loo—only a stable for the animals.

A glance down surprised her. She had expected a dirt floor, but fitted slabs of stone peeked out from under the edges of rugs woven from rags. A pair of windows on either side of the door flooded the space with light and warmth from a southerly direction. The bright day revealed the home's spotlessness. Unattached shutter boards that fit over the windows leaned against the wall beneath them. The solid stone dwelling with dried herbs and baskets hanging from the low ceiling possessed an ancient coziness. Satia stifled a cynical snort. It might be ancient by her standards, but it wouldn't be by theirs.

Mairi placed a wooden cup in front of her and filled it with a golden liquid doled out from the chipped spout of a dark brown crockery pitcher. "Here ye are, lass. I'm sure ye're fair parched."

"Thank ye." Satia sipped at the sweet concoction. It was a pleasant respite from water or whisky.

"Are ye hungry, then?" Mairi set a metal platter covered with a cloth on the table. "We've some fried bread left from this morning." She leaned in with a knowing slant to her brow. "Ye best eat whilst ye can. Whenever the lads are here, there's nary a crumb left from one meal to the next."

"Eat ye out of house and home, do they?" Satia helped herself to the tasty bread that, even cold, was a far sight better than Albie's dry oatcakes.

With a pleased chortling, Mairi toddled around the room, wiping down already clean surfaces and adjusting the black iron pots hung over the fire. "Aye, they do take their fill. But since they always leave behind more than they take, we never complain." The frittering woman finally lit in the chair on the end of the table closest to Satia. "If ye dinna mind me staying, ye have the greenest eyes I have ever seen. Did ye get them from yer mother?"

A tingling prickle of uneasiness zipped through the hairs on the back of her neck. Satia struggled to remember the story Rob had told his sisters so she wouldn't contradict it. While living on the streets between foster homes, she and Breanna had discovered the best way to tell a convincing lie was to weave in little bits of truth. It made it more convincing. "I dinna remember the color of my mother's eyes," she finally said, then added a faint shrug. "I was only six the last time I saw her." That was the truth.

"Bless ye, lass. I am so sorry." And she was. Mairi's expressive eyes revealed her every emotion. She looked contrite and pained. "Who cared for ye? Where did ye live?"

"The church placed me in a few places. All over. Sometimes England. Sometimes Scotland." She offered Mairi a consoling smile because the more she talked, the more the soft-hearted woman looked as though she was about to leap around the table and smother her with a motherly hug. "Scotland was always the best, and as ye can see, I turned out just fine."

Mairi clutched her cleaning cloth to her mouth as though it were a kerchief to stifle sobs. "Until those bastards laid their hands upon ye. I am sure ye werena fine then."

"Aye." She couldn't say much about that since she did not know what details Rob had fabricated. "But Kane saved me." There. That was a truth, too. Sort of.

Mairi didn't speak for an uncomfortable span of time. Then she reached out and rested a hand on Satia's arm. "Ye canna know peace in yer life 'til ye find a way to lay hold of yer pain and toss it out, lass."

"What?" The woman's gentle advice made the hairs on the back of her neck stand even taller.

"I see yer troubles. The suffering. 'Tis all right there in the green of yer eyes." Mairi's brows drew together, knotting with concern and worry. "I've known a bit of pain, m'self. I am sure Kane told ye, did he not?"

Satia wasn't sure what to say, so she made herself busy with another sip of wine, then stared down at the dredges shimmering in the bottom of the cup.

"'Tis all right, lass. He warns everyone." Mairi's smile eased into a pensive frown. "'Tis how he protects me. A good man, that Kane is, a good man indeed." She pushed herself up from the table, went to the doorway, and aimed her troubled scowl outside. A gentle breeze carried the faint sound of children's laughter to them. "I wanted to die after it happened," she quietly mused. "And when the bairns first moved inside me, I hated them as much as I hated the man who put them there."

Satia bit her lip and remained silent, afraid—no, absolutely certain—if she said anything, it would be wrong. She had never experienced such a violation herself, but Breanna had, or at least come close. If Satia hadn't surprised that priest by jabbing lit candles into his eyes, twelve-year-old Bree would have been his next victim.

Mairi meandered back to her seat, her serenity returned as

she settled into the chair and folded her hands atop the table. "But when I held my sweet babes and saw the trust and innocence in their eyes, I loved them with all my heart and soul." Her smile blossomed even more as she bowed her head. "I found my peace and came to realize I could never punish them for the sins of their father."

"I admire yer strength, Mairi."

The woman smiled and tucked an escaped strand of hair back behind her ear. "We women are the strength of this world." She winked. "Dinna let anyone ever tell ye otherwise."

"Nay, stay out here," said one of the sisters just outside the window. "'Tis a fine morning for ye to help me find our best ewe. She had twins, and another is due to lamb at any time."

With a dramatic eye roll, Mairi shook her head. "Laoiri never learns."

Satia knew immediately what Mairi meant. "She loves Kane, does she?"

"She thinks she does." Mouth pursed in disapproval, the woman shook her head again. "Laoiri wishes to escape our life here and believes marrying Kane is the only way to do it."

"He said she's verra kind," Satia offered, tensing against the ridiculous jealousy stirring in her gut.

"Kane has sworn to live and die by the sword, serving the Bruce, or wherever battle is needed." Mairi stole a glance out the window, then leaned closer. "But if ye ask me, 'tis his mother's trials and her mother's before her that keeps him married to his blade rather than a woman. 'Tis the curse. Even Albie says so."

Satia couldn't resist. Besides, she could tell Mairi was dying to tell her. "What curse?"

"Kane's mother was born out of wedlock, as was he," Mairi whispered. "Both his mother and grandmother were gifted healers and followers of the old ways." She looked back at the door, then continued, "'Twas rumored their striking beauty made the old gods lust after them with so much yearning that they gifted them their amazing healing knowledge in return for their favors."

Satia's fingers wrapped tighter around her empty cup as she leaned closer. "Were they put to death for witchery?" She both dreaded and hungered for the answer.

"Nay, lass. Worse." Mairi blew out a heavy sigh. "The grandmother wasted away and died after her lover cast her aside. Kane's mother did the same. Albie said 'twas because those vile men broke their hearts. Lied to them. Always promised marriage whilst they were young and lovely. But in the end, when their beauty faded, as all beauty does, the men spurned them and said they had been nothing but whores who spared them the trouble of traveling to find a brothel." After one last glance at the door, she continued, "Kane himself said his grandmother cursed their bloodline to never know lasting love or a good marriage. She uttered the spell with her dying breath. His mother repeated it with hers."

"Wow." Satia couldn't think of anything else to say. So much superstitious belief to explain the sad consequences of two beautiful women trusting the wrong men.

"Wow?" Mairi repeated. "What is *wow*?"

"It means *oh my goodness how awful*. I picked it up in London." Satia mentally kicked herself for using twenty-first century slang.

Mairi nodded. "*Wow*, indeed."

"Does Kane have any idea who his father is?"

"'Tis believed to have been the Black Comyn though Kane has never said." Mairi gave a meaningful nod. "Scottish nobility itself, that man was."

Satia leaned back, sorting through all she had read about Robert the Bruce. "So, Kane serves the man who killed his half-brother? The Red Comyn?"

Mairi twitched a brow, her expression one of accepting karmic justice for what it was.

Jennet and Anne entered before Satia could comment further. She had always thought the past a simpler time. How deluded had she been?

"'Tis a sin to gossip," Anne gently scolded, her sternness riveted on Mairi. "Rob and Jac have taken the wee ones to help Laoiri bring in the sheep and goats. Albie's repairing the stonework of the cook pit, then says he'll be cooking us a fine venison for supper if Toff has a good hunt."

Satia noticed Anne didn't mention Kane and bit her tongue to keep from asking, since their sister had apparently called dibs on him long ago. The McBride women were sharp as double-edged blades. These women missed nothing.

Jennet retired to a low stool beside the fire and started peeling the knobby carrots and turnips she had picked from a corner basket and tucked into her apron. Before slicing into the first vegetable, she leaned forward and tapped her small knife against the iron arm holding the pot over the fire. She didn't stop clanging until everyone looked her way. Then she pointed the blade at the door and tipped a nod toward Satia.

"She wants me to leave?" Satia wondered what she had done to offend the silent Jennet.

"Nay, lass," Anne reassured. "She's merely reminding me that Kane asked if ye would join him outside—if ye feel rested enough. He said he would like to speak with ye." She cleared her throat, then gave Jennet a tight-jawed look filled with meaning. "With everyone gone to tend the sheep and us inside...ye will have a rare bit of privacy if ye see fit to talk with him now."

"I thought he was going to help find the sheep, too?"

Anne adopted the same disapproving pucker that Mairi had given her earlier. "Laoiri has enough help whether she realizes it or not."

Her attention returned to her vegetables. Jennet gave a curt nod, adding her silent agreement that the three of them considered Laoiri's efforts to snare Kane ridiculous.

That made Satia feel some better. She had never worried about being liked by anyone, but with the McBride sisters, she did. She admired them. Their friendship would be a gift. As she scooted out from the bench, she picked up her cup. "I'll give this a rinse while I'm out there."

"Nay." Mairi snatched it out of her hand. "We have a wash bucket right over there that's pining for something to clean." She shook a finger as she hurried over to a narrow table beside the hearth. It consisted of a single plank set atop a pair of large, upended logs. "And as I told ye before, ye are a guest, and guests dinna do chores." A small wooden tub sat on the makeshift counter, along with a pile of folded linens and small crocks sealed with waxed cloths and twine. Mairi swirled the cup down into the bucket, wiped it dry, then placed it on the shelf with the others. "All done. Quick as can be." She shooed Satia toward the door. "On wi' now. Best see what he wants. Men get cranky as greetin' bairns if they think they're being ignored."

Satia paused, studying each of them. She got the distinct impression they all knew more about what Kane wanted than she did but weren't about to betray their protector's trust. "Not even a wee hint from ye?" she asked Anne.

The lass's eyes flared wide, and Jennet snorted. The first sound she had made other than the racket with her knife.

Still wiping her hands on her apron, Mairi shooed Anne away with a toss of her head. "Best get started with more bread, sister. Ye ken how Jac loves it."

Anne beamed a smug smile, then hurried to the shelves to gather what she needed, acting as if Satia no longer stood in the middle of the room.

Mairi patted Satia's shoulder and nudged her toward the door. "Go and have yerself a nice visit with him, lass. I'll bring yer clothes in here beside the fire where they'll dry faster, ye ken?"

"Dinna be trying to hear what they say, Mairi!" Anne turned from the corner housing the storage shelves and glared at her sister.

Jennet thumped down a half-peeled turnip and her knife on top of an upended basket in use as a table. She darted out the door, then returned a moment later, arms filled with the wet clothes. She shoved them into Mairi's arms, then returned to her seat and vegetable peeling.

"Well, there's that done," Mairi said. She draped the garments over the rope holding the cloth curtains that divided the room. With a glance back over her shoulder, she gave Satia a pointed look. "On wi' ye now. He's a waitin'."

Satia headed out the door, completely overwhelmed by the not-so-subtle form of communication between the McBride sisters.

CHAPTER SIX

S ATIA PAUSED JUST outside the open doorway and soaked up the warm sunshine softening the bite of the blustery March day. She overheard Anne shaming Mairi for positioning herself to eavesdrop. The door closed behind her with a soft, firm thud, making Satia smile. Anne might be the youngest of the four women, but she was the motherly conscience for them all.

Loch Avon rippled a stone's throw down the gentle slope. Far enough away that if snow melt and heavy spring rains made the water rise, the dwelling should still be safe. Hands shoved in her jacket pockets, she picked her way across the rocky ground. A glance to the right revealed nothing but stark Highland wilderness, but a look to the left made her catch her breath.

Kane stood farther down the shoreline with his hands propped on his narrow hips. The southerly wind rippled the worn material of his léine tight across his muscular abs, outlining every hard, sculpted edge. Feet planted in a stance that challenged the world to doubt him, he stared across the waters, lost in his thoughts.

His long black hair whipped in the breeze, adding to the broody darkness of his scowl. She longed to brush it back and secure it either in a braid or a man bun. But she supposed that would be wrong. Too intimate. The bleak realization of just how much she would miss this man shoved her back a step. She liked Kane. Too much, too soon. And she didn't understand why. This wasn't something as simple as lust. It was a need to be with him. A yearning to be his, and for him to be hers.

She shook herself free of the dangerous soul searching and strode toward him with a forced smile. "'Tis my understanding that privacy is a rare thing in this place. Ye best hurry and tell me whatever ye wanted to say."

The smile she had hoped to trigger didn't come. If anything, his troubled expression darkened. "I promised to tell ye Albie's thoughts," he said, his voice low and ominous. He held out a hand. "Come. Walk with me."

"He's afraid I'm a danger to the group, isn't he?" Hoping to head off the storm brewing in his eyes, she took his hand, finding comfort in the strong, calloused grasp. "And I understand that." She didn't want him to think she wasn't aware of just how precarious her existence here was. "Maybe I should head back to *An Lochan Uaine* when the rest of ye continue on south." As much as it made her stomach clench to say the words, instinct told her the longer she stayed here, the harder it would be to leave—even with her reasons for returning constantly nipping at her heels.

"He isna afraid ye are a danger to the group," he said quietly, coming to a stop and turning to face her. "He is afraid ye are a danger to me."

"I would never hurt ye." But she knew that wasn't what he meant. Dangerous things flickered in his eyes. Longings that made her heart pound harder with a choking mix of fear and excitement. "I would never hurt ye," she repeated more for herself than him.

"Ye already have." He pulled in a deep breath and released it with a heavy sigh. "Yer talk of leaving pains me with the ferocity of a new blade."

"Come with me then." Why hadn't she thought of that before? It made perfect sense. Life would be grand with both Kane and Breanna in the same timeline.

He gave a frustrated snort. "This from the woman who's nay even certain she can make it back?"

"I havena tried yet. Ye wouldna let me, remember?"

"Why do ye wish me to come with ye?"

Satia swallowed hard. So far, they had danced around the proverbial elephant in the room, but now he seemed determined to make her say it. She tried to turn aside and look out across the water, but he stopped her.

"Satia." The gentle urgency in his tone made her shudder. "Why did ye ask me to come with ye?"

Fine. She would face this thing head on. "As lame and trite as it sounds, no one has ever made me feel the way ye do." She flattened a hand against the center of his chest and steadied her emotions by counting his heartbeats. "My sister would say ye have a pull to ye." She stared at her hand. The fear of baring the truth to the harsh light of day made her bite her bottom lip. "Ye are like a mag—" No. He might not know what a magnet was. "Ye are the lodestone, and I am the iron that's drawn to ye." She stole a glance upward and immediately found herself trapped in his dark gaze. "I dinna want to leave ye, but I canna stay. My sister's life might depend on it. Other lives, too." She didn't bring up the need for revenge. Somehow, that no longer seemed important.

"What do ye mean when ye say yer sister's life *might* depend on it?"

And that was another frustrating kink in the works. With any hope, Breanna's cancer might never return. But it could, and they needed to be prepared. "She was sick before. They think they cured it, but it could come back," she said. "I'm so close to a discovery that could counter it if it does. It would save her life and the lives of so many others, too."

"But ye've nay yet discovered this cure?" Poor man. He was trying his best to understand. If his brow furrowed any deeper, his expression would lock in place. Nobody had ever tried that hard to understand her before. Nobody.

"No. I havena discovered it yet." She let her hand slip from his chest. "But I am so close. I feel sure the algae from the Green Loch is the key."

"But ye are not sure?"

"Why do ye keep saying that?" She needed him to understand. Even more important, she needed him to agree to come with her. "I'll find the answer. I just need a little more time."

"But I need ye here. With me." His hands moved to her shoulders. "I canna leave here and abandon those who depend on me. Those I've sworn an oath to." He leaned in until the warmth of his breath brushed across her. The golden flecks in his rich, brown eyes sparked with dangerous fires. "Yer sister may live out her years with nary a problem. Ye said so yerself." He grazed the side of his thumb along her jaw, his gaze still locked with hers. "But my duty here is far from over."

The cold, hard irony hit her, making her eyes sting with unshed tears. "But with what I know, the difference I can make for others, I have a duty, too. In my time. Whether my sister benefits from it or not. What was that ye said about being a prisoner to pride and duty?"

"What about love?" His tone and bluntness made the word sound more like a dare than a question.

"The only love I have ever known is what I have felt for my sister." That was a lie. "Well, my sister and my little brother, Seanie."

"That is nay the sort of love of which I speak, and ye know it. I see it in yer eyes." He cupped her chin and kept her from looking away. "What about love?" he demanded.

"It scares the hell out of me because I neither know it nor trust it." She returned his fierce glare, refusing to back down. If it was a battle of wills he sought, then he would have it. "Today is only the second day I have known ye, and yet ye expect me to forget everything I have ever known. Ye want me to follow wherever ye go when ye stood right there and said ye dedicated yer life to serving others. Putting them first. Even before yerself, and I'm damned sure it would be before me, too. Why should I believe in love when it doesna even appear to be a close second on yer list of priorities? Pride, duty, and those to which ye've sold yer soul—all those come before love, aye?"

His jaw flexed, and the fullness of that kissable mouth of his twitched, telling her she had scored a direct hit.

"No answer? Tell me this then—what about yer family curse?" The last thing she wanted was to drive him away, but it had to be done. Inside, she wept for the loss of something so elusive she had never hoped to know it. But there was no other way. She had known lust. Known infatuation. She had only read about love, and that was always fiction.

With a frustrated growl, he tossed her over his shoulder, spun about, and charged back toward the cottage.

"What the devil do ye think ye're doing?" She pushed and kicked, trying to escape his hold even if he did end up dropping her. "Set me down! Now!"

"Nay, woman. If it's back to yer land ye wish to go, then go ye shall."

Before she realized what he meant, he had already planted her in the saddle and thrown himself up behind her. His blood-curdling roar carried across the land, echoing off the rocks. She didn't understand what he said. All she knew was rage and intent fueled that Gaelic cry, making it sound dark and ominous.

They raced back across the land. Northward. Back to *An Lochan Uaine*. It wasn't far. Satia guessed it at a little over seven kilometers, nearly eight. *Méirleach*'s ground-eating stride returned them a lot quicker than the previous trip going southward. Or at least it seemed that way to her.

He halted the beast just past the six burial cairns, leapt to the ground, then reached up and pulled her down. With a firm hold on her wrist, he half walked, half dragged her to the shoreline, then freed her with a hard toss of her hand. "There's yer precious loch, m'love. Godspeed to ye."

She stared at him. The hurt in his eyes burned into her heart like a strike of lightning. "Why are ye being this way?" She sidled away, not realizing she stepped into the shallows until the chill of the water lapped at her ankles. "Why are ye being so cruel? I never promised I would stay forever. Not once."

"Aye, but I thought…" His voice trailed off, and he turned and stared down at the ground.

"Ye thought what?"

"I thought ye might come to love me," he growled, sounding like a cornered beast. He glared at her with his teeth bared.

"I think I could," she admitted, knotting her fists against her middle. "But I canna abandon everything I have ever known. Not yet. You of all people should understand that."

Without looking up, he agreed with a jerking nod. "I do understand." He lifted his gaze to hers. "And I hate it."

"I do, too," she said. "And I never thought I would." She stole a glance at the dark green depths that had brought her to this impasse. "But I will come back. I promise."

"Nay. Ye will not. But I understand." Defeated resignation dripped from his words. "I am as locked to my time as ye are to yers."

Words made things worse, so she lunged forward and clung to him. Her heart broke when she realized he wasn't hugging her back. Eyes shut tight to stop the tears, she cursed fate for playing yet another cruel trick on her. Apparently, she existed only to be tormented by the gods or whatever power ruled the world. Reluctant to let him go, but knowing there was no other way, she released him, then turned and charged into the deeper water. With a hearty intake of air, she dove.

Eyes open, she swam downward into the darkness. She had no idea how deep to go. Either until she drowned or shot forward in time, hopefully, the latter. Her lungs warned her with the familiar burn. The will to survive urged her to relent and push back to the surface, but she ignored it. No. Besides, she had set fire to that fourteenth-century bridge. Determined to see the flashing lights behind her eyelids, she swam deeper, welcoming the return of the cold, numbing darkness.

Heartbeat pounding in her ears, she realized nothing felt the same as before. No flashing lights. No confusion or strange sense of displacement. Just the building terror that she was about to drown. Every fiber screamed for oxygen, bellowing to survive. She couldn't do this. Wasn't brave enough. She rolled and fought upward, not only hoping it was the right direction in the inky blackness, but also hoping she found the surface in time—no matter what century it might be.

KANE STARED AT the water, wishing he had done something, anything to stop her. He should have tied her up and thrown her over his horse. She would've hated him for it, but at least she would've still been here.

The bubbles where she disappeared beneath the surface became fewer and fewer. As each bubble frothed across the ripples and popped, his spirits did the same. He dropped to his knees and bowed his head, cursing whatever vile forces had brought him to this.

A loud, flailing splash followed by a choking sob yanked him from his inner turmoil. He sprang to his feet and charged into the water. "Satia!"

She reached for him, wheezing in great gulps of air between frustrated cries. "I couldna last through it. It wasna the same."

"Thank God." He gathered her up, kicked back to shallow water, and held her. "Thank God," he rasped again, burying his face in her wet hair as he clutched her to his chest.

"But what about Breanna? What about my research? I am so close." Her frustrated sobs held so much despair his heart broke for her. "What if she suffers because I canna get back?" She hit him, thumping her fist against him over and over. Her keening sobs shattered the peacefulness of the glade.

"Find it here." The thought came to him as if an angel whispered it in his ear. "Cure people in this time. If ye make it happen in this time, will it not make it through the ages to yer Breanna?"

Her sobbing diminished to hiccupping intakes of air. She lay against him with a hand knotted in his léine. She was plotting all she needed to do. He felt it as surely as he felt her heartbeat.

"Maybe what ye find here will grow even better over the years and prevent yer sister from getting ill the first time." He would say anything to give her hope. To help her accept staying with him. Nay, not merely accept it, but be glad of it. "Can ye not do yer work here? Somehow?"

"I am not a physician," she said, but her tone seemed less despondent. "I have no equipment. Nothing to isolate the strand."

He didn't understand but also didn't care. She was back. That was all that mattered. "Ye're a canny, lass." He nudged a reassuring kiss to her forehead. "Wiliest woman I know. Ye will find a way. *We will* find a way."

She peered up at him. A calm determination appeared to be taking her over. "Do ye know of any healers I might work with? Someone with an understanding of physiology?"

"Physiology?" The words she uttered reminded him of the dreaded Latin his mother had tried to teach him. "What is *physiology*?" It sounded like a fatal ailment.

She didn't answer, just looked aside, her lovely mouth tensing into a worried line as she stared off into the distance.

"Satia?"

"Let's get out of this water, aye?" A violent shivering shook her in his arms. "Can we build a fire?"

He carried her to shore. "I'll get us a blaze going in no time. Stand here next to *Mèirleach*. He'll block the wind off ye." With a yank of a strap, he freed a pair of rolled blankets, shook one out, and wrapped it around her. Before stepping away, he tipped her face up to his. "I willna lie and say I am sorry ye are still here.

Even though I know ye suffer with all ye've lost. I am sorry for yer pain, but I wouldna give ye up because of it." He gently touched his forehead to hers and closed his eyes. He knew his words sounded as though he didn't give a damn about anyone but himself, but he couldn't help it. "Forgive me, Satia. I fear I have become a verra a selfish man because of ye."

"It's all right." She rested a hand on his arm. "I miss Breanna. My work." She gave a soft sniff. "I miss silly things I never thought I would ever miss." A heavy sigh escaped her. "But I am glad I havena lost ye after all."

He offered her the kiss he had hungered for since the last one. One tasting would never be enough with Satia. "Ye willna regret it," he promised, whispering the oath against her mouth.

"Aye, but ye might." She pushed away and gave him a half-hearted smile. "Build us a fire so we can get these wet clothes off, aye? This is two days in a row I've been chilled to the bone."

He paused, unsure how to tell her he had no dry things for her. Upon their arrival at the McBrides', Rob had relieved the horses of their extra baggage, offloading the goods and supplies brought for his sisters. All that remained behind the saddles were the rolled blankets strapped to them. The sisters always insisted on giving each man's things a good wash and mending if needed. 'Twas their way of showing gratitude and a matter of pride to them. "I have no dry clothes for ye this time."

With a meaningful glance, she gathered the blanket closer. "I guess we'll have to wrap up tight together until everything's dry."

Her suggestion spurred him to gather wood and tinder at a fast gallop. With his fire steel, flint, and a bit of spongy touch-wood, he knelt and peeled off a fine smoldering spark with the first strike. Satia dropped beside him and blew on the glowing strands until a tiny flame erupted.

With a sideways glance at him, she smiled. "I thought I would help. Ye dinna mind, do ye?"

If it got her out of those clothes faster, she could do anything she liked. But he didn't say that. Instead, he smiled his encouragement and fed small sticks, then larger pieces of wood to the flames. As the blaze crackled and popped, growing ever larger, he peeled off his léine and spread it across the nearest bush. He had started the fire as close as safely possible to a semicircle of young pines and tangled undergrowth sturdy enough to hold their clothes.

A flash of creamy white skin beside him made him turn and lock in place.

With her puffy surcoat, her faded tartan tunic, and the strange, long-sleeved shift slung over one arm, Satia was bare from the top of her trews up. All except for a delicate band of lace and ribbon encasing the mouth-watering temptation of her breasts. Smallish but more than enough to make his palms itch to caress their roundness.

He swallowed hard as she spread the clothes across the bushes. His mouth went dry as she undid her trews by rubbing on a strange bit of metal that hissed like a tiny adder guarding her crotch. As she peeled them down off her body, shook them out with a snap, and draped them across the limbs, his cock hardened to the point of making him bite back a groan.

With nothing but an inviting smile, the flimsy covering across her breasts, and a teasing bit of silk and lace cradling her lady parts, Satia hugged herself, scrubbing her arms for warmth. Before she turned back and faced the fire, he caught sight of her nipples puckered to tantalizingly hard points. He almost dropped to his knees.

"We'd both be much warmer on the blanket," she said, reaching toward the flames as she walked around the blaze. "Or are ye staying on that side to dry out?"

He kicked off his boots, shucked his trews, and met her on the second wool plaid she had spread for them to share. "I am nay a fool, love." He took her in his arms and lowered them both to their knees. Her pensive look gave him pause. "Tell me, Satia. Let there be no secrets between us."

She rested a hand on his cheek, running the tips of her fingers along the edge of his jaw and tickling her nails through the stubble. "I will never be the sort of woman ye are accustomed to." She studied him as if weighing every word she was about to say. She shook her head. "I will never be like the McBrides." She added a soft, sad snort. "I wish I could. I admire them."

"I dinna wish ye to be anyone but yerself." He struggled to make her understand. "I canna imagine ye trying to mold yerself into anything ye're not—nor would I want ye to do so."

One of her dripping curls released a bead of water, sending it rolling down her cheek. He brushed it away, then pushed her hair back from her face. "Just be yerself and let me love ye."

Her eyes widened, and her pale pink lips parted. "Love me?" Her shock surprised him.

"Aye," he said, pouring every ounce of sincerity he possessed into it. He eased her back onto the blanket, settled over her, and challenged the uncertainty dancing in her eyes. He would remove all doubt between them. "Let me love ye," he repeated in a soft whisper. "And I nay merely speak of bed play."

"Ye dinna even know me. We just met." She slid a leg around him, tickling his calf with her toes. "How can ye speak of love already?"

"I know enough when I look in yer eyes." He paused and pressed a tender kiss over each of them. "I see the woman I met just a day ago, and yet I have known ye all my life. All my lives, in fact, down through the ages." He nibbled across her parted lips. "I know nothing of ye, and yet I know everything. And I know I need to love ye." He lifted his head and locked eyes with hers. "Or be forever lost."

"My Highland warrior," she murmured, arching into him as she wrapped both legs around him and squeezed. "So, I have won ye then?"

He couldn't resist a grin as he reveled in the soft, feral length of her beneath him. She was brash and fearless, but beneath it all, she had a vulnerability he couldn't resist. She needed him as much as he needed her, whether she admitted it or not. "Ye have most certainly won me, m'lady."

"Woe be unto ye, my brave man." She framed his face with both hands, then slid her fingers into his hair and pulled him down for a kiss. "Love away my pain then," she whispered. "Help me through the loss of my precious sister and all I have left behind. Distract me."

He didn't answer. Instead, he did as she bade, trailing his hands across the velvet of her skin. Chilled by wind and water, she warmed to his touch. Her heartbeat tapped faster against his lips as he nibbled his way down her throat, across her collarbone, then peppered kisses along the border of the lace barrier covering her breasts. He raised up the slightest bit and studied it. No laces. How the devil did the thing come off? It was like a part of her. A layer of tantalizing armor meant to addle him.

"It unhooks," she explained with a wry grin as if enjoying his dilemma.

"Unhooks?"

She pinched the front of it, then twisted where the pale pink ribbons crossed. "Unhooks," she repeated as the sides sprang away, revealing all her glory.

"Ye can show me more later," he said and set to skimming the tip of his tongue across her, reveling in the sweetness of her taste.

Her subtle giggling vibrated the smooth firmness of her breast against his mouth. She cradled his head in her arms, helping him find his way. "There's verra little left to show ye, sir. All the covering I have left are my panties."

"Panties," he repeated, mouthing the word around her nipple. He slid his hand down her torso, caught his fingers in the barrier of lacy nothingness, and yanked them off.

"Ye've ruined them," she scolded, but sounded more pleased than angry. "Now what shall I do for panties?"

"Ye will wear none." An appreciative groan escaped him as he sank into her slippery, hot wetness. She raked her nails down his back and clenched his buttocks with both hands, emitting a breathless growl as she did so. He took that as encouragement to move faster. Pound harder. She agreed, meeting him thrust for thrust.

Belatedly, he remembered he had intended to love her slowly. Savor her. But nay, not this first time. He burned to possess her, claim her fully, drive all doubt from her. And he needed. God, how he needed. He bellowed her name.

"Yes!" she answered, clenching tighter.

Head thrown back and arms locked, a guttural roar exploded from him. Every fiber pulsing with excruciating ecstasy, he shuddered and spent himself inside her. He collapsed, taking care not to crush her as he buried his face in the crook of her neck.

She wrapped her arms around him and held him tight. The pounding of her heart paired with her gasps for air made him attempt to roll off her, but she stopped him. "No."

"I dinna wish to crush ye, m'love."

"I like the feel of ye pressing down on me. Covering me." She tucked her cheek tighter to his. "I feel safe like this." She paused, then added so softly he almost didn't hear, "Dinna leave me."

"I will never leave ye, dear one. Not ever." Sparks popped from the fire, catching his attention. He heaved a despondent sigh. "But the fire needs more wood."

"Leave it a little while longer." She tickled her fingers up and down his sides. The renewed hunger in her eyes was unmistakable. "We can warm ourselves another way, then fetch more wood. The coals will still be hot enough to catch."

"That they will, m'love," he agreed and lowered his head for a long, slow kiss. Who was he to argue with the lady?

CHAPTER SEVEN

"WE COULDHA SPENT the night at the loch." Satia relaxed back against him, much more at ease than her first time on the horse.

"Ye're stomach kept growling." Kane nuzzled through her curls to flick his tongue along the soft, sweet skin just behind her ear. "We'll reach the McBrides' in time for supper. I'll nay be accused of making ye go hungry."

"I've gone hungry before and lived to tell about it." She spoke as though such a thing was commonplace.

"When?" It came to him that other than the strange words about her labors and her sister Breanna, he knew very little about her. She had also mentioned a brother. But only once.

"Breanna and I lived on the streets of London for a while. As young teens."

"Young teens?"

"Actually, preteens. I think we were eleven or twelve." She shifted with an uneasy shrug. "Not a happy time, so I try not to think about it."

"Ye had no family or clan to care for ye?" What little she revealed about her past explained the occasional flinty hardness to her gaze.

"Seanie was my only family. For a little while anyway."

"Seanie?"

"My little brother." She flexed, arching her back as if the memory cut through her middle. "He was three and I was six when the care workers took us away." Even though he couldn't see her face, he heard the angry scowl in her voice. "Seanie got adopted straight off, and I never saw him again." Her shoulder twitched another tensed shrug as if shaking off the uncomfortable memories. "The carers said I would never get adopted. Too mean and nothing but trouble." She snorted a humorless laugh. "Turned out they were right." She pulled in a deep breath and blew it out. "At least the system paid for my time at university, though. A good part of it, anyway."

The more he learned about her, the more he wanted to hold her and heal her from all she had suffered. He tightened his arm around her waist. "I have always loved troublemakers," he said, trying to ease the tense silence that had settled around them. Ghosts of the past were strong, wicked things that couldn't be allowed to linger, lest they taint the present.

"Well, I am one." A shudder rippled her against him as if she shook herself to shed the troubling conversation. "What about ye? Mairi told me about yer Mam and Grandmam."

"I am sure she did. That woman's tongue wags at both ends."

"Aye, but she's good-hearted. I think she did it to make sure I understood ye weren't an average Scot."

"An average Scot?" He wasn't sure if she meant that as an insult or not.

"Ye know—castles, clans, and cèilidhs." Her head tilted to the side, a sure warning that whatever she was thinking was about to come out. He had already discovered that about her. "Seems to me, ye're as much an orphan as I am."

"I suppose so." He would rather agree than delve into the memories of growing up with a father who never called him anything but bastard and also toyed with his mother until he found a younger mistress. Time to change the conversation. "We usually tarry a few days at the McBrides'. Ensure they have everything they need. Help with any repairs they canna do themselves."

She didn't answer. Just straightened again, as though suddenly uncomfortable.

"D'ye need to stop, lass?"

"No." She fidgeted again. "I guess I'm bracing myself for the inevitable." She tossed a glance back at him, sharing her frown. "Albie willna be happy to see ye've returned with me and neither will Laoiri. Far as I'm concerned, Albie can bugger off, but I dinna wish to make the McBrides unhappy. I like them."

"The sisters ken well enough that Laoiri's hopes about my affections are in vain." He had politely declined their sister's advances, but the lass refused to listen. The other three seemed willing enough to accept that he considered them sisters. He wished Laoiri would accept it, too. "And I will have words with Albie."

"I understand his concerns," she said, easing back against his chest once again. "I've read about the witch hunts."

"With proper clothing and minding yer words, there'll be nothing for any of us to fear." He hoped. Her foretellings had both thrilled and frightened the men, and they gossiped worse than a gaggle of old washerwomen.

"The clothes aren't what worry me." She cast another leery glance back at him. "Keeping my mouth shut could be a problem. I have never done well in that arena."

He knew better than to comment. His mother had not raised a fool.

"I dinna remember ye saying if there were any healers I might work with," she said, thankfully changing the direction of the conversation.

Kane pondered the matter. Mam and Grandmam had been the best healers he had ever known. Sadly, their arts had been lost upon their deaths. He supposed the next finest healer would be the friar who not only tended the Bruce but also took care of injured men after battles. "The Bruce keeps Friar Law. That man uses herbs and poultices. And finer stitching to close a wound can nary be found."

"Friar Law," she repeated. "That's an odd name."

"Fits the man. He's odd as they come." The thudding gallop of an approaching rider made him halt their pace. "I need ye behind me, lass. Now."

With impressive agility, Satia held tight to his arm and swung around to settle in behind him. "Scoot up, will ye?"

"Ye are an amazing woman." He gave her more room while drawing his sword.

"Aye, well, remember that the next time ye feel like snapping my neck because I've angered ye." She peered around him. "Isn't that Albie?"

The sun glinting off the man's bald head gave him away every time. A deadly mix of alarm and dread churned through Kane as he debated whether or not he should keep his blade readied. For Albie to seek them out, something had to be wrong. "What is it, man?"

With a scowl as dark as a thundercloud, Albie came to a halt and glared at him but didn't speak.

"Tell it now. All of it." Kane read the old fool as easily as he read the stars, but he would hear the words from the man's own lips.

"I came to see with me own eyes the decision ye made." Lips pulled back in a sneer that wrinkled his thin weathered cheeks, Albie glared at him. "I warned ye, and yet, here ye are. With her."

"I have known ye since I was a wean." Kane rested his hand on Satia's arm, where it wrapped around his middle. "Ye brought food to Mam and Grandmam when we had none. Always saw us taken care of." He struggled to keep his tone even. He owed Albie a great deal but didn't owe him his chance at future happiness. "But in this, ye are wrong and have no say in it. Do ye understand me?"

"Ye will risk everything for her? Ignore the curse and end up suffering for it?"

"*Her* is not deaf or mute," Satia said, leaning around to poke a finger at him. "And curses only have power if ye give it to them. If ye dinna believe in a curse, it will die and go away."

"Ye are wrong, woman." Albie spit on the ground, then bared his yellowed teeth even more.

"Not this time," she countered.

The frustrated man tossed up a hand and turned his horse. "Do what ye will, then. The both of ye. Ye've been warned."

"So, ye were tracking him down to see if he needed help getting rid of the body? Is that it?" Satia taunted Albie like an angry bairn spoiling for a fight.

"Dinna nettle him, lass." Kane gave her arm a gentle pat. "Albie means well."

"Bollocks." She went quiet for the moment.

"I came to console him, if ye must know." The growling old Highlander turned his horse again and faced them. "I know the pain of a love that doesna happen." He cast another surly twitch of his eyes their way. "Them McBride sisters didna tell me ye had ridden away until I finished repairing the cook pit. I heard yer roaring, but when I cast a weather eye all around and saw nothing amiss, I shrugged it off, figuring ye had finally seen sense about the woman."

"My name is Satia. Stop calling me *the woman*. I know what ye mean when ye say that. Ye might as well call me a bitch to my face and be done with it. Or do ye not have the bollocks for it?"

Kane clenched his teeth to keep from laughing. Albie didn't respond to confrontation with females well. 'Twould be interesting to see how he reacted.

The man's eyes flared wide, then narrowed to angry slits. His face turned a bright red as he sputtered and spit. "I am off to the McBrides' ahead of ye. I have venison to put on the fire." With a guttural roar, he thundered away at a hard gallop.

"Arse!" Satia shouted after him.

Kane bowed his head. "I need a promise from ye, lass." He

braced himself, hoping she wouldn't turn on him next.

"He doesna like me, so I willna like him. Not ever."

"All I ask is that the two of ye try to be civil, ye ken? If he doesna try, I shall handle it. I ken he's a foul-tempered, rude bastard, but he's a braw warrior, a fine cook, and a somewhat talented healer. We need him traveling with us."

"I can be civil." But she didn't sound as though she believed it herself.

"'Tis all I ask." He could tell by her tone that it would be futile to ask for anything more.

"Well, at least the Albie confrontation I was dreading is out of the way," she said. "Reckon Laoiri will be as pleasant as he was?"

"Who's to say." As they emerged from the pass, he noticed several sheep and goats dotting the hillside behind the McBride dwelling and close to the stable. With the animals brought in so close, that meant Laoiri would be waiting to greet them. "It appears we are about to find out."

He tethered *Mèirleach* with the other horses, noting they had already been brushed and fed. "If ye wish, go inside whilst I see to the lad here." He bent to unbuckle the saddle.

"Ye have lost yer mind if ye think I'm going in there alone. Hell hath no fury and all that rot, remember?" She peered closer at what the other horses were eating. "What is that?"

"Horsebread. And what do ye mean *Hell hath no fury and all that rot?*" He nodded toward a cloth sack hanging from a stub sticking out of a nearby tree trunk. "Fetch him three. He's a big lad with a hearty appetite."

She fished three loaves from the bag, brought one close to her nose, and sniffed. "Interesting." Then she shrugged. "I dinna ken if it's been written yet. Probably not. But the saying goes, 'Hell hath no fury like a woman scorned.'"

That made perfect sense, and he heartily agreed. He slowed the brushing; might as well enjoy a bit of peace before the storm.

"So, do I break them up and put them on the ground in front of him?"

"Aye, lass. That'll do nicely." The longer he brushed the horse, the more cowardly he felt. When the guilt became too great to bear, he tossed the brush back to the base of the tree and fetched the sack of feed. If not kept in the dry, the horsebread would grow moldy and unfit for the animals to eat. A strong, healthy horse was as important as a well-honed blade. A heavy sigh escaped him as he waved Satia forward. "Come. Let us get this behind us."

"Be tactful," she said with a pointed glance.

"Tactful," he repeated, shooting a hard look right back at her. "So, now ye're an expert on tact?"

She grinned. "No. Just a casual observer."

He opened the door and held it. "Tactful," he muttered a second time under his breath.

Satia landed a sharp elbow in his gut and paired it with a warning arch of a brow. Then she came to a halt and clamped her mouth shut as if to stop a torrent of words even she knew she shouldn't say.

Kane followed her line of sight and immediately understood. Laoiri sat on the bench with her right leg stretched out in front of her and her foot bared. Ever quiet Jac sat behind her, holding her steady as Albie wrapped a steaming bandage around her ankle. "What happened?"

"I twisted my ankle trying to get that fool goat to come down from the point," Laoiri said. Her eyes went soft, and she leaned back to cradle Jac's furiously blushing face in her palm. "Dear Jac here carried me all the way back. I dinna ken what I wouldha done without him."

"'Twas n-nothing, really." Jac stared at him. Something akin to fear and pleading shone in his eyes and shouted from the set of his shoulders. "I couldna leave her there."

"She'll be fine." Albie gave a curt dip of his grizzled chin, then stood and carried the bowl to the window and emptied it of its murky contents. "I sent Rob to find her a sturdy stick to help with her walking for a day or so."

"I'll be needing help with the animals." Laoiri lounged even more across poor Jac. "Ye'll help me with them, aye?"

"Aye, mistress." The ruddy-haired man swallowed hard and looked as though he'd rather march to the gallows. "Leastwise 'til it's time for us to head to Edinburgh."

"I think we can stay here a day or so longer," Kane said, not giving one whit that doing so would doom Jac to Laoiri's cloying attentions. Better the lad than himself. Better by far, indeed. "In fact, if ye wish to stay on here for a bit instead of joining the Bruce in Edinburgh, I feel sure we can spare ye."

"That would be so helpful." Laoiri scooted back tighter against the poor lad. The lass was ready to close in on her prey. "So verra helpful."

Mairi rounded the table with a knowing scowl aimed at Kane. She knew exactly what he was doing and why. "We shall see. Serving the Bruce is a great deal more important than keeping track of goats and sheep." She took hold of Satia's arm and steered her toward the curtained-off area of the room. "The things we washed for ye are good and dry now. Jennet even looked them over for any extra mending they needed. Come, lass, I'm sure ye're more than a little ready to get back into proper attire rather than those things ye're wearing."

If Satia's smile tensed any tighter, the lass's lovely face would surely shatter. Kane gave her a polite nod, not trusting himself to speak. He had grown accustomed to her strange, immodest clothing, but if they were to keep her safe, she had to dress like a proper Highland woman. *A proper Highland woman.* He allowed himself a grin. Satia would never be a proper Highland woman, and he was glad.

"SHALL I BURN them?" Mairi held up Satia's favorite jeans, studying the metal zipper and brads. "And they're wet as can be.

Did a rain catch ye? It didna rain here." Before Satia could attempt an answer, she continued, "Such strange fastenings. Wonder where those murderous dogs came up with these?"

Satia unfastened her bra, wiggled it off before removing her thermal shirt, and shoved it under a pallet before Mairi turned to gather the rest of her clothing. She could never come up with a story to explain the bra. She wasn't that creative.

"I dinna ken where they got these clothes." She peeled off the shirt, handed it over, and covered herself as best she could with her folded arms. "I was just thankful to have them."

Mairi gave a slow nod and scooped up the down jacket, plaid flannel shirt, and thermals. "Too true. There is always something to be thankful for." She ran her thumb back and forth across the slick nylon material of the jacket. "We should keep this for ye." Then her eyes flared wide, compassion shimmering in their depths. "Unless it would haunt ye with troublesome memories. But a good warm coat is always a boon, ye ken?"

"I think I could bear to keep all the clothing. Waste not, want not—right?" She hoped Mairi would agree. Thermals and jeans under her skirts in the dead of winter would keep her warmer. The idea startled her, then sank to the pit of her stomach and triggered a sickly gurgle. She really was trapped in the fourteenth century. A hard swallow did little to sway a sudden onrush of nausea.

"Waste not, want not," Mairi repeated. "Well said, indeed." The matron hung everything to dry on the roped wall of cloth.

"Mama!" The hanging blankets rippled as if about to be pulled back.

Satia snatched up the linen shift and covered herself as best she could.

"If ye open that curtain, I'll smack yer bum for ye, Gara Elizabeth. We have men in this house, remember?" Mairi blocked the way, fisting the panels closed with such a tight grip her plump knuckles whitened.

"Greer willna let me pet her lamb," the tot whined.

"Tell yer Uncle Rob." Mairi turned and winked at Satia. "He'll know right what to do about that."

"Unca Rob!" The wee lassie's pattering steps faded off into the distance. The slamming of the door completed her departure.

"Will Rob know what to do?" Satia had to ask since Rob seemed barely capable of taking care of himself most of the time, much less refereeing a battle between the twins.

"Nay. He willna have a notion what to do." Mairi's wicked, sisterly chuckle set her to jiggling. "But it's good for him. Readies him for when he has bairns of his own." She held out a pair of stockings and knitted ribbons. "Anne knitted these. Wool came from our verra own sheep. Their first shearing. Have ye ever felt such softness?"

"Oh my." Satia remembered the unaffordable price tag on the fine cashmere scarf she had lusted after every time she passed the shop window on her way to the lab. While these stockings weren't cashmere, they felt just as soft. She tried to hand them back. "I canna take these. They're much too dear. I can wear these socks once they're good and dry. 'Tis no trouble. I promise."

"A proper lady must have her stockings." Mairi pushed them back. "Now slip them on and get the ties good and tight whilst I get the kirtle ready to slip over yer head." She added a pleased nod toward the shift Satia had already donned. "It fits ye better than any of us. Almost as if it was made for ye."

As Satia smoothed her hands down the crisp stiffness of the cloth, she realized the generous women had provided her with the newest linen shift they possessed. It would take several washings for the undergown to soften. "Ye've been so kind," she said. "All of ye." She wished she could make them realize just how much their kindness meant to her. After securing the hosiery with a tight bow above each knee, she pulled on the slippers Jac had made for her back at the camp. Still a bit damp but dry enough, the sight of the soft leather shoes made her smile. "Jac made these. If Laoiri catches him, she'll never want for fine footwear."

Mairi cast a weary gaze heavenward. "God help that poor lad. He'll nay be able to slip her noose as easily as Kane did." With the dark blue kirtle bunched over both her arms, she wiggled her fingers, motioning Satia toward her. "Bend forward, and I'll slip it on over yer head. This one's a mite snug on all of us but should do well enough for yer trim figure."

Satia wasn't all that keen on being dressed like a favorite doll, but while wiggling into the fitted bodice and tight sleeves, she was grateful for Mairi's help. She wasn't all that sure she could've managed this alone. Which made her wonder who she could recruit for help once they left the McBrides. A wicked idea tickled a smile across her lips. Kane could help her.

"Ye're grinning like my wee ones when they think they've gotten away with sneaking into the dried fruit." Mairi glanced back at the entry to the curtained-off room and stepped closer. "Dinna hurt him, lass. Please?" Her motherly smile faded. "He hasna had an easy way of it and is the kindest man ye will ever hope to know."

Satia didn't answer, just stared at the woman.

"I see how he looks at ye," Mairi said. "We all have. His men included." Her tone held the ominous ring of a stern warning.

"So, who do ye side with?" For the first time since meeting the woman, Satia guarded her words more closely, fearing they would somehow be used against her. She had figured the McBride sisters to be potential friends. Perhaps she had relaxed her leeriness too quickly. "Are ye in Albie's camp?"

"Camp?" The matronly lass cocked her head. Confusion knotted her feathery brows. She stepped closer and lowered her voice. "I dinna ken of what camp ye speak. All I know is that we cherish Kane and care about him. I told ye of his mam and grandmam, and the lonely curse he's lived under since he was a bairn. Now I'm pleading with ye to be kind to him. If ye love him and keep him safe, we McBrides will be yer greatest allies. But if ye use him for whatever purpose suits ye, then ye will find us quite the enemy."

"I would never purposely hurt him." Guilt pricked at her conscience as she remembered the failed attempt at returning to her time. "I care about him, too."

"Do ye love him?"

"I havena known him long enough to love him." If not for the fact that Mairi had her cornered between a pair of cots, she would end this interrogation by fleeing. As it was, unless she dove around the wide-hipped maid and bounded across the narrow beds, she had no escape. "I do care about him," she repeated, hoping that would make the bull-doggish woman heel and leave her alone.

"Love doesna take a set amount of time to take root." Mairi widened her already broad stance by planting her fists on her hips and flaring her bent elbows like the wings of a cargo plane. "Does he have a pull to him? Does he draw ye in?"

"A pull?" The idea of launching herself across the top of the beds grew more appealing by the minute.

"Aye, a pull." Mairi shifted as if sensing Satia's plan. "A kinship with him? As if ye've known him longer than a mere few days?"

"Well...yes, if ye must know. I've felt that way since I first laid eyes on him." She shooed the woman off to the side, doing her best to sidle around her. "Can I go now? Ye're making me claustrophobic."

Mairi's triumphant smile shifted back to the confused puckering of earlier. "I am making ye what?"

"Trapped." Satia struggled to recover from the slip. "It's sort of Latin for panicking when in a small space."

"Latin, ye say?" Mairi tipped her head to one side as though impressed. "So, ye're an educated woman, then?"

Uncertain whether that was good or bad, Satia finally relented and managed a shy nod. "Some."

With a firm shake of her head, Mairi angled to one side and made more space between them. "Ye would do well to hide that, lass." Her tone rang with sincere warning. "Men dinna like it when we seem smarter than them." She leaned closer and lowered her voice again. "Even when we are."

"I will bear that in mind." Satia remembered that many men and women back in her time still fostered that mindset. She rubbed her knuckles across the tight weave of the medium-weight wool gown that had been dyed the deepest shade of blue. This, too, would be quite the pricey item in her time. "Thank ye for everything, Mairi. I know I seem a bit odd, but I do appreciate ye opening yer home to me and sharing yer things."

"Ye're nay odd, lass." Mairi pushed back the curtains, opening the space to the rest of the room. She glanced back and smiled. "Ye're special. And that's exactly what our Kane needs. A special lady." She turned to those still gathered in the room and spoke louder. "The blue makes the green of her eyes even lovelier. D'ye not think so?"

Still trapped by Laoiri lounging back against him, Jac agreed with a quick nod, then froze when he spotted Laoiri's narrow-eyed scowl. Poor man. He might as well marry her and get it over with. Anne and Jennet gave approving smiles, and Albie stomped out the door, then slammed it behind him.

Kane strode forward, scooped up her hand, and kissed it. "Loveliness itself," he said in a voice meant for her alone.

"Thank ye," she whispered, amazed at how sinking into the depths of his gaze could make everything around them disappear.

"Shall we go for a stroll, m'lady?" He tucked her hand into the crook of his elbow before she even agreed. "Nothing makes a supper taste so fine as a brisk walk before it."

His mention of supper booted her conscience. "Should I not help with the preparations?"

"Albie's seeing to the meat," Mairi said while lifting a cover off the pot on the fire and stirring whatever bubbled within. "Jennet's vegetables are coming along nicely, and Anne's bread will soon be done." She straightened and cast a scathing look at Laoiri. "And Laoiri can lay the table, whether she believes it or not. That is, if she can stop draping herself across poor Jac." Mairi clapped her hands and made her sister jump. "Up off him now, Laoiri, afore ye cripple the dear lad by cutting off the feeling to his legs. I've seen ye limp through twisted ankles afore." She aimed an arched brow first at Satia, then at Kane. "I believe she twisted her fine fat foot once last summer and had to be carried back by Kane—did she not?"

Kane grinned and headed out the door without answering. Once outside, the tensed muscles of his arm relaxed beneath her fingers. "God help, Jac," he said as they ambled toward the shoreline.

"That's what Mairi said." Satia plucked at the folds of her gown while trying to lean forward to see if it dragged across the rocks. The last thing she wished to do was muddy the hem. That would just be rude. "Should I hold it up so it doesn't brush the ground? I dinna want them thinking I dinna appreciate their generosity. Do ye know how much a gown like this would cost in my time?" Without waiting for his answer, she held up a fold and ran her thumb across it. "This fine a weave with such a rich dye and authentic to the time period would cost well over a hundred and fifty pounds."

He came to a halt and frowned down at her. "As amazing as that is, ye must not speak of it, ye ken? For yer own safety."

His gentle scolding hurt. Not because he seemed cruel, but because he was right. And because he cared. "Sorry." She smoothed out her skirts and stared downward. "I know ye're right." She shrugged and slipped her hand from his arm, edging sideways to put some space between them. "I shall try to do better."

"Satia."

"Dinna say my name like that. I am not a child." She sidled farther away, locking her gaze on the clear, rippling waters. Treating her like a child brought back the memories. The abandonment. Not knowing what would come at her next. Old demons she knew all too well. "I dinna belong here, Kane. I shouldha tried harder to stay under until it sent me to my time."

He stepped behind her and hugged her back against him. "Ye said yerself it wasna the same. If ye had stayed under any longer, ye wouldha died." His embrace tightened, and he rubbed his cheek against hers. "This world would be a darker place without ye." His whisper made her shiver. "I dinna want to think about that," he added so quietly she almost missed it.

No one had ever said such things to her—not even when trying to take advantage of her or run a con. His words both thrilled and terrified her, and she hated that as well. She always prided herself on never being afraid of anything, but damned if this century and this man didn't scare the living shite out of her. "This place makes me afraid," she confessed. "There's nothing I hate more than a cowardly person, and I have become one here."

He shifted with a heavy sigh, the warmth of his breath tickling against her neck. "I have known many a coward in my time. Trust me when I say ye are not one of them." He stepped back and turned her, tilting her face up to his. His voice deepened to a sorrowful pitch, like the tolling of a death knell. Pain and loneliness shadowed the richness of his brown eyes. "I am not enough for ye. Am I?"

"Dinna say such a thing." An avalanche of emotions caught in her throat, burning her eyes with stubborn tears that refused to be abated. She never cried, and she hated that, too. "Ye are more than I deserve." She cupped his cheek and rested her thumb in the cleft of his chin—easily finding it through the stubble of his beard. "Ye are a lot more than I deserve. Trust me."

With a swipe of his fingers, he wiped the wetness from her cheeks and gifted her a sad smile that made her weep even harder. "Ye are mine," he said softly. "And I am yers. That is all that matters. We will find our way to a steadfast love. Together."

She buried her face in his chest and hugged him with all her might. By jings, she would conquer this century one way or another for Kane.

CHAPTER EIGHT

"HOLD IT LIKE this." Satia held up her hands with her fingers outspread. A single loop of dark blue yarn wrapped around the thumbs and pinky fingers of both her hands and stretched taut between them. "Now slide your middle finger under the loop across this palm, then this middle finger under the loop across the other palm. Now, pull yer hands back apart. See? Ye've made a cat's cradle."

The twins watched her intently, then mimicked her moves. Gara succeeded. Greer's string slipped and got tangled in her chubby little fingers. "Shite!"

"Greer Marianna!" Mairi rose from the bench, snatched the child up from her stool, and swatted her bum. "To yer cot with ye. Young ladies dinna use such words, and ye know it."

"But—"

Mairi silenced her with a stern look and pointed at the sleeping area beyond the curtains. After the wee one stomped out of sight, Mairi spun and cuffed Rob on the back of his head. "How many times have I told ye to watch yer tongue around them?"

With an agile move to keep from getting hit again, Rob pointed at Toff then Jac. "I didna do it. 'Twas one of them, ye mean cow." He turned and nudged Anne. "Tell her, Anne. Did ye not hear their coarse talk earlier?"

"Fight yer own battles, Rob," Anne said without looking up from her mending.

"Jennet?" Rob rose from his seat and angled himself between her and Laoiri for protection.

Jennet rolled her eyes and pushed him away.

Before he continued, Laoiri shoved her hand in his face, then reached over and patted Jac's shoulder. "Ye need to be more like my Jac, here. Sweet-tempered and soft-spoken as the day is long."

Satia noticed that soft-spoken Jac looked ready to vomit. "Are ye all right, Jac? Did yer supper not sit well?"

The redheaded hunk pried himself free of Laoiri's clutches and hurried to the door. "I need to step outside for a bit."

A moment later, Kane entered with an armload of wood. "Jac doesna look well, Albie. Reckon ye could fix him a tonic?"

Adjusting the angle of the small chunk of wood beneath the blade of his knife, Albie kept his focus on his carving. "No tonic exists that'll help that lad."

Mairi nudged Gara up from her stool and shooed her toward the sleeping area. "Off to bed with ye, as well, my wee one. The hour is later than I realized."

"But I didna say *shite* like Greer did," the little one whined, locking her legs to slow her mother's progress in getting her to her cot.

Mairi crossed herself while muttering under her breath as she scooped up the lass and carried her the rest of the way.

Satia neatly piled the loops of yarn on the table, then angled for a spot beside a window, hoping a little fresh air might waft in through the narrow openings around the ill-fitting shutter. Upon their arrival, she had thought the small cottage cozy and comforting, but with all of them crammed inside the one room, it reminded her of the London Underground during rush hour. "I think I'll step outside for some air, too."

"Stay away from my Jac," Laoiri called out, her tone sharp with jealousy. When she realized everyone's attention had shifted to her, she cleared her throat and continued in a much softer voice. "He is shy a lad, ye understand. If he's ill, I'm sure he'll wish to be alone and not burden ye with his troubles."

"I promise I have no intention of bothering Jac." Satia hurried to the door to keep from saying that the man would eventually escape unless Laoiri chained him to her bedpost. For Jac's sake, she didn't need to give Laoiri any ideas. The woman might try it. As the chilly night breeze hit her, she pulled in a deep lungful and smiled.

"Are ye all right, lass?"

She turned and waited for Kane to catch up, pleased and not at all surprised that he had followed. "I'm fine. Just felt it was a little crowded in there." With a glance back at the small dwelling, she instinctively pulled in another deep breath as if fighting for enough air. "Do ye think they'd be offended if I slept outside? I'm sure the cook pit is still giving off some heat. The night isna that cold. I could make a pallet beside it. I'm quite used to camping. Did it a lot during research trips."

"Ye canna sleep outside. It wouldna be proper."

"I have never been accused of being proper." She eyed the house again. "Where will all of ye sleep? Draped across the table and benches?"

He looked up at the blue-black expanse of sky dusted with a shimmering trail of stars. "Since it's a clear night, the lot of us will sleep outside rather than up in that cramped loft."

"I never figured ye for a hypocrite." She perched on an up-ended log not too far from the water's edge. "I canna sleep outside, but ye can? Bollocks, I say."

"It willna be that crowded once all of us are outside. 'Twill merely be yerself and the rest of the women."

"Ye are a chauvinistic hypocrite." She refused to let up on this, and he might as well accept it. Granted, this century might hold her captive, but that didn't mean she agreed to embrace all its mindsets. Apparently, he knew what chauvinistic meant because he fixed her with an offended scowl. Without hesitating, she added, "Of course, I say that with love."

His demeanor immediately shifted from insulted to more than a little pleased. "With love, ye say?"

"I didna mean to say that." And she hadn't. That saying was something she and Breanna had shared ever since they were children. They used it to tease each other when they traded gentle insults during friendly banter. Like a sisterly inside joke.

"Then why did ye say it?" His self-satisfied grin was unmistakable even by the light of the waning moon. With a swipe of his hand, he pulled a log closer, upended it, and sat beside her. "And what does chauvinistic mean? I ken well enough what a hypocrite is."

"Chauvinistic means ye discriminate against women."

"I dinna do that." His offended air returned, puffing him like a great toad.

"No? Ye dinna think we are equal."

"Equal to what? Of course, ye're nay equal. All women are different."

"Never mind." She leaned forward, propping her elbows on her knees. The man was impossible, and she was too bloody tired to cover over seven hundred years of female versus male issues.

"But ye said it with love," he repeated, softly bumping his shoulder against hers.

"I swear ye're like a dog with a bone when ye get something in yer head." And the sad thing was she liked that about him. It strengthened the strange connection she had sensed from the moment they first met. She straightened her spine and fired off a heightened dose of her own stubbornness. "I am not sleeping in that house."

He gave her a sly look coupled with a decisive nod. "Fine, then. We shall gather Jac inside with the rest and announce that we have mutually consented to live as man and wife for all the rest of our days."

His victorious smirk made her seriously consider spitting in his eye.

"What say ye to that?" he prodded.

"I say ye've lost yer freaking mind." Marry? Was he serious? And besides, how could they marry without a registrar or a church or some sort of contract or something? Hadn't they used contracts in this time? Handfasting? Is that what he meant? A year and a day and at the end, they would be free to go their separate ways if they so choose? Bugger that. Women always got the raw end of the deal in that situation. "I will not handfast. 'Tis not in my best interest to dedicate a year of my life just so ye can go skipping away at the end with no strings attached. And especially not so I can just sleep outside instead of shoved together with the McBride sisters like biscuits in a tin."

A dangerous smile curled one side of his mouth and sent a chill down her spine. "I didna speak of handfasting, m'love. In Scotland, when I say ye are my wife in front of witnesses, I am claiming ye as my own." He leaned closer. "Of course, God Almighty is the one true witness to a marriage for all time." He took her hand and laced their fingers together. "Then ye claim me as yer husband, and we are considered married by mutual consent. In front of God, the McBrides, and my men. 'Tis quite legal."

"Ye lie."

"I do not, m'lady."

She stared at him for a long moment before realizing her mouth hung open. She closed it with a snap. "Why on earth would I agree to such a thing?"

He shrugged. "So, ye could sleep outside with the rest of us. Preserve yer good name, ye ken? Ye slept among us before because of dire circumstances. Anyone would understand that. But now..." He gave a slow shake of his head. "Now it wouldna be proper." He lowered his voice to a tone so deep and seductive it made her swallow hard. "Even though we've already consummated our union. No one else knows that."

"Just so I could sleep outside," she repeated, struggling to keep her libido in check. This was no time for unfettered lust.

"And so ye would always have my protection—officially for all to know." He brushed a kiss across her knuckles. "Well, what shall it be? Sleep inside in the stifling confines on the pallet between the McBride ladies or out here under the stars with yer husband." He leaned closer and lowered his voice back to that tone that made her clench her thighs tighter together. "As I said before, after what we did earlier today…" He stopped himself and gave her a smile that made her wet her lips. "After what we did several times, in fact, we are actually married in the eyes of God."

"Ye are an impossible man who is doing his best to take advantage of the situation."

He pulled her closer and nibbled a searing trail along her throat to the sensitive skin behind her ear. "Call me anything ye like, m'love, as long as ye call me husband." The tip of his tongue tickled her pulse line. No way could she camouflage the pounding of her heart.

Determined not to cave for principal's sake alone, she pushed him back. "I have changed my mind. I will sleep inside." She expected an argument, or at least a grand show of disappointment.

All he did was tilt his head and shrug. "As ye wish, m'love." He feigned a ridiculous stretch and a yawn. "Ye best get inside and get settled then. We rise early tomorrow and head for Edinburgh, ye ken?"

"I ken, all right." She flounced inside, which irritated her even more. With all these skirts, she couldn't even manage a proper raging stomp. Instead, she flounced like some silly character out of a fairy tale.

"There ye are, lass." Mairi smiled and waved her in, pointing to the wide pallet on the floor that the four sisters shared. The twins slept together in one cot. The other narrow bed looked to be piled high with extra clothing and wraps. Jennet and Anne took up the left side of pallet, each of them wrapped in a blanket and well on their way to their dreams. Mairi tossed a blanket around her shoulders and settled down on the floor beside the twins.

The narrow space remaining between Mairi and Anne made Satia swallow hard and seriously contemplate Kane's offer. After all, she was trapped here. And such a thing wouldn't really count, would it? Just saying they were married? It couldn't be real. She wasn't versed on Scotland's history of marriages, but how could such a thing be legitimate? And as he said, they had already *known* each other in the biblical sense of the word.

His deep, rumbling laugh echoed not too far from the window, kicking her stubbornness into overdrive.

She dove into the spot, flipped to her back, and stared at the shadows flickering across the low ceiling. Silence fell across the cottage. Well, as close to silence as the night would get with four snoring women and two toddlers tossing and turning so much that the cot's joints creaked and whined.

Then she noticed a smell that increased to suffocating proportions with the heat of so many bodies in such a small space. Not that they stunk, but heaven help her, what she wouldn't give for some deodorant and industrial-strength body spray right now. The women were clean by the time's standards, but they possessed a female earthiness that made Satia breathe through her mouth. A horrifying thought hit her. How long would it take for her to smell like that? She covered her face with both hands and stifled a groan.

With Anne's back to her right and Mairi's plump behind to her left, there was little room, so she crossed her arms over her chest as if ready to be laid in a coffin. Then both sisters rolled closer, exhaling their heavy snores in her face and narrowing her spot on the floor even more.

"I can do this," she muttered through clenched teeth while holding her hands on either side of her face to block their ale and stew-scented breath.

Then both sisters threw an arm and a leg across her and groaned. One, she had no idea which, cut loose a long, loud popping fart that gagged her.

"I canna do this." She dug her way free, clapping loudly as she made it to her feet. "Everyone into the kitchen! Now!"

"Wha's wrong?" Mairi jerked upright and checked the children. Once she saw them safe, she floundered to her feet. "An attack, lass? Did ye hear something? We have weapons hidden in the loft."

"Nothing is wrong." Satia ripped back the curtain and pointed at the bench. "To the kitchen, please, whilst I rouse the men."

"What is it, sister?" Anne muttered as she and Jennet helped Laoiri rise and limp across the room.

"I dinna ken. She willna say." Mairi caught hold of Satia's arm as she yanked the door open. "Tell us, lass. Did ye have a vision? Rob mentioned ye have the sight."

"Ye might say I have had a moment of clarity I wish to share." She brushed Mairi's hand away, stepped outside, and bellowed, "Get in here, Kane Macpherson, and tell them I am yer wife."

"I am right here, lass," he said from where he leaned against the house beside the door. "I'm impressed. Ye lasted longer than I thought."

"Ye are an unbelievable arse."

With another rumbling laugh, he caught her close. "Aye, that I am." After a glance at all the faces, he spoke louder. "I am also yer husband."

He kissed the tip of her nose and jostled her in his arms. "Yer turn, dear one."

"I am yer wife," she said with an irritated huff. "May God have mercy on yer soul."

The men cheered, and the sisters clapped, making Satia wonder if they had been in on Kane's plan all along.

KANE BRACED HIMSELF, knowing when she spotted the cook pit ablaze with a fresh load of wood, she would figure out his carefully laid trap and, more than likely, be a tad irritated. A cannier lass he had never met. Nor a feistier one. Satisfaction filled him. Feisty, canny, and fiery she was, and now—all his.

Silhouetted by the firelight, shoulders tensed, and hands fisted, Satia looked ready to brawl as she turned and faced him. She pointed at the fire. "Even Albie went along with yer little farce?"

"Farce?" He tossed the extra blankets onto the thick pallet he had prepared for their wedding bed. "We are married, Satia, just as surely as if we spoke the words before a priest." With a tip of his head toward the dwelling behind them, he allowed himself a cocksure grin. "Every soul in there witnessed our vows and will attest to our union in any court ye choose."

Her soured expression called him a liar. Either that or she was pondering how best to kill him.

"I swear," he promised with a light-hearted pat of his chest.

Without a word, she turned back to the fire and glared down at the flames, hugging herself.

An inkling that maybe he had gone too far sobered him. He staunched the urge to gloat any further as he stepped up beside her. Close but not touching, he waited for either a rant, tears, or worse—uncomfortable silence. The tensed set of her jaw and her puckered brow warned a storm was imminent.

The longer he waited, the more his conscience shamed him, filling him with guilt as stinging as a nettle. Perhaps he shouldn't have used this opportunity to trick her into marriage. But surely, with time, she would see it as the well-intentioned thing that it was. Now, he could better protect her. Even though he had no lands or titles, he could still keep her safe. And when the skirmishes came, she could shelter with the McBrides. They had already said as much even though he had yet to tell her.

After what felt like forever, she cast a sideways glance his way. "So, tell me, Kane. What does a nomadic warrior without a pot to piss in want with a wife?" Even though she spoke in a calm, quiet tone, her words hit him like a hard cuff across the mouth.

"I can protect ye." The excuse sounded feeble even to him.

She ignored his answer, sidling another angry glare his way, looking ready to kick him. "Sex? Was that it? We already had that. And would've probably done it again without the aid of an official union. Why the need to trick me into marrying?"

"Dinna speak in such a way." He hated the detached harshness she used to describe their loving. "Ye make it sound like a common, dirty thing, and what we shared—was not."

"No, it wasn't," she admitted, her fury seeming to lessen a bit. With her gaze still locked on the flames, she massaged her temples as a weary sigh escaped her.

"Good then. At least we agree on that." This was not how he intended this night to go. "And dinna fash yerself, whenever the Bruce sends me into battle, ye shall stay here with the McBrides. They've already said as much." He forced a smile. "See? It doesna matter that we dinna have a pot to piss in. Ye have a home right here whenever ye wish it."

She cut him another narrow-eyed look. "Did it ever occur to ye to ask me first? Find out what I want to do when ye go jaunting off to play yer war games?"

Actually, it had not, but he wasn't about to admit it. "I was protecting ye, planning for yer safety."

"I am not a pet to be kenneled when ye're required to travel for work!"

"God's beard, woman." He scrubbed a hand across his face. "Do this for me, aye? When we quarrel, can ye at least use words I'm more familiar with so I've half a chance at defending myself?"

"Fine." Her eyes sparked brighter with renewed fury. "I am not a horse to be stabled until ye decide to return and ride me."

"Satia!"

"Ye asked for it." She flipped a hand as if dismissing him and turned back to the fire.

He had asked for it. That point, he could not argue. With a heavy sigh, he lowered himself to the ground and sat on the end of the pallet. This most definitely was not how he intended this night to be. Defeat weighed heavy on him, tasting as bitter as burnt bread. He stared up at her, wishing for the wisdom to make things better between them. "What do ye want from me, Satia?"

She plopped down beside him, sitting cross-legged with her skirts bunched around her. With her elbows propped on her knees, she bowed her head and continued rubbing her temples. "I have no idea what I want, Kane. I have never had a husband before. Nor have I ever lived in the fourteenth century." She met his gaze, looking as weary as he felt. "What am I *supposed* to want here?"

"A roof over yer head. Food in yer belly. Safety. Children. Love?" A dismal cross between a huffing snort and a groan escaped him. "Those were the things Mam and Grandmam always longed for."

"Appears to me, they had them." She leaned forward and snapped off a stalk of grass growing out from a crevice between two of the larger stones making up the base of the oblong cook pit. "Yer mother and grandmother loved each other. They loved ye. Had a roof over their heads. Lived in safety. Since ye grew into such a good-sized man, I'm assuming ye had enough to eat most of the time." She tossed the grass into the fire, smiling as it crackled and burst into flames. "Roof. Food. Safety. Children...well, a child. And each other's love."

"Aye, that is true." Then he realized that even though they always had what they thought they wanted, they never perceived it. "It appears they never knew what they had. Not ever."

"That's true of a lot of us," she said. Her fury calmed once again. "We dinna ken what we have until it's too late." She blew out a heavy sigh that rivaled his. "Dinna decide things for me unless I'm unconscious or for whatever reason canna decide for myself, aye?" Her frown appeared more solemn than angry. "As a child, they shuffled me around like a piece of unwanted furniture. I have outgrown that. Do ye understand?"

The shadows in her eyes said so much more than her words. With a hesitancy spawned from all the other mistakes he'd made this night, he slipped his fingers under hers and slid her hand into his. "Ye are not a horse, a sword, or a favorite dagger to be carried close to my heart. Ye are my wife, my love, my helpmate. The one I need at my side as we walk through this life together." He rested his other hand atop hers. "Forgive me, Satia. I never meant to make ye feel…less."

She didn't respond, just stared up at him with such sadness that he dreaded what might come next. He feared the marriage he had so carefully orchestrated was about to end before it ever started.

"I am tired," she finally said. "And my head is splitting." Ever so gently, she pulled her hand free, settled across the length of the pallet, and curled onto her side to face the fire.

He took that as a dismissal, and rightly so. Served him right for treating marriage like something to be seized and then acting like a cocky bastard. He unfolded one of the extra blankets and spread it across her, tucking it in close around her neck. After a tender kiss to her temple, he rose and stepped away, unsure where he was headed but giving her both the peace and space she sought.

"Where are ye going?" she called out.

He paused and looked back at her. "Away…I guess."

"Away?" She rolled over and pushed up on an elbow. "What do ye mean *away*? Is that yer way of saying ye're going for a pee?"

"Ye said ye were tired and unwell." He stood there, opening and closing his fists, feeling the greatest sort of fool.

"Aye, that means I want to sleep. Ye said we were leaving early for Edinburgh tomorrow—right?"

"Aye." He stood there. Still unsure what she wanted from him. He had erred so badly earlier. He was extra leery now. But even in the shadows, he picked up on her shaking head. "What?"

"Husbands sleep with their wives, aye?" She spoke slowly as if he might not understand the language.

"Aye."

"Then if ye aren't going for a pee, why are ye going *away*?

Isn't this sleeping arrangement how this all got started?"

She made a fair point. He returned to the pallet but didn't settle down beside her. "Does this mean ye forgive me?"

With a fluffing of her blanket, she laid back down and rolled to once again face the fire. "I forgive ye on one condition."

His heart lifted. "And what might that condition be?"

"The next time I give ye a case of the red arse, and I will, mind ye, ye best remember this marriage deal was yer idea and not mine. I accept no responsibility when ye realize ye've stuck yerself with a shoddy wife."

He stretched out behind her and fit his knees into the crooks of hers as he pulled her back against him. "Ye'll nay be a shoddy wife. Ye're already finer than fine, and I thank whatever powers brought ye to me."

She hugged his arms around her and rooted back into his embrace until her head rested on his shoulder. After a jaw-cracking yawn that would do any man proud, she patted his hand. "We'll consummate the union tomorrow, aye? It's been a verra long day." Her words slurred with drowsiness. "Besides, we had that fine tumble earlier, right after I nearly drowned."

"That we did, my love." He buried his face in the silk of her hair and closed his eyes, breathing in the scent of her. She smelled of pines, crisp Highland air, and the cleanness of an icy loch. He inhaled deeper. And woman. She possessed that mouthwatering fragrance of woman.

"Stop sniffing me and go to sleep."

He held his breath to keep from chuckling. She was scolding him again. A good thing. That meant she forgave him for certain.

SHE AWOKE WITH a start, fought to sit up, and wheezed in long, deep breaths as if they were her last. Heart pounding so hard it almost choked her, she clutched her throat, gasping for more air.

"Satia?" Kane sat up beside her. Firelight illuminated the concern on his face. "What is it? Tell me what is wrong."

"Terrible…terrible dream," was all she could get out. With her mouth dry as dust, her tongue refused to work. She forced a swallow and focused on slowing her labored breathing. With a shove of the blankets, she rolled to her feet and stumbled to the water's edge. She knelt and splashed overflowing handfuls across her face and to the back of her neck. The cold water helped. Breathing evened out, and her knotted muscles gradually relaxed.

"Are ye better now?" Kane crouched beside her. The caring weight of his hand on her back helped center her.

"Much better." After one last splash of water, she rose and immediately lost her balance, teetering to the right.

Kane caught her up and carried her back to the pallet. "Saints alive, lass. Ye're hotter than banked coals." He pressed a hand to her forehead then her throat. "Burning with fever. Wrap this blanket around ye. I'll get ye inside."

The thought of the crowded dwelling suffocated her all over again. "No!" She grabbed hold of the front of his tunic and pulled him back down beside her. "I canna breathe in there. Out here. Fresh air. Keep me out here in the open. Please." When he didn't answer, she fisted her hands tighter in his shirt and yanked. "Swear it. Swear ye willna take me back inside. Not tonight."

"I swear, lass, I swear." He wrapped another blanket around her, settled down beside her, and rested her head on his shoulder. "We will stay here as long as ye wish. I promise."

With her forehead pressed to his strong, safe chest, she closed her eyes. Big mistake. The unreasonable panic returned, fighting to control her again. "Dinna let them bury me," she said, the words bursting free of her. The dark remnants of the vicious dream flashed back, trying to suck her back down into its terrifying spiral. "I canna breathe when they bury me." They…she couldn't remember who *they* were…had put her in a box and buried her alive. Shovels of soil and rock had hit the lid over and over. Bits of dirt sifted through the cracks of the cheap wooden coffin. The dust had choked her, robbing her of precious air. And then water rushed in. Icy water showered down through the lid. Its level slowly rose until it covered her face. She gulped for more air, wheezing in the great mouthfuls as fast as she could. "They buried me alive," she gasped. "Then tried to drown me. Keep them away!"

"Shh now, ease yerself. Ye have plenty of air now, and no one will ever bury ye or try to drown ye again. I swear it, precious one. I've got ye. And here in my arms, ye will stay."

"It seemed so real." She dug the blanket away from her throat and shoved it off her shoulders. "I need air, but I'm so cold." Her bones ached as if shards of glass had ground into her joints.

"Albie!"

Kane's bellow increased the hammering inside her head. She clamped both hands over her ears, holding tight to keep her skull from splitting in two. "Why are ye calling Albie?" she whispered. Her own voice seemed too loud.

"Ye need a hearty tonic to keep that dream from coming back. At the verra least, ye need a strong cup of willow bark tea to fight whatever this is that's taken hold of ye." He pressed his hands over hers, helping her cover her ears, and roared again. "Albie! Hie yerself out here! Now!"

She swallowed hard at a raw aching lump in her throat. What was wrong with her? Nightmares didn't cause fever. Or migraines. Or throbbing in the bones. The scientist in her struggled to reason out the possibilities. Bacteria. Had to be some sort of bacteria she'd picked up. As much loch water as she'd inhaled and swallowed during her trip through time, who knew what sort of antagonistic germ she'd sucked in? With no antibiotics to be found, she prayed her immune system, as well as all the vaccines she'd had over the years, would help her overcome it.

"What is it?" Albie loped toward them.

"Not so loud." She clutched her head. Every sound caused more pain. "Please tell him not so loud." A jaw-tingling throb behind her ears warned vomiting was imminent. She rolled to her hands and knees and barely made it off the pallet before heaving out every meal she had ever thought about eating. Elbows locked as she waited for the next round already churning in her gut, she couldn't quite make out what the men were saying. The only word she clearly picked out was *curse*. She didn't have the strength or the time between puking sessions to correct them. Of course, maybe they were right. It damn sure felt like a curse.

A cool wet cloth appeared out of nowhere and gently daubed across her forehead, then the back of her neck. Hands held her as she dry heaved over and over until she felt turned inside out. A cup pressed to her lips, but she turned away. "No. It'll just come back out."

"Aye, but it'll give ye something to toss back out and ease the harshness of yer dry gagging," Mairi said, pressing the cup to her mouth again. "Please, m'lady. Ye must try. For yer own sake."

Not having the energy to argue, Satia sipped at the water to make Mairi leave her alone.

"Please let us bring ye inside," Mairi asked, finally taking the cup away.

"No." Satia blindly reached out. "Kane?"

"I am right here, dear one." He lifted her up and settled her back down on the pallet, and lay beside her. "Give me the cloth for her head."

Water splashed somewhere nearby, then the blessed coolness of the linen gently fell across her eyes. "Thank ye," she whispered, pressing her hand across it and holding it there. "I am so sorry I've been so ratty to ye." And she was. He had been nothing but nice and kind, and she had been a royal shite, per her usual. "I dinna ken why I'm such a shite to the ones I love. God knows poor Breanna suffered my rudeness for years." Behind her closed lids, her eyes stung with feverish tears. "I miss her, Kane. She's the only one in the world who ever loved me."

"Not anymore, dear one," he gently corrected. "Not anymore."

CHAPTER NINE

"YE SHOULDHA GONE with them the last time." Propped upright among rolled blankets and every threadbare pillow the McBrides possessed, Satia looked like a weary angel fallen from Heaven.

"We have talked of this already." He filled the spoon with a healthy dollop of parritch and held it out. "Eat. Yer strength needs building. Ye've wasted away to nothing."

"I can feed myself." She turned her face aside, dodging the food.

He adjusted his approach and nudged the spoon closer to her mouth. "I enjoy doing it. Now, eat, my fussy wee hen."

She wrinkled her nose and shoved herself deeper into the pillows to escape him. "I dinna like oatmeal."

"Ye're a Scot."

"What's that got to do with it?"

"Scots eat their parritch." Just to prove his point, he popped the bite into his mouth, then licked the spoon clean. "Wonderful stuff." He scooped up another bite and headed toward her mouth again. "Now, eat."

"No."

"Satia...ye promised." He pushed the spoon closer and gave

her a stern look along with it. While it might not be chivalrous, he wasn't about to let her forget anything she had said during her raging bouts of fever. She had told him she loved him, apologized again and again for being a wee shite, and promised to do better—which she had agreed meant listening to her husband when he had her best interests in mind. And he had witnesses. He would bring them in if he had to, and she knew it. "Mairi added extra butter and honey, then made it even richer with cream." He arched a brow and waited.

"They dinna have a cow. How can they have butter and cream?"

"Goat's milk. Now eat."

With a dismal huff, Satia leaned forward and closed her mouth around the spoon. She swallowed, then relaxed back into the pillows while licking her lips. "That is better. Help me remember to thank Mairi for her efforts, aye?"

"I will, dear one." He offered another spoonful, pleased when she didn't resist, but meekly ate until over half the contents of the bowl were gone.

As he scraped down the sides to offer her more, she held up a hand and shook her head. "No more for now. I feel as full as if I've eaten a side of venison."

He set the bowl aside and wrung out a square of linen resting in a basin of water. Crushed mint leaves floated on the surface. "Here's the mint, 'case ye start feeling sick again."

She accepted the cloth and patted it all around her mouth while inhaling the crisp, fresh scent from the crushed herb. "I'm not nearly as queasy today."

Her wan smile and the bluish circles beneath her red-rimmed eyes made him doubt her words. "I hope ye are feeling better, lass. Truly."

"What day is it?" Her pale brows twitched in a weak attempt at an inquisitive frown.

"Eighteen April." He wished he could tell her otherwise. She had fought for her life for well over a month, and there had been several times when they all feared she would lose the battle. But each time, when he thought her knocking at death's door, he had held her tight and begged her to stay. And now she was healing. Finally. He owed God a fine herd of Highland cows at first opportunity. 'Twas the boon he had promised to the church if the Almighty would just allow her to live. At her startled expression, he retrieved the cloth, wet it again, and pressed it to her temples. "It's all right, lass. Ye've fought a long hard battle. All that matters is that ye're still here with us, ye ken?"

She stared off into space, her eyes moving back and forth as if reading some invisible text. "I've lost over a month. I canna imagine what sort of virus or bacteria I couldha come across that would take me down that long. Has no one else been sick?"

"No. All of us are hale and hearty." And there were those words again. She had mumbled it a lot during her fevers. "What is *bacteria*? Or *virus*?"

She frowned. "Well, bacteria are things we need in this world, but the problem is there are so many kinds. Tiny little things. So wee ye canna even see them without special equipment that's not been invented yet. But they are there. Some good. Some bad. They can either cure ye or kill ye. Viruses are just nasty wee beasties." She went quiet, staring at him as though pondering. "Edinburgh Castle. Did it happen?"

A shiver tingled up his spine and raised the hairs on the back of his neck. "Aye. Exactly as ye said it would. Rob brought word of it. He's out helping Laoiri with the animals. I'll have him come inside and visit when they're done if ye feel up to it." They had kept her isolated, curtained off in one end of the sleeping area. It had taken them hours that first night to convince her to allow them to bring her inside.

"Is everyone else all right? Toff? Jac?"

He grinned. "Aye, and so is yer favorite in all the world. Albie's scouring the land for more herbs to replenish Mairi's stores."

She ducked her head with a sheepish look. "Please tell me that was a hallucination brought on by fever."

"Nay, love. Ye broke his nose with that bowl." He scooped up her hand and kissed it. "Ye have quite good aim even with one foot in the grave."

"I dinna even remember now why I threw it at him." She grew thoughtful again. "I canna believe that little wooden bowl broke his nose."

"As I said, good aim, and ye caught him with the edge." He pushed up from the stool beside the cot, bent, and kissed her forehead. "Rest now. If ye feel well enough later, I'll carry ye outside for some sunshine. Would ye like that?"

"That would be nice," she whispered, her eyelids already dipping low. Poor lamb would be asleep before he even stepped beyond the curtain. As he moved into the main living area, he quietly pulled the cloth divider shut behind him.

Mairi and Anne, sitting at the worktable chopping vegetables, glanced up with expectant looks. "Still improving, I hope?" Mairi asked, her knife hovering above a parsnip.

"Aye." He took the bowl and spoon to the wash bucket after scraping the leavings into the scrap bowl meant for the chickens. "Ate almost all the parritch and said ye made it taste grand."

Mairi beamed with a proud smile and bobbed her head. "I am glad of it." She pointed her blade at the wash bucket. "Leave that be now. I'll wash them up in a bit once I finish with the parsnips."

Anne cleared her throat. Her tensed glance at the door gave him pause. "The lads are waiting for ye outside. Best see to them."

He knew without asking what they wanted. 'Twas the same thing they had wanted the other two times they returned from Edinburgh. The Bruce had sent messages along with them. In the first, the king had expressed his concern and made a gentle inquiry. The second, he had worded somewhat stronger, wanting to know when Kane would rejoin his liege and the fight for Scotland's independence. The men outside didn't wish to return to Edinburgh again without him and face the Bruce's temper on his behalf. In all fairness, he didn't blame them. This was not their affair, and nor should they suffer for it.

As soon as he stepped out the door, Rob, Toff, Jac, and Albie lined up in front of him, their faces grim. Albie and Jac nudged Toff, bumping him forward. Apparently, the man had lost and been chosen as spokesman.

"Ye must come to Edinburgh, Kane." Toff took another hesitant step toward him, staring at the ground for a long moment before sliding his gaze upward. "We canna manage the Bruce for ye any longer. He needs to speak with ye about his plans. Ye ken well enough how ye talk him through strategies and weaknesses he doesna see."

"Satia isna strong enough to travel yet. 'Tis a week's journey in fit weather, and this being spring, that could change at any moment." He resettled his stance and lifted his chin, silently warning them to tread lightly. "If I go to Edinburgh without her, who's ta say when I could return and fetch her?"

"We made the trip in a mere three days each time," Toff defended.

"That was riding hard and stopping only long enough to rest the beasts." Kane knew better. He had done it himself. Satia could not handle such a pace. Not yet. "Do ye deny it?"

"Ye ken what happens to those who anger the Bruce," Albie said, apparently unable to remain quiet any longer. "Yer own brother paid the price for crossing him, even when he thought himself safe on holy ground."

"Half-brother," Kane corrected. "And we dinna speak of the Comyns, old man. I willna warn ye again."

"Might ye at least speak to her about the trip?" Rob asked. With a sheepish glance downward, he stubbed the toe of his boot deeper into the loose rocks. "Sometimes we hear the two of ye talking when she's awake. Seems she's a mite calmer and more understanding of things than she used to be."

"She's still weak. That makes a body less ill-tempered." The more they nettled him, the more he struggled to hold his anger. He understood their side, but they needed to understand his. He couldn't—nay, he *would not* abandon her.

"We've seen to everything that's needed doing here," Albie said in a resigned tone. "We leave tomorrow. I advise ye to come with us." His eyes narrowed, tightening the wrinkles of his weathered face. "For yer own sake, man. Think of yer future." His hardened gaze shifted to the cottage, then returned to Kane. "For her future, too. Ye've a strong connection with the King of Scotland. A fierce man of power. Eventually, will ye not wish for a bit of land to build yer wife a home? Ye please the Bruce now, and he'll give ye that. He's a generous man. Ye ken that as well as I."

Albie made a convincing argument even though it pained Kane to admit it. He pulled in a deep breath and whistled it out through his teeth. "Damn ye, man."

Albie nodded. "I understand. But I promised yer mother I would always counsel ye, whether or not ye found my words pleasing."

"I will speak with Satia." He scrubbed his face with both hands, wishing for a better answer than leaving her for an undetermined amount of time. Since he had been gone from the Bruce so long, instinct told him it would be a long while before his liege would see fit to spare him again.

"What if we found a wagon?" Jac asked. "Or maybe even a carriage? That would be better. We could fix Lady Satia a fine, comfortable pallet inside. Think ye she could travel that way? Might do her good to see Friar Law, since she's been ailing so long. Ye ken the man's got the best poultices and tisanes. He might could help her."

Kane stared at the man. In all the time he had known Jac, the man had never strung so many words together at one time. He was a quiet brute of few, if any, words. "What's come over ye?"

"What do ye mean?" Jac stared at him, his bushy red brows drawn together.

"Ye've never said so much in all yer life."

Jac stole a look all around, then took a step closer, waving for the others to follow. Once all the men stood in a tight circle, he leaned in and lowered his voice. "I canna keep coming here so much. Laoiri's determined to make me her husband, and the more we visit, the worse she gets." He straightened and looked all around again before ducking back down. "No offense, Rob, but I'd rather marry one of them feckin' sheep than her." He gave each of them a meaningful dip of his chin. "She's an ill-natured cow and sure to get worse as she ages."

Kane understood the man's dilemma since he had been Laoiri's target at one time. "I will speak to Satia and see what she thinks about traveling."

"'Twould be good if one of the sisters could ride inside the carriage with her," Toff said. "'Case she needed something during the journey."

"Not Laoiri!" Jac paled.

"Anne or Jennet, then. Mairi canna do it because of the bairns." Rob shifted in place as though excited to put their plan into motion. "Anne would be best. She's calm as a saint and mean as a nun. No one will bother Satia with her around."

"Fine. As soon as Satia wakes, I will speak with her." If the fair weather held, the trip might even do her good. She had already regained enough strength to complain about how tiresome and boring her wee sickroom had become.

"Kane!" Mairi's call made him turn. "Yer lady wife says she's ready for some sunshine."

She'd not napped but a few moments. The realization both pleased and filled him with dread. Now he had to speak with her—just as he'd promised the men. Then it came to him that all this talk of carriages had not included where exactly such a conveyance might be found. The McBrides owned nothing more than a small, two-wheeled cart. He turned back and singled out Jac. "And where did ye plan on getting this fine carriage equipped with a comfortable pallet?"

Jac gave him a sly grin. "Never ye mind. The less ye know of it, the better." He clapped young Rob on the shoulder. "Come on. Ye can be my lookout."

"They'll hang ye if they catch ye," Kane warned, wondering which affluent member of Inverness's society was about to part with their carriage.

Jac winked. "We're merely borrowing it for a while. Dinna worry."

"Dinna worry," Kane muttered as he swung around and strode back inside. He knew Jac's history. The man never got caught. But there was a first time for everything.

As he crossed the threshold, he noticed the curtain to Satia's area had already been pulled back, so she could see out into the rest of the room. "Look at ye. Wide awake after just a few moments of closing yer eyes."

"A wee catnap was all I needed." She smoothed the covers across her lap and smiled. "And after Anne helped me wash my face and visit the chamber pot, I felt wide awake. Can we go outside now?" A spark of liveliness pinked her cheeks and brightened her eyes. "Ye promised—remember?"

"Aye, love, I remember." He wrapped a heavier shawl around her shoulders, then scooped her up into his arms.

"I should try to walk. Ye know that—right? The less I do, the weaker I get." With a pat of his chest, she graced him with a gentle smile. "Ye canna cosset me forever."

"Now there's where ye're wrong." He kissed her cheek, then headed toward the door. "'Tis my place to *cosset* ye. Forever and a day."

As soon as he stepped outside, Satia lifted her face to the sun and smiled. "Sunshine makes ye feel grand, doesn't it?"

"That it does." He seated himself on the bench against the front of the house and settled her on his lap. "Since the cottage faces south, ye'll be plenty warm here." He scanned the horizon. Not a single cloud marred the brilliance of the bright blue sky.

"With one arm still around his shoulders, she angled a per-turbed look his way. "Ye know I could sit beside ye on the bench."

"Aye. Ye could." He leaned back and squared her more comfortably on his lap. "But I like this better."

"Ye sound like a spoilt bairn."

"With ye, I am spoilt." He smoothed his hand up and down her back, pained by the bony ridge of her spine bumping against his palm. She had thinned out far too much. A powerful gust would carry her away. "There is something I need to ask ye," he said, forcing out the words. Best get the unpleasantness over with.

"Yes. Ye can go. Have I not told ye that already?"

"Let me finish." He snatched up her hand and pecked a scolding kiss across her knuckles. "I dinna wish to leave ye here for any length of time."

"That's exactly what ye planned to do when ye married me. Ye said so yerself."

"Aye, well…things change." While fighting to keep her alive, a burning protectiveness for this wee hellcat had grown within him, taken him over. He knew now he could never entrust her care to another. Nor could he bear to be away from her. At least not yet. "I know the McBrides would take fine care of ye, but I canna in good conscience or the wants of my heart leave ye here with them." He settled her back and rested her head on his shoulder. "I need to see ye every day, Satia. Need to know ye're hearty and hale."

"As much as I hate to admit to weakness," she said, then interrupted herself with a frustrated huff. "Ye know I canna make the ride to Edinburgh. Not yet, I'm afraid."

He slowly nodded. "I agree, love. And if the weather turned, another drenching could verra well be the end of ye." He combed his fingers through the silkiness of her hair, glad that Anne hadn't yet bound it in a braid or bun. The coolness of the curls slipping across his palm mesmerized him.

"So, when do ye leave?" she asked, interrupting his reverie. "Because ye must," she said. "Dinna think I havena laid on that cot and heard a great deal of what's been said."

"Do ye think ye could manage the trip to Edinburgh in a

carriage?"

"In a carriage?" She raised up and eyed him as though he had threatened to dump her out of his lap. "What sort of carriage do they make in this century? I verra much doubt it has the lush, padded seats of Cinderella's enchanted pumpkin."

"Now I'm certain ye're fully on the mend because I have no idea what the hell ye just said."

"It's a fairy tale about a…oh, never mind." She loosened the shawl around her shoulders and once again lifted her face to the sun, closing her eyes as she soaked in the warmth. "Where is this carriage? I have not seen it."

"Jac and Rob are procuring it."

"Stealing it, ye mean," she said without opening her eyes.

"Jac used the word *borrowing*."

A lazy laugh escaped her. "Aye. That's the word I used to use, too." She lounged back against him and bent her legs, balancing her bare feet on his knees.

He fluffed out her shift and blanket, resettling their folds to ensure she was properly covered. "They should have it by tomorrow. Or so I expect."

"I thought the Bruce stayed in the Dumfries and Galloway area, mostly," she said, the question of the carriage apparently ended. "I understand he took the castle just last month, but that's no reason for him to still be in Edinburgh. Of course, in June, there will be Bannockburn and Stirling. I guess Edinburgh makes sense if ye keep that in mind. It's not all that far."

"Do ye feel strong enough to make the trip in a carriage?" She had never answered, and that worried him. Would she be honest? With herself, as well as him?

"All I can do is try." She opened her eyes, leveled a somber gaze at him, then shook her head. "But we need a backup plan. If things go sour, what could we do? I couldna verra well drive the carriage back here."

"I shall bring ye back."

"That defeats the whole purpose." Her somberness turned to that flinty sternness he had come to know so well. "One way or the other, it's time ye returned to the Bruce." She looked away, staring off into the distance at nothing in particular. "I've read accounts of the man. Some respected and worshiped him. Others feared and hated him. Either way, I dinna think he's one to be ignored or crossed." She turned back to him. "Have ye ever heard the saying *keep yer friends close and yer enemies closer?*"

"No. But it makes a good deal of sense." He tucked back her silvery blonde curls that kept blowing into her eyes. "If ye canna make it, I shall have Rob bring ye back. Then I will return to ye as soon as I can." It killed him to say it, but her intense stare pulled the words from him. It was what she wished to hear.

"I will do my level best to make it," she promised. "My stubbornness has fueled me before when my body wanted to give up."

"With any luck, it'll take Jac and Rob a day or so to *borrow* a carriage. That'll give ye a wee bit more time to work on yer strength."

"The pampering must stop then. Understand?" She wiggled out of his lap and plopped onto the bench beside him. When she frowned and shifted from side to side, he leaned forward and studied her.

"What is it, lass?"

"Apparently, my arse has become quite bony. I dinna remember this bench being so hard." She pushed to her feet and held onto his shoulder to steady herself. "Come. Walk with me a bit. It'll do me good."

While he agreed with her intent, he wasn't so sure strolling around the loch barefoot and wearing nothing but her shift and a shawl was the best way to go about it. "Perhaps ye should dress first. The ground's still damp and cold enough to chill ye."

She looked down at her toes, wiggling them atop the packed dirt in front of the bench. "Perhaps ye're right. It does seem a mite on the cool side." With a determined dip of her chin, she turned and headed toward the door. "We should tell Mairi and Anne so they can help me get ready." She stopped and frowned. "I'm going to miss the twins."

"We're nay leaving forever," he reminded. "Just until we can sort out the Bruce and convince him to reward me with the land he's been promising all these years. After all, we need our own home to fill with our bairns."

"Bairns?" she repeated, not only looking leery but ready to run.

"Aye. Do the women in yer time not wish to become mothers?"

"Some do. Others don't, and I know from personal experience, that those who dinna wish to have children, shouldna be pressured into doing it."

Her tone echoed with uncertainty and something else he wasn't so sure he liked. Was she saying she didn't wish to have his child? He tried to read her expression. Shadows subdued the vivid green of her eyes. Nothing told him what he wished to hear.

She stared at him. Her troubling expression shifted to a worried frown. "Now is not the time for us to have this discussion. Our first order is to get ye sorted with the Bruce, then we'll figure out the rest." She reached for him. When he took her hand, she squeezed it. "Ye had to have known that a life with me wouldna be easy or uncomplicated." She paused, then peered at him more intently to pull the answer from him. "Ye understood that, aye?"

"Aye, I knew that." He gently pulled her into his arms and held her. "And I dinna regret my choice for a moment, dear one. Not for a blink of an eye do I regret it."

She rested her head on his chest as if weary beyond measure. "I'm glad," she whispered. "Most have always given up on me." She shifted, lifting her face to his and stirring his heart with a loving smile. "But not my fine Highland warrior." She patted his chest. "Now, give us a kiss, then help me inside so we can speak with Anne and Mairi about our plans."

Her supple lips tasted sweet as ever. Sweeter, if possible. Once the kiss started, he hated to end it, but her health came first. She barely possessed the strength to walk across the length of the cottage. Lovemaking would wait until she was stronger. He ached in anticipation.

CHAPTER TEN

"ARE YE COMFORTABLE? Enough pillows and blankets?" Kane tucked the throws and shawls around her, fussing worse than a mother hen tending her first clutch of chicks.

"I am fine." Satia caught hold of his hands and leaned forward. "Now give me a kiss for luck and go get on yer horse."

His face, a storm cloud of worry, he leaned closer and framed her face with his hands. "I dinna need luck. I need yer love and good health. That is all."

"Ye have it." She struggled to keep her lips from trembling as she tried to placate him with an encouraging smile. How could she already love this man so hard, and he really love her back? "I love ye, my fine warrior. Now, let's get on with this trip."

He kissed her again, slow enough that his reluctance to start the journey flowed into her. As much as she hated to, she gently pushed him away. "Go. Now. I'm sure the lads are getting antsy."

"Antsy?"

"More than a little ready to get going."

Understanding filled his face. "Aye, I'm sure they are." He turned and fixed Anne with a pointed stare that betrayed his concerns even more. "Call out if she has need of anything at all, ye ken? Dinna listen to her. Do what she needs to keep her safe and comfortable, aye?"

"Ye know I will." Anne gave a gracious nod, then shooed him away. "On wi' ye now, or ye'll wear her out before we even get started."

With a curt dip of his chin, he stepped down from the boxy, four-wheeled contraption, closed the door, then tested the latch to make sure it caught before striding out of sight.

"I swear that man worries worse than a new mother," Anne said. "I've never seen him fuss this way." She cleared her throat and settled more comfortably into the pillows on her side of the carriage. "Ye couldna ask for a better husband, ye ken?" She offered a faint smile as she drew her knitting from a bag beside her.

"I'm beginning to understand that." Satia peered out the window, quite comfortable, lounging with her legs stretched across the seat. A cushioned seat even. Jac and Rob had *borrowed* well. Thank goodness they'd not gotten caught. They had postponed the trip to Edinburgh for a few days while they scraped away the red tint from the carriage's sides. They dulled it even more with a drab black concoction mixed with fat and other questionable substances to make it waterproof and lasting. By the time they finished, she had to admit, the conveyance looked nothing like it had when they showed up with it.

She liked the wide windows with the leather flaps rolled up and secured to let in the breeze and sunlight. If the weather turned, the shades wouldn't keep out all the rain, but they would be dryer than the men on horseback. She adjusted the knitted fingerless gloves that reached to her elbows, keeping her forearms cozy and warm. "These are lovely, Anne. Such a soft blue. Thank ye again."

"Ye are quite welcome." Anne didn't lift her attention from her knitting. "With not a bit of fat on yer bones, ye'll chill too easily, even with it being almost May. I thought them proper and needed." She looped the yarn around the tips of the long wooden needles, worn smooth and stained a dark brown with much use.

"What are ye making now?" Satia found Anne more difficult to talk with than Mairi. While the young woman possessed a kind temperament, she had no use for frivolity or mindless chatting, and she wouldn't hesitate to tell you so. "Is it a scarf?"

"Not exactly." Anne held up her creation. It looked like the beginnings of a cowl-necked sweater Satia once owned. "'Twill stay around yer neck and shoulders with no pins, ye ken? Ye can even pull it up to cover yer head if ye wish."

"Verra grand, indeed." And it was. Satia couldn't imagine attempting to make such a thing.

"I can teach ye, if ye like." Anne glanced up from her work, her perception perking like a cat spotting a mouse. "But ye wouldna like to learn, would ye?"

"I'm afraid I wouldna have the patience for it." Satia gave a faint shrug. "Sorry."

"Dinna be sorry." Anne returned her full attention to her knitting. "Ye are who ye are." Her lips pursed as her head tilted slightly. "But ye will need to learn knitting and sewing so ye can do for yer bairns, ye ken? Babes need their caps and blankets."

There it was again. Bairns. Was procreating such a priority in this century? It occurred to her that since she had now been in the fourteenth century for well over a month, any prescription measures to level out her hormones as well as prevent pregnancy had long since weakened to the point of being useless. As a fertile young woman, or so she assumed, if she didn't wish to become a mother, she better figure out a means of birth control.

"Ye dinna want bairns," Anne noted, her knitting needles pausing mid-stitch. It didn't sound like an accusation, merely an observation.

"Not really." Honesty seemed best with Anne, even though it might make or break any chance of friendship with this particular McBride sister. If it quelled their friendship, she'd be down to two: Mairi and Jennet.

Anne's dark brows rose until they nearly touched her light brown hairline. "I see." Without another word, she returned to her knitting.

"Ye see?"

Her forehead puckering with concentration, the lass brought her knitting closer and squinted at what appeared to be a difficult stitch. "Aye. I see," she repeated, sounding distracted.

"No preaching?" Satia needed the woman's approval, for what reason she couldn't fathom.

"Preaching?" Anne frowned at the knitting, pulled one needle free of the yarn, and unraveled several rows of stitching. "Do ye mean scolding?"

"Aye. Scolding that I should do my best to pop out as many babies as Kane can father." Perhaps she could have worded that better, but it was too late now. She heaved a grand sigh and folded her hands in her lap. "I dinna wish to have children because I dinna wish to ruin them the way my mother ruined me."

Her expressive brows quirking again, Anne stared at her for an uncomfortable amount of time, then looked back down at her yarn. "Ye dinna seem ruined to me." Her head tipped to the side with another twitch of her shoulder. "I will admit ye are a mite odd, but I wouldna say ruint." She paused her stitchery and looked back up. "Why do ye think yerself unfit to be a mother? The twins love ye like another auntie, and ye seem to like them well enough. I've never seen ye do anything ill against them."

"It's complicated." Satia wasn't about to rehash the details of her childhood, both for Anne's sake and her own. Some pasts were better left unvisited. She lowered her voice even though the loud, squeaking rattle of the carriage bumping across the rough ground would hide a conversation better than a soundproof room. "How do women in this time *not* have children?"

"They dinna lay with their husbands—or any other man for that matter."

"Well, obviously." Anne wasn't making this easy. "But if they *do* lay with their husbands, then how?" Satia hoped the woman would come out with something other than prayer or wishful thinking.

Anne stole a glance out both windows as if about to commit a crime. "Seeds of the wild carrot. Ye must chew them within a few hours of bed play. Or a bit of wool soaked in tansy oil. Put it up inside ye before ye lay with him. If ye canna find tansy, they say vinegar works, too." She leaned forward, looked out the windows again, and checked all directions. "But ye must never speak of such things with anyone other than myself or my sisters. The church forbids it, and they have accused many a woman of witchery when, in fact, she's done nothing more than try to control her own life and her body." Her scowl hardened. "And even the seeds dinna always work. Mairi's bairns survived them." She hurried to lift a forefinger and shake it. "Now, dinna think I dinna love those two wee mites more than life itself. But when Mairi first discovered she carried them, we sorely feared she would end her life because of it. Every time they moved, it reminded her of that cruel bastard and what he had done."

"It had to have been a terrible time." She did her best to put Anne at ease. "I'm honored to know all of ye. Ye're some of the strongest women I have ever met."

"Ye possess a fair bit of braw canniness yerself." Anne gave a friendly wink. "All the lads fear ye. Ye must tell me yer secret someday, so I might use it myself."

Satia laughed. "Ye're more powerful than ye realize. Not a one of them would cross ye."

"Well, we must keep them in line." With the errant stitches corrected, Anne reinserted the rod of wood back into the yarn and returned to her work, the rhythmic dance of the needles mesmerizing.

"I do want to make him happy," Satia said, needing Anne to understand. The admission somewhat surprised her. It wasn't that she wanted him unhappy; she had just never expected to have a husband. "I'm afraid I'm ill-equipped in this centur—I was never taught that much about being a married woman." She bit her tongue, hoping Anne would be gracious enough to ignore the bungling near slip.

Anne didn't. The dance of the knitting needles halted. "What did ye start to say and then stop yerself? Mairi and I noticed ye do that a lot, but we thought it might be confusion caused by the fevers. Is that so, or have ye always been this way?"

Satia took the easy out. "The fevers." She bobbed her head with a quick nod. "Definitely, the fevers. Seems like my thoughts get all jumbled while I'm trying to talk."

Anne gave her a commiserating look. "Poor lamb. I'm sure that'll get better with time."

"I hope so." Satia meant that more than Anne could ever realize. "I can sew buttons and stitch rips and tears," she said, trying to veer the subject back to safer ground.

"That'll be more than a little handy." Head bowed over her work, Anne's nimble hands moved the needles faster. "What about cooking and cleaning?"

"Well, of course, I can clean." Satia flipped a hand at the silliness of the question. Of course, there was no risk of Anne ever seeing the jumbled state of the flat she and Breanna had shared.

"And the cooking?" The lass's hands stilled again as she pinned Satia with another stern look.

"I canna cook worth a shite."

Anne's stern look melted with a soft giggle. "A lady doesna say shite."

"Aye, well, I have never claimed to be a lady. That was Kane's doing."

"So, ye're not of high birth then?" The knitting needles remained motionless in Anne's lap.

"No. I am not." Satia wouldn't lie about that. The most believable lies kept as close to the truth as possible. "But I'm not a whore either. I stayed in the wilds mostly, studying nature, only going into town when I needed supplies." That was sort of the truth. Her research had kept her afield much of the time.

"Ahh." Anne gave an understanding dip of her head. "A follower of the old ways. I understand now."

Satia didn't, but that didn't matter as long as Anne seemed satisfied. "Do ye think ye could teach me?"

"Teach ye?"

"Aye, how to cook and whatever else I need to learn." She clutched her hands in her lap, worrying her thumbs across her knuckles. "Kane's talking of a place of our own someday, and I dinna have a clue how to keep house to suit him."

With a knowing grin, Anne leaned forward. "Keep him happy in the bed and food in his belly. That's all any man really wants."

"I can manage half of that right now."

"Then perhaps I should stay with ye longer than this trip to Edinburgh." Anne's lively brows arched to her hairline again. "It appears ye will need my help for quite some time."

"Would ye really do that?" Satia couldn't believe Anne would leave home for her. "Ye'd consider leaving yer sisters and the two weans?"

"Those three can manage the weans and homeplace just fine." She huffed out a soft laugh and took up her knitting again. "Often, there's too many of us minding that house." With a lopsided smile, she added, "A gaggle of women, even close as we are, can be a heavy cross to bear at times." She fluffed out the cowl and measured it by spreading her fingers and counting the times she could easily stretch her thumb and little finger across it. "Three hands. Nearly done." She gathered it back up and took to knitting again. "Have ye no kin, m'lady?"

"Ye dinna have to call me *m'lady*. We covered that remember?"

Anne gave a knowing tip of her head. "If ye mean we talked of it, aye, 'tis true. But 'tis safer for ye to be known as a lady of high birth rather than a white lady of the woods."

"A white lady of the woods?"

"Aye, a witch. A practicing pagan." She shrugged. "I dinna give a whit that ye're not a Christian, but some would." Her nonchalant air shifted to one of warning. "Dangerously so, if ye get my meaning."

Satia's stomach clenched, whether from Anne's warning or the rocking conveyance she wasn't sure. She swallowed hard and nodded.

"Ye've gone all peely-wally of a sudden." Anne reached down and picked up a wooden mallet concealed beneath the folds of her skirts.

"What's that for?" With a quick glance at the door, Satia wondered how badly jumping out of the carriage might hurt.

Anne rolled her eyes, then banged the mallet against the wall of the carriage above her head. Hard. Three times. The sway of the wooden box slowed to a stop. Hoofbeats thundered close, the latch rattled, then the door flew open.

"What is it?" Kane gripped both sides of the doorframe, ready to launch himself inside. "Are ye unwell?"

"I'm…I'm fine." She pushed away the blankets piled across her, suddenly very warm. "I'm overheated. Just…too hot." She wasn't too hot, she was worried. If Anne thought her a witch, and the men believed her to be some sort of fairy queen, how long would it take for the wrong person to get hold of that news and decide to roast her?

"She's gone whiter than my best linen," Anne said. "Let's get her a bit of air and let her stretch her legs, aye?"

"Come—Anne's right. Ye dinna look well at all." Kane took hold of her hands and gently pulled, leaving her little choice.

"I'm fine. Really."

"Anne doesna think so, and neither do I." He eased her into his arms, lifted her down, and steadied her as he set her on her feet. Tucking her hand in the crook of his arm, he gave her a stern nod. "Come, m'lady. We shall walk a bit and get ye some air."

As soon as they'd gotten out of earshot of the others, Satia leaned against him as though needing more support. She didn't, just wanted to give everyone that impression. "She thinks I'm a witch," she whispered up to him.

Kane's jaw hardened, his tensed muscles rippling beneath the darkness of his neatly trimmed beard. "Does she?" After a few more steps, he added, "And why might that be?"

"I told her she didna have to call me *m'lady* because—I'm not. I explained that I mainly stayed in the wild studying nature and only traveled to town when I needed stuff. But I didn't tell her what *century* I did it in or exactly where." When he didn't comment, she added, "The best lies stay closest to the truth as possible."

With a pained scowl, he scrubbed a hand across his forehead. "Aye, but the way ye described yerself made ye sound like a white lady of the wood."

"That's what she said."

He still didn't comment, just glared straight ahead as if wrestling with inner demons.

"But she said she didna care that I wasna a Christian and would keep calling me *m'lady* to protect me."

He came to a halt, planting his feet as though about to be hit by a massive force. "Are ye pagan?"

"No." To be truthful, she didn't know what she was. She'd had too many run-ins with cruel, two-faced Christians that made the tenets of Christianity a joke. "I think I believe in God, but I dinna think we're on speaking terms right now. I'm fairly sure He's forgotten I exist. But if Anne thinks I'm a witch, and yer men think I'm some sort of loch fairy queen that foretells the future, how long is it going to be before I'm roasting on a spit?"

"No wonder ye went pale." He drew her into a tender hug and held her. "Ye can trust Anne. And the lads. Ye're safe with them." He kissed the top of her head. "Ye can also trust that I will never allow ye to roast on a spit, ye ken? Just mind yer words, m'love. Mind them closer than ye ever have before."

"I'm trying, but I am so not good at this." Her stomach went all queasy again at attempting to filter everything before it came out of her mouth.

"Ye told me ye survived on the streets for a while. Yerself and yer sister?"

"Aye."

"Did everyone know who ye were and what ye were doing? Did they not find it strange that two young lassies, not even women grown, had no one looking after them?"

"No. We conned them." She understood then what he meant. Gaze locked with his, she nodded. "So, ye're saying I'm running the biggest con of a lifetime?"

"And yer life depends on it—that is, if con means what I think it means." He stroked her cheek, seeming calmer but still appearing troubled. "Ye must never let down yer guard, m'love. Not ever. Understand?"

She stepped back and turned away, hugging herself.

"Satia?"

"I'm going to find a bush. Stand watch, aye?"

"Aye." His tone revealed that he knew she didn't really need to pee, but in fact, just needed time alone.

She tromped up the rise toward a cluster of rowan saplings. How appropriate. The tree fabled to protect against witchcraft and enchantment. Maybe if she peed there, they would know her to be just an average human trapped in a time different from her own. She took shelter behind the bushy young trees, hiked up her skirts, and squatted. As she tried to convince herself to pee, she frowned at the clusters of partially opened blooms about to burst into clumps of white flowers that bees, flies, and beetles couldn't resist. She could already detect their distinctive fragrance of slightly rotten meat even though the flowers hadn't fully opened.

Elbows propped on her knees, she contemplated squatting there as long as her legs would hold. If only her return into the loch had worked and sent her back to the future. Kane's rich deep voice rumbled below, floating up to her on the breeze. She blew out a heavy sigh. If she had returned to the twenty-first century, there would be no Kane. No marriage. No more of the most connected lovemaking she had ever experienced, and now she couldn't imagine a life without him. Funny how fast things changed.

"Satia! Be ye all right?" he called out.

"Fine. I just need another minute or so." That was a bare-faced lie. It would take more than a minute or so to figure her new life out. At least, Anne had offered to help. She felt sure most of the men would. Except Albie. That one there didn't like her, and she didn't trust him. Maybe that's why she'd broken his nose while wild with fever. An unleashed subconscious could be a dangerous thing. She managed a pathetic trickle of urine, dried herself with a leaf, and stood. At least she didn't have to lie about that. She had officially peed on the rowan trees. For good measure, she snapped off a branch and carried it back down the hillside with her. Just as she suspected, the men's eyes widened. Even Anne and Kane shuffled a step back.

"It's a shame it's not the time of year for the berries." She swished the branch back and forth. "Course, ye do have to be careful, or they'll poison ye depending on the age of the tree and time of year."

"Yer cheeks are brighter, m'lady," Anne said, completely ignoring the rowan branch. "I knew fresh air and a walk would do ye good." She led the way to the carriage door, hoisted herself inside, and waved Kane forward. "Hand her up, and I'll get her sorted."

"Ye're a canny lass," he rumbled quietly against her ear. "Pray the sight of the rowan works."

"I'll do what I can." She tried to climb up into the carriage by herself but failed. The walk up the hillside, then back down had left her arms and legs trembling. Kane's strong hands gripped her waist and lifted her in as if she weighed no more than a feather. She settled back into the seat, sitting normally rather than with her legs stretched out across the bench beside her. "Thank ye. I'm much better now. So much so, I think I'll try riding like this for a while."

He stepped up and gave her a long, slow kiss that made breathing difficult. Then he turned to Anne and gave a meaningful nod. "Ye know what to do, lass. I beg ye not to fail either of us."

"I will not." Anne spoke with convincing certainty, her chin lifted to a proud slant. "Ye should know that well enough."

"Aye, I do. But I also had to ask. Ye know that as well as I."

She waved him away. "On wi' ye then, or we'll never get there."

He cast Satia one last glance before closing and latching the door. She gave him an encouraging smile, not feeling any more confident about fooling fourteenth-century folk, and she could tell he didn't either.

"I canna stand the smell of rowan flowers." Anne tossed the branch out the window. She dusted off her hands and took up her knitting. "Whatever possessed ye to snap the thing off and bring it back to the carriage?"

"Ye know good and well what possessed me." Satia wasn't falling for that trick.

Anne smiled. "Aye, I do. But ye do realize that doesna prove ye're not a witch? It could just mean ye're the most powerful enchantress this age has seen."

"I am not a witch." Satia gave up, swiveled sideways, and stretched out on the bench. As she pillowed her head on her arm and snuggled against the back of the seat, she twitched a shrug. "I'm just tired and misunderstood." A weary laugh escaped her. "Have been my whole life, so ye'd think I'd be used to it by now."

"Once yer strength returns, ye'll be better," Anne reassured. "I saw the fire in yer eyes afore ye fell ill. Ye're nay one to give up easy."

Satia yawned. "So, will ye teach me to cook and sew?"

"And knit," Anne added in a tone that brooked no argument.

"And knit," Satia repeated with a repressed huff.

"Aye, m'lady, and I will help ye keep house until ye have no more need of me." Focused on her knitting, she smiled. "We shall be friends ye and I. Ye shall see."

"I am sure we will." Satia pulled the covers up over her shoulder and shielded her eyes from the sun's rays flooding in through the window. "As long as ye've got an endless supply of patience, we will be golden."

CHAPTER ELEVEN

Since they would reach Edinburgh tomorrow, Anne convinced Albie to allow Satia to prepare the final supper of their journey. The past few days, over the course of the long carriage ride, Anne had tutored her about the art of frying bread and putting together hearty stews with whatever a successful hunt and the land provided. It all sounded simple enough. Time to put the instructions into action.

She could do this. After all, at university, she'd aced most of her classes with very little study. As long as she paid close attention to lectures, she soaked up information like a sponge. But one sniff of the pot bubbling over the fire told Satia her overconfidence had shot her in the foot. She wafted the steam toward her face and inhaled it again, studying the aroma. It smelled… off. In an acrid, bitter sort of way. "Anne, I fear I've made a feckin' mess of this."

"Ladies dinna say feckin'," Anne said as she joined Satia by the fire. She leaned forward, took a whiff, then wrinkled her nose and backed up a step. "'Tis scorched. Did ye not stir it often like I told ye?"

"How often is often?" Satia couldn't recall stirring the soup at all. She'd been too busy mixing dough for the fried bread, making a mess of that, and having to start over. Twice.

"God help ye." Anne wrapped her hands in her apron, lifted the pot from the fire, and waddled the weighty burnt mess across the camp. She sat it on the ground, found the only other pot they had, and dumped a fair amount of the stew into it. "I think I've saved the best of it. With the blackened part out, it willna be as bad." She cast a dubious glance at the pot encrusted with a heavy layer of charred stickiness. "I'll take that one to the stream and set it to soaking in the hopes of saving it."

"Will the soup ye saved taste good?"

The disbelieving slant of Anne's brows spoke volumes.

"Will it at least be edible?"

"If they're hungry enough." The harried woman placed the recovery pot on the fire and bustled over to the small crate containing their food supplies. "We'll add more spices, fry extra bread, and stir in some fresh spring greens." She gave a decisive nod. "Then we'll tell them to be thankful because many go to their beds this night with no food in their bellies at all."

"I am sorry." Frustrated disappointment made Satia catch her bottom lip between her teeth. How could she have forgotten to stir the pot? She threw up her hands and went back to her makeshift workstation atop a boulder, searching for a way to redeem herself. The sad lump of dough that had failed Anne's inspection caught her attention. "What if we pinch off little pieces of this dough here and make it into noodles or dumplings? Would that work?"

Anne gave a defeated shrug. "Who's ta say? It canna make it any worse."

The youngest McBride sister pulled no punches, but Satia appreciated that. At least the woman was honest. "Sorry again," Satia offered.

"Stop apologizing and get started on yer noodle dumpling idea. I'll do the fried bread tonight. It appears ye've struggled with that as well."

"I warned ye I couldna cook."

With a slow nod, Anne pursed her lips as if struggling to keep her thoughts to herself. Finally, she forced a smile. "Ye did at that, m'lady."

"What smells—" Toff choked on the remainder of the comment as Kane cut him off with a hard backhand across the chest.

"So good," Kane finished with a warning cut of his eyes at the rest of the men as they entered the camp. "What smells so good?"

"Scorched noodle soup," Satia said, lifting her chin with fake pride as she pinched off more dough and stirred it into the broth. "Where I come from, men eat this to enhance their…" She let her gaze linger for a moment on Kane's crotch, then added, "stamina."

All four men turned in unison and stared at Kane as if seeing him in a new light, making Satia realize she had just insulted her husband. "Not that ye have any need of it, m'love," she hurried to add. With a dismissive tip of her head toward the others, she dropped more bits of dough into the now bubbling broth. "But with us nearly in Edinburgh and all, I thought a few of the lads might make use of it." Then she remembered to stir the mess before she scorched it again.

Anne settled down beside her and set to the task of frying bread from the proper dough she'd mixed. "Ye're a canny woman for certain," she said, so only Satia could hear. "'Tis why I am truly proud to call ye friend."

Satia treasured Anne's announcement as the highest praise she could ever receive. She leaned downward and whispered, "How do I know when the noodles are done?"

Anne glanced at her and gave an almost imperceptible shrug. "I dinna ken. I've never made yer noodles."

"Well, neither have I."

"Fish one out and try it. If it's fit to eat, it's done."

Satia stared at the simmering pot, dreading the outcome. Diving in with the long-handled ladle, she stirred and lifted, then stirred and lifted again. "They're gone," she whispered in horror.

Anne popped to her feet and nudged closer, scowling down at

the pot. "Give me that ladle." After several foraging attempts of her own, she shook her head. "How many eggs did ye put in yer dough? How much grease?"

"Shite!" She had forgotten the eggs. And the grease. No wonder the dough disintegrated. All that held the flour together was water.

"How could ye forget both?" Anne gave her an incredulous look.

"I guess I got too wrapped up in putting together the stew, tending the fire, trying to mix the dough, and chopping the herbs. How do ye get it all done at once?" Poor Kane would starve to death whenever they settled in a home of their own.

Anne's mouth tightened, and her cheeks flared even redder than usual. She grabbed hold of Satia's hand and squeezed. "I think there's a wee bit of flour left. Make more dough." Her battle-stance glare tightened even more. "With eggs and grease this time. Then make yer noodles. There's no helpin' it since ye told them it was scorched noodle soup. Ye must make them work."

"I'm on it." Satia hoped Anne didn't decide to back out on her offer to stay and help until she didn't need her anymore. At this rate, she would need the lass forever. There was so much to remember and do, and the heat from a campfire was so difficult to adjust. No simple turn of a knob. Coals had to be shifted. Pots lowered, lifted, or set to the side. What a hot mess. Literally.

With two handfuls of flour, a generous glop of rendered fat, three eggs, and probably too much salt, Satia worked the concoction against the curved sides of the shallow wooden bowl until a not-too-disappointing dough ball formed. Wishing she'd watched more cooking videos, she carried it to the pot and started rolling bits of it between her palms to make the same sort of snaky strands she'd seen children create with modeling clay. After dropping a few into the bubbling pot, she stirred and separated the wicked things that kept trying to glop together.

"They're not disappearing," she whispered to Anne, who had

returned to the chore of frying bread.

"Thank the Almighty." The maid slathered a flat stone with a generous amount of fat, waited until it took on a rippling sheen, then dropped the patted out rounds of dough across it. A happy sizzling filled the air, along with the rich, mouthwatering scent of the deliciously greasy treat.

"Now *that* smells fine," Toff said.

"It's first watch for ye," Kane growled with a threatening step toward him. "Now."

"But I havena had my supper." The fair-haired warrior cast a longing stare at the cooking stone where the edges of the first pieces of bread were already crisping to a golden brown.

"Take ye an oatcake or two." Kane bared his teeth and advanced another step. "If there's any stew or bread left, ye can have it when Jac relieves ye."

"Ye know I meant no disrespect to Lady Satia." Toff squared his shoulders and held his ground. "I didna say anything wrong."

Satia snatched up the first two pieces of fried bread as soon as Anne took them off the stone. "Yer gallantry is appreciated," she said to Kane as she stepped between the men. "But it's not warranted this time." She held out the steaming bread to Toff. "Here. I took no offense, and I am sure there will be soup left."

Toff accepted the offering and shot a smug grin at Kane. "Thank ye, m'lady. 'Tis an honor to serve one who possesses such wisdom."

"Dinna be an arse about it and make me regret my generosity," she warned, remembering too late Toff's tendency to gloat.

Kane lunged toward the man.

She caught hold of his arm and squeezed, tugging him back.

Toff bit off a generous hunk of the bread, spun about, and strode off into the woods. "I canna wait to try the soup, m'lady!" he called back.

Kane started after him, but she pulled him back again. "No. Leave him be. Ye know ye're the better man."

"I'll be thrashing his arse for him." He glared at the spot

where Toff had disappeared into the trees.

"No. Just come and get some bread before it's all gone." She wrinkled her nose at the gurgling pot of questionable soup nestled in the coals. "I'm not too sure about that stew so, trust me, he did not hurt my feelings."

"That is neither here nor there. The man should show more respect." He curled an arm around her and pulled her close. "I willna have ye hurt. Not in any way. By anyone."

Her heart swelled as she leaned against him, reveling in the warmth of his caring strength. "No one has ever taken care of me like ye do."

"And no one ever will."

"Kane!" Toff's shout came from deeper in the woods, and his voice no longer dripped with smug sarcasm. Instead, his tone shot a surge of adrenaline through Satia. She knew Kane felt the same by the way his body tensed beneath her fingers.

"To arms!" Kane bellowed, then gently pushed Satia toward the carriage. "Inside wi' ye, now. Dinna come out 'til I tell ye it's safe, ye ken?" He caught Anne's attention and waved her onward. "The both of ye. To the carriage. Now!"

"'Tis unnecessary to hide yer women from yer liege," advised a deep voice that stopped Satia and made her turn. *Robert the Bruce.* She breathed the words to herself, barely moving her lips. There he sat, her ancient ancestor, proven through DNA testing. The man she had studied in books and online, astride his white horse within a few meters of her.

Kane and his men took a knee.

Satia didn't know whether to kneel, curtsy, or run and hide. She knew protocol for twenty-first century royalty, but not Scotland's legendary fourteenth-century king. After a harried glance at Anne, she mimicked the same deep curtsy and bowed her head.

"Rise. All of ye." The Bruce rumbled a congenial chuckle. "I found myself in need of solitude, so I thought to ride for a while." He dismounted, closed the distance between himself and Kane in two broad strides, and greeted him with a hearty grasp of his forearm. "'Tis good fortune itself that I have come upon ye. My restlessness must have been the Almighty Himself leading me to ye."

"'Tis good to see ye, my king." Kane gripped King Robert's forearm just as hard and clapped his other hand to the man's shoulder.

Satia noted the two men greeted each other more like equals, almost like brothers even, rather than king and subject. As Kane turned her way, she tensed and staunched the urge to back away, knowing he was about to introduce her. *Be careful,* she silently reminded herself, repeating it over and over. Not only to protect herself but also to protect Kane.

Kane motioned her forward and smiled. "Allow me to introduce ye to my wife, the Lady Satia."

She clenched her teeth, managed a modest, respectful smile, then moved to Kane's side with her head still bowed. "Yer Majesty," she said, and offered another curtsy.

"Rise, Lady Satia." The gallant Bruce took her hand and steadied her when she bobbled a bit to one side. "'Tis an honor to meet the woman so able to lead my most trusted advisor astray." Although he didn't inflect resentment into the words, Satia sensed it just the same. The ruler still obviously brooded about Kane not returning to Edinburgh before the siege. The mighty one was not pleased that she existed.

"I beg yer forgiveness, Yer Majesty, but surely ye wouldna respect a man if he turned his back on a damsel in distress?" While she would do her best to show the required respect for Kane's sake, she would not be bullied, not even by the renowned King Robert himself. "What wise king doesna value chivalry as much as loyalty?"

The Bruce's wide smile split his reddish-brown mustache and beard. "Indeed, m'lady. Well said." Settling a sly look on Kane, he gave an impressed tip of his head. "Not only found yerself a rare beauty, but a canny lass as well."

"That is the truth of it, for certain." Kane tucked her hand in the crook of his arm.

Satia acknowledged the compliment with a gracious nod but braced herself, sensing the Bruce had more to say. Perhaps she could delay whatever sparring he intended to continue by escaping to check on supper. King or not, she'd burned the soup once; she didn't want to burn it again.

"I beg yer leave, sire." She eased a step back to make her escape. "I must stir the meal so it doesna burn." *Worse than it already has*, she silently added. No sense admitting defeat publicly.

The Bruce patted his stomach with both hands, lifted his nose, and sniffed. "I knew I smelled a fine meal cooking. Will ye make a king beg for an invitation at yer table, Lady Satia?"

"Why, of course, ye are welcome, Yer Majesty." She hurried to the pot and stirred, wondering what her fate would be if she poisoned the king. What would happen to history? She clutched the ladle tighter and sent up a rare wish to any entity that might be listening. "Dinna kill him," she whispered to the bubbling stew. "And dinna be ruint either."

Heaven answered favorably. The handcrafted noodles hadn't glopped together into a single gummy knot. At least, not yet. She cast a worried eye at Anne, whose soft gray eyes had gone wide with fear. The Bruce would probably order them both beheaded after the first bite. She saw that thought flashing in Anne's face like a neon sign. "Is the bread done? Soup's ready."

"Uhm…aye." Anne hurried to join her, gathering the last of the fried rounds onto a wooden platter and covering them with a cloth.

"Dinna worry. I will tell him I'm to blame." Satia spoke as low as she could, taking care to keep her back to Kane and the king. "He's already ratty toward me because I kept Kane from him. Ye should be safe."

"I willna let ye do that." Anne scowled at her with such reproachfulness it felt like a slap. "Ye are a lady. Act like it."

"Fine." Satia held up a shallow bowl and banged on it with a wooden spoon. "Gather round, lads. Our honored guest is hungry." With a lively swish of the stirring stick, she waved King Robert forward. "Come, sire. As our guest, ye are first." She embraced the live or die decision to treat the man like everyone else. Ridiculed and scorned by pompous souls all her life, Satia learned long ago that some couldn't be pleased no matter how much you bowed and scraped. Never would she do that again. And if this was a poor life choice, at least she would die with her pride intact. "Supper is served!"

Kane flinched and covered his face with one hand; the other men paled, and Satia wondered if Anne was about to faint dead away. Poor lass didn't seem well at all.

"In for a penny, in for a pound." She gave a decisive nod. "Let's do this."

Pale beyond measure, Anne held out a bowl and stared down at the gurgling contents of the pot as if it held a witch's brew.

Satia filled the vessel with an ample portion, added three slices of fried bread for luck, then handed it to the king. "To yer health, my king." What the man didn't realize was she meant it, hoping the concoction wouldn't kill him.

"I thank ye, m'lady." The Bruce accepted his supper with a regal nod, then lifted the bowl to his nose and sniffed. A puzzled look drew his bushy brows together. He sniffed again, then peered at the contents closer. "And pray what do ye call this fine meal?"

"Scorched noodle soup." Satia gave him her best smile, then added a saucy wink. "Where I'm from, it's known to help a man with his…uhm…stamina."

The king's light brown eyes flared wide. With a meaningful rumbling that fell somewhere between a lascivious chuckle and a lusty growl, he turned to Kane and nudged him with an elbow. "I'm beginning to understand what kept ye away so long." Before Kane could comment, he peered at him closer. "Are ye unwell, man? Yer color's gone off."

"Must be the firelight." Kane snatched up a bowl and held it out. "A hearty helping, m'love. My wame's growling for yer fine meal."

Satia bit her lip. Concern about her soup sending this fine man to his ruin filled her. She filled the bowl, added the bread, and placed it in his hands. "Sorry," she whispered, meaning the apology more than she had ever meant anything in her life.

"It will be fine, dear one," he whispered back with such tenderness she almost wept.

"Upon my soul, Albie. Why is it ye never prepared such an offering for me?" The Bruce scooped up another hearty dollop and shoved it into his mouth. "'Tis the best venison soup I have ever eaten, m'lady." He brought the bowl closer to his face and scooped in another bite.

"I shall learn the recipe," Albie said with a dubious look into his bowl. He sampled the contents, tipped his head to the side, then shrugged and settled down to enjoying the meal.

"Praise God Almighty," Anne whispered with a discreet pat on Satia's back. "'Tis a miracle for certain."

"Ye got that right." Satia sampled the thick brown substance laced with the pale noodles. It wasn't half bad with its smoky rich flavor balanced by a not unpleasant acidic tartness. Now, if she could only remember what she did—besides letting it scorch bad enough to ruin the first iron pot.

"A wily beauty. A fine cook. Ye are a blessed man, indeed," the Bruce said to Kane.

"That I am." From his seat on a downed tree, Kane beamed at her with a proud smile.

The king surrendered his empty bowl to Anne with a thankful nod, then settled more comfortably on the log beside Kane. After a long swig from the whisky flask being passed around the fire, he gave Satia an expectant look that warned she wasn't in the clear yet. "Might ye see fit to grant me more details about Bannockburn, m'lady?"

"Bannockburn?" Satia stacked the soiled bowls and clutched them against her aproned waist. "I dinna ken what ye mean, sire, and I really must get these washed. Scorched soup sticks like glue once it dries."

"I shall see to the washing." Anne grabbed the bowls from Satia before she could argue.

"There. Ye see?" A sly knowing glittered in the Bruce's eyes. "The fine Mistress Anne will take care of supper's final chores." He crossed his legs at the ankles and folded his hands across his belly. "Now, Lady Satia, pray tell me every detail ye can about yer vision. It could save lives, ye ken?"

Satia wiped her sweating palms on her apron. Not sure what to say, she turned and stared down into the fire. She had to give the king what he wished. Deep in her heart, she sensed Kane's standing in Scotland, and possibly his life depended on it. "On the first day of battle, on the twenty-third of June, Sir Henry de Bohun, riding a massive warhorse, will charge at ye with his lance lowered to run ye through." She looked over at the horses. "Ye must ride yer nimble palfrey there into battle that day. 'Twill help ye maneuver to the side at the last moment, stand in yer stirrups, and split Bohun's head in two with yer ax." She recited the scene exactly as she had read it on a website, hoping it was true and not a glorified embellishment of what really happened. She hadn't even known what a *palfrey* was at the time but did remember Googling it to find out. Thank heavens, she possessed an almost photographic memory when she applied herself to learning something word for word.

With her gaze still locked on the flames, she nodded. "His death sets the stage for the battle by greatly reducing the English's morale." She finally turned and faced the king, who sat on the log with rapt attention. "But the battle will not be won until the second day. Stirling will be regained, and King Edward II of England will be defeated." She laced her fingers together and clutched her hands at her waist. "That is all I know. Ye must understand I have no control over when I receive such knowledge or what I will be shown at any time." Hopefully, that would deter him from planning to make her his permanent crystal ball.

"I have but one more question. I beg ye to find it in yer heart to answer it." The king paused and scrubbed a burly hand across his mouth. "Do ye ken if I will ever have a son? An heir?"

The pleading in the man's face pried the words from her lips even though she had promised herself not to say another word. "Aye. But not until the year 1324. David Bruce, the future David II of Scotland, will be born in Dunfermline."

The man beamed, nodding so hard he rocked forward on the log. "King David."

"And that is all I know. Truly." She noted the awestruck fear reflected on the faces of the other men, including Kane. If any of them ever chose to turn against her, they would burn her at the stake for sure. "I really must go help, Anne. It isna fair that she bear the brunt of the cleanup."

The Bruce pushed himself up from his seat, closed the distance between them, and took both her hands in his. "Thank ye, m'lady. Ye have strengthened me this night, and I know in my heart our Almighty Lord sent ye to do so." With a regal bow, he squeezed her hands. "I am forever in yer debt. Never hesitate to make any need known to me, ye ken?"

She managed a shy smile and dipped a teetering curtsy. "I am glad I made ye feel better, sire." She eased her hands out of his and fled, hoping she hadn't endangered the future of Scotland by anything she had just said.

HER SHIVERING CONCERNED him. Kane scooted closer and pressed a hand to her forehead. Merely warm against his palm. Praise Almighty God. The searing heat of her earlier fevers hadn't returned.

He leaned over her. "Tell me, love," he whispered, so those sprawled on their blankets close by wouldn't hear. "Tell me what troubles ye."

"I worry about telling so much."

"Telling so much?" He understood. Or thought he did. Just hoped she didn't worry about telling him anything she might need to say.

"What if my talking to the Bruce about what hasna happened yet throws a spanner in the natural order of things? What if it makes something *not* happen that should happen?"

He didn't know what a *spanner* was, but it sounded ill-omened. "Did ye tell him as it actually happened before?"

"I think so. To the best of my studies. But what if the historians or bloggers got it all wrong? What if they embellished? Or made things up to make themselves look more important? King Robert is a legend, ye ken? There are statues and artwork of him everywhere." She shivered again and backed up tighter against him.

Statues? Works of art? Impressive. "What is a *blogger*?" he asked quietly. It sounded like a stable chore. Her deep sigh told him she wasn't in the mood to go into a detailed explanation. It didn't matter. He knew about historians. Instead, he tugged the blanket higher around her shoulders and wrapped an arm around her. "Ye did what ye had to. Ye couldna refuse the Bruce."

"But did ye see Toff as soon as I said all those things? And Jac and Rob?" She resettled her shoulders as if unable to get comfortable. "And I think if Albie still had any hair, it wouldha fallen out all over again."

He had seen their faces and would be reminding them of their loyalties before they set out tomorrow. "They willna betray ye," he promised, knowing that's what she feared.

"I need people to think I'm just an average, ordinary person like anyone else." She sounded so despondent, his heart ached for her. "I'm not the only one at risk here. They could come after ye for marrying me. Sheltering a witch and all that? Ye know how barmy people get about things they dinna understand."

"When England steps down, and they make a truce, we will

build a home off to ourselves. We will be safe. I promise." He had already planned a fine dwelling. All the outbuildings. A sturdy, stable large enough to shelter horses, cows, goats, and sheep through the winter. Roosts for chickens. And two gardens. One just outside the kitchen door for herbs and vegetables and one with fine soft grass. The perfect place for their precious wee ones to play.

She blew out a heavy sigh. "If I remember correctly, the truce isna agreed upon until 1323. That's nine years from now. And the Bruce willna be satisfied with just winning Scotland's independence. He continues poking at the Brits for years by raiding Northern England. In fact, he almost captures York." She clutched his arm. "He will want ye at his side through all of that."

His mother's wisdom came to him, and once again, he was thankful that she had nattered her sayings at him endlessly throughout his childhood. "If we worry about what ill tidings might befall us, we lose sight of all the joyfulness of the present. We willna even realize all the good things we already have." He lifted his head and pressed a lingering kiss to her temple, inhaling deeply as he did so. "Ye smell of fried bread and a warm fire."

"Where will we stay in Edinburgh?" She ignored what he'd meant as a compliment, obviously trapped in her worries.

"At the Bruce's post."

"The castle?"

"Nay, love. Too much destruction there. The Earl of Moray, along with the help of a man named William Francis, excelled in their efforts to please their king. The Bruce inspected it. Said they had done well." Her soft warmth and enticing scent turned his mind to other things. "Ye seem almost as hearty and hale as when we first met." He stretched over her, nuzzling through her curls and nibbling at her ear. "We've nay consummated our vows yet," he reminded as he slid his hand lower and squeezed her thigh.

She gently pushed him away. "And we are not going to consummate them here." The stern scolding of her whisper made him pause. "I willna put on a show for the others."

"They're asleep."

"As we should be, too. I said no." In a more sympathetic tone, she added, "I want ye just as bad as ye want me, but I canna enjoy it with everyone else so close." She wiggled around, turning to face him. Her velvety mouth tenderly rained kisses along his throat as she tickled her fingers through the untied neck of his léine. "I promise to make it worth the wait. Ye willna regret it."

He allowed himself a long low groan, caught hold of her fine wee arse in both hands, and ground her curves against him. "Ye've given me fierce risin', lass, but for ye, I will wait."

"Ye willna regret it," she said, nestling her head against his chest.

"Aye, I will. But I shall do my best to bear it."

CHAPTER TWELVE

"DO YE THINK they'll know what we were doing?" She turned away from him and pointed at her back. "Laces, please."

"I am quite certain they ken exactly what we were doing." Kane brushed her hair aside and trailed kisses along her bare neck and shoulders before tugging the dress closed and attending her ties. He nibbled at the ticklish spot behind her ear, his mouth trembling against her skin with a self-satisfied chuckle. "How could they not? The bed collapsed."

"Aye, well, there was that." The memory of what led up to that crash made her want him all over again, but they needed to get downstairs and do whatever it was that Scots planning an independent Scotland did. While she didn't look forward to the chore, she found herself a great deal more relaxed about it now that she'd kept her promise and properly consummated their vows. Several times, in fact. Belatedly, she wondered if anyone in Edinburgh sold those wild carrot seeds Anne recommended. It was most definitely too late for the bit of wool soaked in tansy oil.

His hands smooth from her back to her front, cupping her breasts with a gentle, suggestive squeeze. "I could send down word that ye're still feeling poorly, and I must stay with ye to ensure ye're resting properly."

"Dinna tempt me." She would much rather stay up in their room rather than go downstairs.

He stepped closer and ground his hard length against her bum. "Do ye find that tempting, m'love?"

She reached back, slid her hand down into his trews, and stroked. "Ye know I do, but we did just finally get our clothes on with all the endless ties and buttons. 'Tis a feckin' chore getting in and out of these things. They really need to get on with inventing zippers."

"If that's all that's holding ye back…" He spun her around and went up against the wall with her. He shoved her skirts up out of the way and drove inside her with such force, she hoped the wall didn't collapse like the bed and send them into the street below.

His powerful hands clutched her arse. With her fingers digging into his shoulders and him pounding with a delicious rhythm, she decided vertical held some lovely benefits. Then a knock sounded at the door.

"Ignore them," she rasped. Eyes closed, she reveled in every sensation. So close. So very close to pure bliss.

"Aye," was all he managed to groan, hammering harder and giving a determined growl that vibrated through her.

The knocking at the door grew louder.

"Go away!" she bellowed, teetering on the cusp of what promised to be another brilliant orgasm.

"Aye!" Kane joined in. "Afore I kill ye!"

Blessed silence followed, and the knocking stopped.

And then she teetered no more. Every nerve ending exploded with such powerful deliciousness, the rest of the world fell away. "Yes!" she shouted at the top of her lungs as wave after wave crashed across her.

Kane shoved in hard and stayed, then roared something in either Latin or Gaelic. She didn't know which and definitely didn't care. All that mattered was that once again, they'd melded into one. She cradled him in her arms as he pinned her to the wall and rested his head on her shoulder, tenderly kissing her throat between gasping breaths. "I love ye, my own," he whispered so many times she lost count.

"I love ye more," she said, meaning it more than he would ever know. She had never loved anyone. Not ever. Not like this. But this man, the way he cared, protected, and bared his soul, demanded she love him back. It would be the biggest mistake of her life to refuse.

She smoothed her hands across his broad shoulders. "I guess we should behave now and go downstairs. I'm sure the king is waiting for ye."

With a reluctant huff, he stepped back and eased her down to her feet. "I'm sure ye're right, but that doesna mean I like it."

"Yer liege *is* waiting for ye," King Robert called out, his voice muffled through the door. "And if ye've finished *resting,* I would appreciate a word with the both of ye."

"He is going to order us beheaded." She shook down her skirts, then made a futile attempt at taming her hair. "Or do they hang in this century instead of beheading?" She couldn't remember.

Kane didn't answer, but his jaw hardened to a displeased line as he fastened his trews, strode across the room, and yanked open the door. "My liege," he said, the respectfulness in his tone sounding more than a little strained.

The Bruce strode in, his face dark as a thundercloud. "I ken how it is with a new wife, but we've duties to attend to. Some of which ye might not be aware of since ye were so long absent from my side."

"That was my fault," Satia said, stepping forward. This legendary man didn't come across as a lofty, untouchable royal. He was just a man struggling to help his country. "If ye wish to be ratty with anyone, be ratty with me. Not Kane."

"Ratty?" Robert repeated, his thick brows knotting tighter as an expression of befuddlement overpowered his scowl.

"Hard to get along with." She shrugged. "Impossible to please." She folded her arms across her chest as she added. "Ye know ye're acting like a spoilt English king, right?"

"Satia!" Kane stepped between them. "Forgive her, my liege, she isna privy to all our ways."

"I thought ye were a Scot," Robert replied, stepping around Kane and peering at her as if she was a lab experiment in a Petri dish.

"I am. By blood." What would be the safest and simplest way to explain? "As a child, they took me from the woman who bore me. Some of my youth was in Scotland, but I spent a good part of it living on the streets of London until I made it back here."

"Why did they take ye from yer mother?" The Bruce's tone had leveled out, and so had the reddish flare across his cheeks.

"She treated me poorly." She would say no more, remembering her promise to herself to tell no one any details. To speak the memories resurrected the pain. She would never utter the dark words. Not ever. "I know I'm not like ye're other subjects, but ye can trust my loyalty even though I nearly fall on my arse every time I try to curtsy for ye."

Thankfully, the man smiled. "Perhaps I should give ye a special dispensation from curtsying as payment for that fine meal ye fed me last night."

"That would be most generous and very much appreciated." She hoped he was serious.

"So be it, then. Now come. The both of ye." He turned without another word and headed out the door.

"He was serious, right?" she whispered, hurrying to keep up with Kane.

"Aye." Kane slowed a bit. "Ye will find the Bruce rarely jests about a dispensation."

He seemed distracted. Worried. She pondered asking him what was wrong, but instinct stopped her. Kane and the Bruce were on shaky terms right now because Kane had placed his own wants and needs over those of his liege. Repeatedly. Politically, that might be lethal. She granted him silence and the privacy of his thoughts. His life could depend on whatever was on his mind.

The long narrow hallways, dimly lit by flickering lanterns, seemed menacing and endless. And it was daytime. Satia couldn't imagine walking here at night without a weapon. While she prided herself on not being the skittish sort, that didn't mean she wasn't alert to possible dangers. The stairs were worse since only a single lantern hung between the landings. Although the Bruce and Kane lauded the inn as one of the finest in Edinburgh, it still felt…questionable, for lack of a better term. Like a member's only den where outcast members ended up murdered. At least it was clean and, near as she could tell, the only people allowed inside were those granted admission by the Bruce himself.

When they reached the low-ceilinged common area that served as dining area, pub, and room check-in, the Bruce strode across the space, ignoring the expectant looks from those sitting at a few of the tables. He headed straight for an open door behind the counter where a pair of barmaids kept the ale flowing.

Satia caught hold of Kane's arm and tucked in close. An eeriness prickled across her like an ominous premonition about to make itself known. As they followed the Bruce into the private room, she immediately understood why. Intuition never failed her.

A tall man wearing the drab robes of a monk stood with his back to them in front of a makeshift altar bearing a crude wooden crucifix flanked by candles heavy with dripping wax. He didn't turn upon their entry, just kept puttering through books and parchments spread in front of him, muttering under his breath as his quill twitched with harried scratchings.

"Friar Law," King Robert said. "I have brought her to ye."

Satia had never studied the Spanish Inquisition but knew enough about it to start backing toward the door to escape any chance of a Scottish version. Then the friar turned and faced her. All thoughts and instincts collided, sputtering to a screeching halt. She knew this man. From the twenty-first century. Her will to survive kicked in before she blurted it out. He recognized her. It flashed in his watery blue eyes.

The friar recovered quickly, making the sign of the cross in midair, as if calling on every saint in Christendom to bless her. "Welcome, m'lady. His Majesty has told me much about ye."

"Has he?" Satia doubted the king could tell her favorite professor from the University of Edinburgh anything that he didn't already know. Professor Lawrence Carruthers had mentored her through some of her most challenging studies. The man was brilliant, devoted to helping his students, and had gone missing several years ago. The entire community had mourned his loss.

The professor smiled his trademark smile that all the students loved. His eyes crinkled until almost completely shut as both sides of his mouth curled high on either side of his bumpy beak of a nose. "Aye," he said. "He has told me much, indeed. He relayed yer prophecy of Edinburgh Castle and also shared what ye said regarding Stirling and Bannockburn."

"I wouldna call it prophecy exactly." Leeriness filled her. She wished she knew Professor Carruther's—or Friar Law's agenda. She spotted Kane's hand resting on the pommel of his dagger, and her heart swelled. He stood ready to defend her even in the presence of his king. "It was all more like a dream, really. I pray everything comes to pass as I dreamt it."

"I am sure it will," Friar Law said with a quirky look they both understood. "God often speaks to us through our dreams, and what better way to help his chosen king and bless the beloved land of Scotland?" His sharp-eyed gaze took in Kane's protective stance. "And this must be yer husband?"

"Aye," she said, deciding to test him with a hint at how she had arrived in the fourteenth century. "He saved me from drowning at *An Lochan Uaine*, and we married days later."

"*An Lochan Uaine*, ye say?" The friar's expression turned thoughtful. "So, the fairy waters brought ye to him?"

"Ye might say that." They needed to talk. Privately. He thought so, too. She sensed it.

"I thought ye might bless their union officially, good friar." The Bruce's smugness betrayed exactly how clever he thought himself to be at bringing them to this point without their knowledge. "God hasna heard their vows in His church, nor has a contract been signed or recorded."

"I would be honored." Friar Law turned, shuffled through his books, and retrieved a palm-sized tome with a tattered black cover. "But I fear I canna help with the contract."

"Not to fear." King Robert pulled a folded square of parchment from an inner pocket of his surcoat. "When my most trusted man's irregular marriage first came known to me, I had this drawn up." He beamed a grand smile at Kane. "I wish ye nothing but happiness, old friend, even though I might behave a bit…" He turned to Satia. "What did ye call it?"

"Ratty."

"Aye. Ratty." He unfolded the document and handed it to Kane. "Ye are a good man, Kane, and ye will find a deed included to a good bit of land there as thanks for yer loyalty."

"I am honored, Yer Majesty." Kane stared down at the parchment, barely shaking his head. "This is most generous."

"Well, of course, it is. I'm nay a stingy bastard with my friends." Robert clapped him on the shoulder. "Sign the papers, man. Ye and yer lady wife. Then the good friar will bless ye officially, ye ken?"

As Kane accepted the quill from Friar Law, it struck Satia that this time, she would marry him for real. Not *pretend*, as she had justified to herself before. She found that somewhat daunting. It was easy to pretend and then if anything went wrong, say it had never been real to begin with. But this—this locked it into reality in both eras because Friar Law had been an ordained minister and a professor in the twenty-first century.

Kane held out the quill. "My love?"

She accepted it, hoping her trembling wouldn't snap the nib or make her drop the feather. She dipped it in the ink, then stared at the line beside Kane's name. Without a doubt, she loved him, but the fear she would fail him made her hesitate to sign.

"Satia?" Kane's gentle whisper and the tender weight of his hand on the small of her back steadied her.

"I'm sorry. Had a dizzy spell there for a minute." With bold strokes, she scratched her name *Satia Nicole Josephine St. Clair.*

"Well done," Friar Law announced, once again making the sign of the cross over both of them. "Since our Lord already heard ye speak yer vows one to the other previously, we willna bother Him with them again." He winked. "After all, the Lord Almighty is verra busy." But he flipped open his book, found the desired page, and tapped on it. "However, I feel it appropriate that I somewhat quote our Lord's word, so ye both realize the importance of yer sacred oath." He wet his lips, took a deep breath, and began, "Love is patient and kind. It doesna envy or boast. Nor is it arrogant or rude. It doesna insist on its own way like a greetin' bairn. Nor does it act irritable or resentful. It abhors wrongdoing and rejoices in truth. Love bears all things, believes all things, hopes all things, and endures all things. Love never ends."

Somewhere off in the distance, a bell tolled just as he finished speaking. Satia swallowed hard, hoping that was a good omen.

"Ye may kiss yer lady love," Friar Law instructed as he closed the book and hugged it to his chest.

Kane tipped up her chin, then paused and smiled down at her. So much love shone in his eyes, it made her tears well and overflow. She couldn't help it.

His brows drew together as he caught her tears with a gentle swipe of a finger. "Weeping?"

"Good weeping," she promised. "Now kiss me."

"Gladly." His mouth closed over hers, making her forget all else in the room. For better or worse, richer or poorer, she was now this Highland warrior's wife—in any century.

"Well done!" With loud clapping, the Bruce strode to the closed door and threw it open. "Whisky, Dorcas! There's a union to be toasted."

"One more thing to be done," Kane said, giving her a sly look. He joined the Bruce at the door, stuck out his head, and bellowed, "Rob!"

"Ye've settled in well," Friar Law told her under his breath.

"Not as well as ye might think," she admitted. "We need to talk."

"Aye. We do." He leaned closer. "I am impressed ye chose to give up the comforts of the future and stay here to be a wife in the past."

"Chose?" She shot him a sharp look. "I didna choose. Nearly drowned trying to get back and finally gave up."

He confused her even more by looking surprised, opened his mouth to speak, then quickly closed it. She couldn't find out anything more because Kane was headed back to her, looking proud as a preening peacock.

"Yer hand, m'lady," he said, waiting to accept it while keeping one of his hid behind his back. "It's nay much, m'love, but I wanted ye to have something." He presented a silver band engraved with ivy leaves and slid it onto the ring finger of her left hand, smiling as it settled into place. A perfect fit. "A good omen, indeed."

Fingers trembling, she touched the ring, then clasped both hands to her heart. "It's lovely." Then she frowned. "Did ye know the Bruce planned this?"

He shook his head. "Nay, dear one. I intended to get this ring the night we pledged our bond, but I couldna do so until we reached town."

"Ye are too good to me." She stared down at the ring. The sudden rush of adrenaline she'd gotten when the friar looked surprised that she hadn't returned home, that there might actually be a way back, made her feel unworthy of Kane's love. "I dinna deserve ye."

He tipped up her face again and cupped her chin in his hand. "Ye fill me with joy, m'love. A joy I have never felt before." He kissed her, long and slow and with a tenderness that threatened to draw more tears. "I am thankful the fairies brought ye to me. More grateful than ye will ever know."

"I'll do my best to make ye happy." She hoped she would never have to choose whether or not to break her word. He gave her more love and contentment than she had ever known, and yet the temptation to return and see that Breanna was okay might prove too great to resist. How could she be so fickle and unfaithful? Her feelings for Kane burned strong, but she couldn't stop thinking about the possibilities hinted at by Friar Law. Guilt about her preoccupation filled her. She looked away, hoping he couldn't see the internal struggle in her eyes. "Shall we toast now?"

"Absolutely, m'love." He kissed her hand, then turned them to the Bruce. "Where's that whisky, my liege?"

"Right here, we were merely waiting for ye to complete yer special moment." The king patted a table that looked more like the desk of a general planning for war. Two bottles of whisky and enough glasses for all waited on the small space not covered with maps, books, or handwritten pieces of parchment. He broke the seal on one of the bottles and poured. Once they all held a glass, he lifted his own. "*Slàinte Mhath!*"

Each of them echoed the same, then downed the burning richness of the golden nectar. Satia welcomed the trail of liquid fire coating her gullet. In fact, she could do with a few more shots, considering what she feared a conversation with the professor might reveal.

The king thumped his empty glass down on the desk and gave her a dismissive nod. "Forgive me, dear lady, but now that we have gotten the pleasantries of yer union past us, might I have some time with yer husband? There is much he and I must discuss with great haste."

This was her chance. She couldn't resist the temptation. "Only if ye will allow me time with Friar Law. I understand he is quite the healer, and I have need of a strengthening tonic since my fevers."

Mischief danced in the king's eyes. "Ye sounded quite strong earlier while I waited outside yer door, but who am I to argue." He turned to the friar. "Take good care of her, wise sir. She has given us much hope for the future."

"It will be my honor, sire." Friar Law pulled open the door to an adjoining room and waited. "M'lady?"

Without a moment's hesitation, Satia grabbed the second bottle of whisky and her glass. She paused beside the altar and tipped her head toward the professor's empty cup. "Ye'll want yers, too, aye, Friar Law?"

"That would be most grand, m'lady."

She paused next to Kane and leaned in for a kiss. "Dinna let him get ye hurt or killed, understand?" Remorse for what she was about to do filled her, making her feel unfaithful to this man who made her feel so loved. "I willna allow ye hurt, ye hear?"

He rewarded her with a tender kiss. "I shall bear it in mind, dear one."

She cast a last glance back at him, then passed into the adjoining room ahead of Friar Law. The inn reminded her of the university library, honeycombed with hallways, alcoves, and rooms within rooms. This one appeared to be used mainly for storage. Sturdy wooden racks lined the walls, filled with barrels, kegs, and bottles, many coated with a thick layer of dust. A small table with two chairs waited in the center of the room. On it, Friar Law placed the three-armed candelabra brought from the other room.

"Is it safe to have an open flame in here?" Satia peered closer at the stamps on the barrels and the wax sealing the bottles. They contained alcohol. What sort, she couldn't tell, since she couldn't decipher the markings.

"Aye. Should be safe enough. An explosion in the heart of Edinburgh wouldha been recorded, and I dinna remember reading anything about such a thing, do ye?" As he seated himself, Law gave her a knowing wink and nodded toward the bottle in her hand. "Pour us a hearty one there, hen, then tell me how ye came to join me in the fourteenth century."

She filled both the cups with a generous slosh, then set the bottle on the table and took a seat. "I was collecting water samples at *An Lochan Uaine* in an attempt to replicate my initial findings regarding a strand of bacteria that could verra well be effective against some cancers. The ledge beneath me gave way; my waders filled and pulled me deeper than I'd even gone with diving equipment. I thought it was all over. Tried my best to swim back to the surface, but I blacked out. When I woke up, I was in the fourteenth century."

With an intense look that made her want to squirm, he slowly sipped his whisky. "And ye said ye tried to go back?"

She nodded and took another sip, swallowing hard at the chilling memory. "The next day, or maybe another day after, I dove as deep as I could and kept swimming downward, but it was...different. And a lot more difficult."

"Different how?" He perked, his long narrow face lit with interest.

"The first time, I distinctly remember flashing lights inside my eyelids and a strange sort of wooziness." She frowned down at the dredges in her cup as she idly traced a finger around its rim. "Of course, I played that off to dwindling oxygen, but now, I'm not so sure. All I know for certain is my attempt to return to the twenty-first century failed, and what I'd felt before was not replicated." She refilled their glasses, tossed back the contents of hers, and swallowed hard again, stoking her courage to ask the question burning hotter than the whisky. "Ye said ye were surprised I *chose* to stay here. Are ye telling me there is a way back?"

He pursed his thin lips and slowly nodded. "I have successfully returned twice now." A self-satisfied grin accompanied his warm chuckle. "Even saw the fine plaque hung in my honor at the university." He reached for the bottle, refilled his glass, and topped off hers. "But I prefer here. I am a ward for this time. 'Tis my duty to help history as best I can without altering the timeline too terribly." His grin became a full-blown smile. "'Tis in our DNA, Satia. Not everyone can dance across the web as we have."

All that he hinted at sent her mind whirling. "Explain."

"I, too, came to this time via *An Lochan Uaine*. But my passage wasna nearly as traumatic as yers appears to have been." He flattened both hands on the table, splaying out his long, thin fingers and thumping them one by one against the wood. "Myself and three interns stood in the shallows that day. Barely ankle-deep, all of us were. There to gather algae samples. Thunder rumbled, and I found myself alone." He locked eyes with hers. "I read the account the interns gave the press regarding my disappearance. They said they turned away for a second, and when they turned back, I was gone."

"I am definitely jealous. Yer trip was a great deal less traumatic." Of course, as in all things of life, she never did things the easy way. "How did ye determine a way back?"

"Data, Satia. How many times have I always told ye to be patient, list all the data, and study it without emotion? Logic only, hen. Logic, first and foremost."

She deserved that scolding because that had always been one of her greatest flaws. Whenever she got close to a solution, she got in a hurry. Impatient. Sloppy. "I admit I havena studied it as I should." She folded her hands and forced her nervously jiggling leg to stop bouncing. "So, what did I miss in my observations?"

"Not only must ye possess the unique DNA that apparently we two have, but the Green Loch is a gateway that can only be unlocked for the merest span of time at a particular point during the waning cycle of the full moon—and only on a full moon of its choosing. Not every month works."

"Bollocks."

"I have returned to the twenty-first century twice in the past five years. How many times have ye successfully gone back?"

"Fair point." She held a hand over her cup when he tried to fill it again. Additional whisky wouldn't help her sort this out, and she'd had more than enough. She needed somewhat of a clear head. "How did ye discern the exact point in the moon's phase since we both apparently traveled during the daytime and not at night? And how do ye ken which month?"

With a sheepish grin, he shrugged. "My observations are nay an exact science as yet. Ye have to make certain the moon has begun the waning phase, then sit with yer feet in the waters and wait." Both his brows ratcheted up to his thin, gray hairline. "But it works. For instance, on my last trip back, I heard how that wee shite Cameron Stote stole yer research." With an angry shake of his head, he added, "I canna believe the council sided with that lying little bastard instead of yerself."

"He is a *rich* liar, remember? And his father is on the council." With some surprise, she realized the raging inferno Cameron's betrayal once unleashed within her burned no more. The useless maggot would reveal his ineptitude one day since all he knew was how to steal—not study. "How do ye know ye'll hit the right timeline whenever ye give the loch another dip of yer toe?"

He shook his head, then propped his chin in his hand. "That I canna tell ye. Near as I can surmise, we must possess some sort of physical time stamp that draws us to a particular time. Perhaps a bloodline?"

"That doesna make sense," she said. "We'd have a bloodline connection as far back as our origin ancestor, and yet ye say ye've gone back and forth between this timeline and the future twice?"

He shrugged. "The only other reasoning I can offer is Divine Providence, Fate, or the wishes of the Faeries. Take yer pick."

"I wonder if I could go back and see Breanna?"

His mouth tightened, and he peered at her with the same disapproving look he'd used when she was a student about to do something foolish. "And how exactly would ye explain that to the man ye just professed yer love to?"

"He knows I'm from the future." Well, he didn't exactly know, but he blindly accepted whatever she told him. That unconditional love made her misgivings even worse. How could she even contemplate leaving him even for a little while? "But if I went, I'd have to be there until the next cycle of the moon, right?"

"At least. Ye could be gone for even longer. As I said, 'tis not an exact science, and I've nay narrowed down which month the loch chooses. It changes." He leaned back in his chair and eyed her. "And while I have traveled back and forth with no issue. I canna guarantee ye would do the same. I only know my experience." He shook his head. "Ye might make it back to him, and ye might not."

So much to think about. So much to weigh. She massaged her temples, then let her hands drop. "Does the Bruce plan on staying here in Edinburgh for a bit?"

"Aye. Why do ye ask?"

"Because ye and I have a lot more to discuss."

He patted her hand away from her glass and topped off their drinks one more time. With his lifted in a toast, he smiled. "To knowledge."

She nodded, clinked her cup to his, and downed the liquid fire, feeling as though she had just made a deal with the devil.

CHAPTER THIRTEEN

WITHOUT OPENING HIS eyes, he reached for her as he rolled to his side. His touch found nothing but the coolness of the bedclothes. He opened his eyes and scanned the dark room, lit only by the dwindling fire flickering in the hearth and the silvery moonlight streaming through the window. There she was, sitting in the window seat, hugging her knees to her chest.

He pushed himself upright and leaned back against the headboard, studying her. Whatever her thoughts, they had to be deep because she hadn't even noticed his movement. With her long, tousled hair illuminated by the moon, she reminded him of a fairy queen, no matter what she said about the silliness of such notions. The perfection of her subtle curves softened the silhouette of her leanness through her shift. He ached for her all over again. Never would he get enough of this woman. Not in a thousand lifetimes.

"Satia?"

"Aye?" She kept her gaze locked on whatever lay outside the window.

"What is it, love?" They had been in Edinburgh almost a month now, and with every passing day, she became more distant. "What troubles ye so? Ye've nay been yerself in a fortnight."

"Do ye remember me telling ye about my studies to help my sister's health?"

He couldn't remember all the strange words she had used, but he recalled the conversation. "Has Friar Law provided ye with helpful information?" The two had become inseparable. If not for the fact the friar was old and sworn to celibacy, Kane's jealousy would rage unchecked. And were he honest, he still struggled with all the time she spent with the man. But it seemed to please her and give her purpose, so he forced himself to tolerate it. Of course, he made sure Anne and Rob were with them much of the time. He wasn't a fool. "The man is a renowned healer. Did he understand what ye sought and why?"

She turned, her face hidden in shadow with the window aglow behind her. "He's from my time, Kane. He was my professor at university."

Envy bordering on a surge of uncontrollable jealousy made Kane shove back the covers, rise from the bed, and join her on the window seat. "From yer time," he repeated to make sure he hadn't imagined it. Now, he could see her face and wasn't too sure he liked what he saw. Her expression gripped his heart with an iciness he couldn't shake. She looked…guilty.

"And he's returned there twice. He unlocked the secret to traveling back and forth." She hugged herself, sitting ramrod straight as though waiting to be backhanded, acting as if she expected it even though he had never and would never strike her. "And his way is a lot easier than what I thought had to be done."

"Ye wish to leave me." The realization hit him like a gut-wrenching blow. "I see it in yer face."

"He helped me isolate the origin of the strand." Her feathery brows took on a pleading slant. "It's the leeches, Kane. I thought it was the algae or the chemical makeup of the water, but it's the secretions from the leeches in the Green Loch."

"Ye said ye couldna discover any of this without the tools from yer time." He wanted to shake her. Make her forget this foolish quest and any thoughts of leaving.

"On his last trip, he brought back a small microscope. Keeps it hidden, and while it's basic as they come, it showed me enough. I'm right about that strand."

"Ye wish to leave me," he stated again, realizing she had never answered the first time he'd said it. He caught hold of her shoulders and yanked her closer, trying in vain to make her look him in the eyes. "After everything ye've said to me, all yer words of love, ye wish to go back to yer time and cast aside all I thought we shared?"

"No." She squeezed his arms. "I mean, yes, I want to go back and share my findings, but then I'll come back here. I do love ye, but I really need to do this."

"What if ye canna come back? If Law is wrong—or lying about traveling back and forth at will? What if he is the only one able to do it?" But the biggest *what if* he left unsaid was, what if once she returned to her time, she changed her mind and no longer wished to return? "Ye canna do this, Satia. I beg ye not to do this to us."

"It would only be for a month." She squeezed his arms again. "The loch only works when the full moon begins waning. Near as we can tell, a few hours after it reaches its fullest point."

He released her shoulders, pushing her away as he did so. "A month in yer time." He jumped to his feet and strode to the hearth, leaning against the mantel to stare down at the fire. "Ye expect me to believe ye would return after spending a month back where ye belong?" He shot a hard look at her, willing her to see his pain. "I am not a fool." Then he snorted out a bitter laugh. "Nay. Mayhap I am. After all, I was fool enough to give ye my heart."

"Ye know I'll come back." She rose and eased toward him. "Ye know I will."

"How do I know this?" He thumped a fist against the mantel hard enough to rattle the candlesticks on each end. "I thought I knew ye loved me, loved *us*, but obviously, that was wrong."

"That isna fair." She took another step closer. "Ye know I

love ye."

"I know no such thing. Not anymore." It came to him he had been too lenient, granting her the independence to do whatever she wished because it seemed her right. Even the Bruce had commented that such a headstrong woman needed taming to become a proper wife and helpmate. He raked a hand through his hair, tempted to forbid her from ever seeing Friar Law again and also from ever going near *An Lochan Uaine*. But he didn't want a captive wife. He wanted one who loved him with all her heart and wished to spend the rest of her life at his side—willingly. His grandmother's curse had come to fruition after all. He would die alone. He turned away, gathered his clothes off the chair, and threw up a hand. "Do as ye will."

"But Kane—"

"Stop!" He faced her as he yanked on his trews. "Dinna ask for my blessing on this because ye will never have it. Ye have made yer feelings known, and now ye fully understand mine." He threw on his shirt and shoved his feet into his boots. "I willna take ye back there. The Bruce needs me here."

"I will come back," she said, the pitch of her voice filled with sorrow and pleading. She stood with her hands clasped in a knot. "Please try to understand. I promise I'll come back. I'll only be gone a month."

"In this time, Mistress St. Clair, wives stay at their husbands' sides. They dinna leave them for months at a time because they understand that life is precious and short, and they might never see them again. I bid ye Godspeed in yer travels." He stormed out the door and slammed it behind him, gritting his teeth when the creak of the hinges warned she had yanked it back open.

"So, it's fine for ye to leave me when ye go to battle, but I canna leave ye for a short time to save lives?" She threw the door open wider, bouncing it back against the wall. "Ye're a feckin' hypocrite, ye are! Ye know that, right? A feckin' hypocrite!"

A frustrated roar escaped him as he charged back, grabbed hold of her, and poured all his fury into the last kiss they would ever share. Chest heaving as he broke free, he shoved her away. "Aye, I am a feckin' hypocrite all right. One who loved ye more than anyone else ever will. Remember that when ye're back in yer time laughing about how ye tricked an ancient man into caring for ye with the entirety of his heart and soul." Then he turned and left, cursing the day he had been born.

NO MATTER HOW much they acted as though they accepted it, Satia knew neither Anne nor Rob believed her pathetic lie about needing a spiritual pilgrimage to *An Lochan Uaine* with Friar Law. Neither had the Bruce until the friar had hinted that perhaps she might receive more prophetic dreams if allowed to make the journey. That tipped the needle in their favor. They were packed up and sent off with the Bruce's blessings within a day's time.

But Kane hadn't seen them off. In fact, she had not seen him since their fight. Her heart ached with a hurting she had never known before, but she strengthened herself, knowing that once she returned, she would win him back. He would realize she hadn't abandoned him. At least, she hoped it worked out that way. They would patch things up and be happy once again. *She hoped.* And even tried to pray. Rob's stories about Kane's ability to hold a grudge to his grave concerned her.

"The moon looked pretty full last night," she said as she and the professor strolled around the shores of the Green Loch. She pointed at a shadowy point off the bank. "That's where I went in the first and second times. Deep as possible."

"I canna imagine trying to drown yerself, but I guess that's all the data ye had to work with." Friar Law shielded his eyes and squinted up at the sky. "By my calculations, tonight the moon hits its fullest point at just after midnight. After that, we must touch the water at all times to ensure we dinna miss the gateway."

"I wonder what Rob and Anne will think when we disappear?" She spotted Anne stirring the fire on the other shore while Rob hunted for their supper.

"Since our mounts will still be here, they'll either think us drowned or carted off by ne'er do wells." With his hands clasped to the small of his back, he peered at her with a look that made her shiver. "Ye are certain ye wish to do this? Ye seemed quite happy with yer husband before the subject of returning to yer time came about."

He didn't have to remind her of how contented and happy she had been. She remembered full well and hoped with everything in her she hadn't ruined it forever. "I feel it my duty to pass along my findings."

"Because ye wish to clear yer name and make yer mark in the scientific community?"

"No. I dinna care if I get any credit for the discovery at all."

"That doesna sound like ye."

"I know. But a lot has changed. Including my priorities." She picked up a rock and skimmed it across the surface. "All that matters is that people are helped, especially Breanna."

"A month is a short time to get one's research made known for a cancer study." Friar Law tried his hand at rock skipping but failed. The stone hit the water with a dismal *kerplop*. "There will be announcements and press, more testing required, papers to be written."

"I'll do what I can, then give Breanna everything else." She had it all planned out. Breanna was a gifted researcher, too. She would accept the torch and take it across the finish line. "I promised Kane I'd only be gone a month. I canna stay any longer than that."

"Ye should not have promised him a month. I told ye it might be longer. Are ye certain he will accept ye back when ye do return?"

"No." She wouldn't lie to the professor or herself. "I'll not know that until I'm back."

"And if he doesna?"

"I'll worry about that when it happens." It would not happen. It couldn't. She could not lose Kane forever. But then, why was she doing this? Why would she risk the greatest love of her life? A heavy sigh escaped her but didn't help with the burden of indecision. She did this because she had to. Something inside wouldn't leave her alone until she completed this task. Time to change the subject before she crumbled into a pile of uncontrollable tears. "What will ye do while we're back home?"

"Visit the library. Lurk about and see what I can. Perhaps I shall visit with Breanna, too. After all, the two of ye made quite the pair in all my classes ye took together." He skipped another rock, improving enough to make it skim almost across the width of the loch. "This will probably be my last trip back to the future. Each time I go, I am reminded how much I dinna belong there anymore." He shook his head. "The world of the future is a frightening place. I fear it willna last much longer."

"This time is much simpler," she admitted. "But it has its dangers, too. I guess every time does."

"Aye. I suppose that's true." With an indulgent smile, he turned them back to camp. "Come. Perhaps Anne needs help with the preparations, and if not, we should nap. Tonight will be a long one."

Satia agreed with a nod but looked out across the land in the direction they'd just come. "Please keep him safe," she whispered, knowing that before she returned, the battle of Bannockburn would take place. She hoped he'd be careful but knew in her heart he wouldn't. She would try prayer again for his safety, then find out if the prayers worked when she returned.

AN EXPECTANT SHIVER stole across her as she stared at the bright blue-white orb glowing overhead. "It's definitely full, so our window should be approaching." She hugged the bag containing her twenty-first century clothes and stepped into the shallows. "Are ye sure we shouldna wait until right after dawn? That's when I came through the first time."

"That was March, and this is June. Ye know as well as I that everything shifts with the time of year." Friar Law held a bag of his own.

She assumed it held appropriate clothing as hers did. "How do ye keep from being recognized? All yer students loved ye."

"Ye are most kind," he replied with a humble nod. "Whenever I return, I dress as one of the homeless. They are invisible to most people because folk fear if they look too closely, they will see their own future."

Sad but true. How many times had she looked away when coming across a homeless person on the streets? "Do ye feel woozy or see lights behind yer eyelids?" She needed to know what to expect.

"I believe that was a side effect of yer near drowning." He looked up at the moon, studying it as if seeing it for the first time. "There's a bit of disorientation, then ye regain yer footing as though ye slipped across an icy patch of pavement." He shrugged. "Leastwise, that's the best way I know to describe it."

"But it'll be the same time of day there as it is here, right? The timelines run parallel?" She tried to remember her first trip, but the unconsciousness from almost drowning fouled her data.

"Aye. Completely parallel from what I have observed."

She glanced across the way at the campfire and the blanketed lump that was Anne dreaming her dreams. "I hope they dinna get too upset." Anne had been such a loyal friend and taught her so much. She hated causing the lass any trouble. And even though Anne *knew* things weren't right between her and Kane, she hadn't nagged or pried. Just supported her with an occasional stern glance or two that let Satia know right off that she didn't agree with her making the trip to *An Lochan Uaine*. But again, Anne hadn't commented, just gone along. Fidgeting in place, she turned to Friar Law. "Do ye think they'll be upset?"

He gave her a perturbed look. "How many times are ye going to ask me that? And does it really matter? Ye didna mind upsetting yer husband to follow yer *duty*, as ye called it. Why do ye fret so over yer friends? Will ye not do it if ye fear it will cause them discomfort?"

"Ye never were one to coddle, were ye?"

"Not in the slightest." He rolled up on the balls of his feet and set himself back down on his heels with a soft splash. "But ye've always known that about me. And since when are ye such a sensitive soul? Ye know the professors and I often referred to ye as the Iron Maiden?"

"I thought it was Ice Queen?" She had taken pride in the nicknames. Then. Now, things had changed. Kane had awakened her heart, shattered the wall around it, and at this precise moment, she didn't know whether to kiss him or kick him for it. To *feel* was not always a good thing. "Or the Dragon. I really liked that one."

"There was a vote, and we settled on Iron Maiden," he said. "After all, we needed pet names for some of the other students, too."

She resettled her bundle and surrendered to a jaw-cracking yawn before widening her stance to ensure she didn't nod off and topple over. "I wonder what Kane's doing?" she whispered to herself, willing the moon to see her love for the man and carry it to him. She swallowed hard at the knot of emotions making her throat ache. This place held too many memories. She turned to the friar. "Can we not sit with our feet in the water?"

"I dinna ken." He shrugged. "I've never tried it that way." He nodded to the right and waved her forward. "Walk in the shallows. That's what I did last time to stay awake."

With as little sloshing as possible, Satia made her way around the loch in the ankle-deep water. The professor was right; concentrating on not slipping on the rocks helped keep her awake. By the third lap, she noticed a pinkish-white light spreading across the horizon to the east. Anticipation made her stomach gurgle and clench with the realization that dawn would soon be upon them and probably the opening of the gateway.

"Let's stand here for a bit," Friar Law advised, obviously sensing the moment almost at hand.

She kept her gaze locked on Anne, barely making out the gentle rise and fall of the blanket covering her. Dear Anne. She was leaving her without saying goodbye. At least Rob would keep his sister safe and get her back to the MacBride homestead.

Her vision blurred as if her eyes had gone all goopy with allergies or sleepiness. She blinked to clear them and rubbed the gritty inner corners. As she did so, her balance faltered, making her stumble to the side. She caught herself and adjusted her stance on the slippery rocks. "Mercy! Sunrise is messing with my balance."

Friar Law didn't answer. She turned to see why, and her heart shot to her throat. No one stood beside her. Friar Law was gone. "Bollocks! He went without me?" She turned all around, searching the landscape. Then she realized Friar Law was not the one gone. She was. Anne, Rob, their horses, and the camp had disappeared.

The viewing platform, the carved bench, the stone bordered path coming down from the road. All the things from the future had returned. She was back. Or at least, she was at some point in the future.

She sloshed out of the water, took shelter behind a cluster of pine saplings, and changed her clothes, taking care to repack her fourteenth-century attire for use on her return trip. If she had landed back in her time, the Glenmore Visitor Center wasn't that far. The café inside should have a phone she could use, or surely, someone would loan her a cell once she told them hers was lost.

As she walked along the road toward the center, the only risk she could think of was that they'd think her homeless or a tad on the barmy side and shoo her out before she could contact Breanna. She needed a cover story. A mugging or something. Aye, that would do. She rubbed dirt on her face and bit her bottom lip hard enough to make it bleed and swell, hoping not only to validate the mugging tale but also elicit some sympathy and help. A limp might help, too. She adopted one immediately. The only thing she couldn't manage was fake tears. Tears on cue had been Breanna's strong suit.

"You there! Are you all right?"

Brilliant. Not even into the visitor center's car park, and some kind soul had already noticed her. With the most distraught face she could manage, she turned and almost fell out of character. A parks constable. They possessed the full authority of the police. "Thank heavens for ye, constable. They got my money. Identification. Phone. I barely escaped with my life."

"There now, miss. You're safe now. How badly are you injured?" The middle-aged Brit's kindly gaze swept across her appearance as he gently herded her toward a nearby bench. "Shall we make a trip to hospital?" He unclipped his radio mic from his shoulder and rested his thumb on the button.

She shook her head, then covered her face with both hands, wishing she could eke out some tears. "I just want to go home, but they took my car, too." A high-pitched whining keen added authenticity. Or at least, she hoped so. "My friend. I need to call my friend. She'll come and get me."

"We should go to the station and file a proper report," he said, shuffling in place as she increased the volume of her caterwauling. "There, there now. You're quite safe now, I assure you."

"I just want to call my friend," she howled, hoping that rubbing her eyes had made them look red enough. "She'll take me home. I won't feel safe until I'm home. P-please. Just let me call my friend."

"But I must file a report, miss. We can't allow those hooligans to go unpunished."

She unleashed another high-pitched sob. The kind-hearted man was on the edge of doing what she wanted just to get her quiet. She could see it in his eyes. Especially since a few early arrivals to the car park had started gathering around and staring.

"She can bloody well use my phone," said a grandmotherly woman who looked ready to wage battle with the constable. "Can ye no' see how upset the wee thing is? Shame on ye, man! Have ye no heart at all?"

The elderly woman settled down beside her on the bench and wrapped an arm around her. "Here now, lass. Call yer friend." She pressed the cell phone into Satia's hand with an encouraging nod. Then she rose and shooed the onlookers away, including the constable. "On wi' ye now. Give the lass some privacy to make her call. Who knows what the poor wee kitten's been through." The plump matron herded everyone several paces away, then glanced back and gave Satia a nod. "Go ahead, love. Make yer call. I willna let them bother ye."

A distinct sense of remorse for tricking the sweet lady filled Satia as she tapped in Breanna's number. But it couldn't be helped. She only had a month or so to accomplish quite a bit. On the third ring, the voice that Satia feared she would never hear again answered. "Hello?"

"Breanna?"

"Who is this?" Sharp, cold, and filled with suspicion. It didn't sound like Breanna at all. Well, it did. But Breanna only sounded that way when on the defensive.

"It's Satia." She spoke low, hoping her friend would believe her.

"Whoever ye are, this is pretty feckin' low." Then she hung up.

"Shite." She hadn't considered that Breanna might not accept that it was really her. She tapped out the number again, praying her friend would pick up rather than decline the call.

"I dinna ken what cruel game ye're up to, but—"

"Breanna, I swear it's me, and I can prove it. Remember how we used to steal cigarettes out of Sister Mary Evangeline's stash that was hidden in the bottom of the baptismal, and she couldna rat us out because she'd be ratted out, too?"

Silence on the other end, but at least she hadn't disconnected the call.

"And remember the song I used to sing to piss off Sister Martha Elizabeth when she came every night to beat any kid whose skin was darker than hers?" Satia hoped Breanna was still listening. "And I'd sing until she beat me? And I'd keep her beating me until her asthma kicked in, so she couldna breathe enough to beat anyone else?"

"I remember," Breanna whispered, her tone hard and filled with bitterness. "Ye were the death of that wicked cow, ye ken? Pushed her right into that heart attack that night."

"And who blinded a priest because ye're the only sister I've ever had, and I'd do anything to protect ye?"

"Where are ye, Satia. Where the hell have ye been?"

"Glenmore Visitor's Center. If ye'll come and get me, I'll try my best to explain everything."

CHAPTER FOURTEEN

"H E HAS RETURNED. Without her." Albie stood with his hand on the latch, and his head stuck partway in, waiting for orders. All the men, even the Bruce, had steered clear of Kane since Satia left. Especially after he had given into his rage and destroyed every stick of furniture, ripped every pillow, and torn all the blankets in his room. But the furious destruction failed him. The delicate scent of her still lingered, filling the space and driving him beyond madness.

"Where is he?" Kane turned from the window that faced north, the direction in which she had gone.

"In the altar room." Albie backed into the hallway as Kane approached. "Mind yerself, man. Ye canna kill him. The Bruce will nay allow it."

At the moment, Kane cared little for what anyone would or wouldn't allow. He stormed out of the small room he had taken after destroying his own and thundered down the stairs. When he entered the common area, everyone at the tables and those loitering near the walls went silent. Out of the corner of his eye, he noted that Toff and Jac joined Albie, falling in step behind him.

He kicked open the closed door behind the counter and drove into the room. Friar Law's eyes widened. He lifted his hands, shielding himself as he backed away. Kane grabbed hold of the man by the front of his robes and slammed him against the wall.

"Give me one reason to let ye live," he forced through clenched teeth.

"I have none," Law said. "Do what ye will."

"Kane." The Bruce's tone held quiet warning. "Killing him willna bring her back."

"If not for him, she would still be here." Kane bounced the friar off the wall again. "Why would ye tell her the way back? Why?"

"I have known yer lady love for many years." Law reasoned in a voice that infuriated Kane even more. "Trust me when I say she would have discovered it on her own—eventually. She is a stubborn wee minx who's never given up on anything that's ever puzzled her. That is where her brilliance lies."

As much as he hated it, he knew the holy man's words to be true. Which meant only one thing. He had not been enough for her. Their love, or what he had thought had been their love, meant nothing to her. Only her work mattered. And her sister. He shoved the man aside and stepped back.

"She loves ye." The friar tugged his robes back in place, then laced his fingers together, folding his hands across his narrow middle. "And will return."

"How can I compete against all that awaits her in her world?"

"Trust me when I say I am not muttering platitudes to save my neck. She loves ye and will return. I have known that stubborn hen for many years, and never have I seen her look at any man the way she looks at yerself." He gave a decisive nod. "She will return as soon as she finishes the task she has set for herself."

Kane turned away, lifting a hand to quell the holy man's preaching. 'Twas more than a little clear; the only reason the friar spewed such things was to save himself, no matter what he claimed.

"Come, man. Let us drink our sorrows away. Perhaps, someday our wives will be restored to us." The Bruce led him to a chair beside the table covered in maps and parchments. "Edward holds my Elizabeth prisoner, and yer wife's quest with the Green Loch imprisons her." He shoved aside the clutter and motioned for one of the men near the door to bring libation to ease their pains or at least numb them until they sobered.

Toff fetched four bottles and set them on the table.

Jac supplied enough glasses for everyone in the room. "Thought we'd join ye, aye?" he said. "Pains us to see our chief suffering."

"I'm not yer feckin' chief." Kane lowered his head to his hands and dug his thumbs into his throbbing temples. "I am nothing." Without her, an aching emptiness filled him.

"We will drink to yer sorrows," the Bruce said as he filled their glasses. "But we willna wallow in self-pity. Ye're a braw, canny man. Loyal. Fiercest warrior I have ever met, and I couldna gain our beloved Scotland's independence without ye." He set the bottle on the table and leaned closer. "Now tell me, where is this place yer lady love has gone? The way Law and yerself speak, 'tis like she is no longer in our world."

"Ye wouldna believe me if I told ye." Kane tossed back the drink, wishing he could ride off into the Highlands and never see anyone or anything ever again. But he couldn't. He would not desert his king as Satia had deserted him.

Robert refilled his glass. "Try me." His expression along with his tone made it clear the question had changed to an order.

Albie caught Kane's eye. He gave the barest shake of his head. A subtle warning.

While the Bruce might find traveling across the centuries impossible to believe, the man swallowed myths, legends, and signs from nature with the same routine comfort as eating his morning parritch. Kane leaned back in his chair and downed his second glass of whisky. "I am sure ye ken the tales of *An Lochan Uaine*, the Green Loch?"

The Bruce's eyes narrowed as he refilled both their glasses

then handed the bottle to Toff to refill the others. "Aye. They say Glenmore is home to the king of the faeries himself."

"Satia is of that royal line." Kane watched his liege over the rim of his glass, waiting for the man to either swallow the lie or challenge it.

King Robert paused with his cup halfway to his mouth. He stared at Kane, then looked to all the others in the room, even Friar Law. "What say the rest of ye about this claim? Especially yerself, Law. I heard ye say ye had known the lady many years."

Friar Law wet his lips, then pinched them into a hard, flat line. After a long moment of silence, while he poured himself another glass, he nodded. "She is not of this time or place, and the loch is the doorway to her home." Then he crossed himself and drained his glass.

Kane erupted with a bitter snort. For a holy man, Friar Law danced around the truth as well as anyone. He upended his glass and thumped it down on the table. In his current mood, he needed no more whisky. "I weary of this subject. What is yer next plan of attack?"

The Bruce eyed him, then dipped his chin in an understanding nod. "Stirling Castle. We shall prepare for the battle yer lady wife prophesied to be our greatest victory." He reached across the table and dragged a map closer, then tapped on it. "Here. A mile south of the castle. We shall dig trenches along the Bannock Burn to funnel the English and disable their horsemen." He sat back in his chair and fiddled with his empty cup, turning it in circles on the table. "And I have commissioned every smithy I can find to ensure we have additional pikes as well as other weapons when we face Edward and his forces."

"I shall see that they follow all yer orders." Kane pushed up from the chair, ready to be shed of the room in which he and Satia had signed their marriage contract. If the document hadn't already been filed away, he'd rip the lying piece of parchment to shreds. "Trenches. Weapons. Anything else I should know?" He paused at the door, itching to leave and immerse himself in the life that never rejected him. The life of a warrior.

"Aye." The Bruce stood and locked a fierce scowl upon him. "Mind yerself. I willna have ye taking foolish risks because ye no longer value yer own existence, ye ken?"

Kane promised nothing on that front. "All I can do is live until I die, my king. Nothing more." And with any luck, the dying would come sooner rather than later. Because at the moment, the cold darkness of the grave held the only peace to be found.

⫸⫷

BREANNA STARED AT her. Now and then, she blinked, and her confused frown tightened. Then her brow would smooth, and she would stare some more.

Satia poured herself another cup of tea, added a slice of lemon, then settled back in the threadbare armchair too plush and comfortable to get rid of no matter how shabby it became. "I swear, Bree. Every word."

"I saw ye drown." Breanna's confused look remained as she paused and sipped her steaming tea. "Ye went under and never came back up."

"But they never found a body, aye?" Satia leaned forward and scooped up one of her favorite shortbread biscuits. "And ye know as well as I, when water temperatures change, bodies surface."

"No. They never found a body." Breanna rose from her seat on the couch and meandered back and forth across the small sitting room of their shared flat. She cradled her teacup between both hands as she obviously struggled to grasp the concept of time travel. "The year 1314?" She stopped her pacing long enough to stare at Satia again.

"Aye. And I met Robert the Bruce."

"*The* Robert the Bruce?"

"Aye." Satia helped herself to one more biscuit. She had forgotten how good they tasted. "In about three weeks, he will wage the battle of Bannockburn and reclaim Stirling Castle."

"How is it they didna kill ye for being a witch or something?" Breanna placed her cup on the tray on the coffee table and plopped back down on the couch, folding her legs up under her and tucking her feet into the cushions. "Ye've been gone nearly three months, and last I checked, ye weren't enough of a history buff to play such a part. How did ye survive?"

"My husband," she said quietly, dreading the inevitable on-slaught of more questions. She set her cup back on the tray and braced herself.

"Yer what?" Breanna leaned forward, scooping her dark curls behind her ears as though that would improve her hearing. "Did ye say, husband?"

"Kane Macpherson." Satia swallowed hard, forcing herself to hold her emotions in check. "The kindest, most understanding man I have ever loved."

"Ye have never loved."

Satia stared down at her hands and twisted her wedding band. "Ye're absolutely right. I have never loved. Only yerself, dear sister. Never anyone else. But Kane helped me find my heart." She snorted out a bitter laugh. "Damn him straight to hell."

"Then why did ye come back? Or did the time warp thing toss ye back against yer will?" Breanna leaned forward, her elbows propped on her knees, as she listened with rapt attention. "Does he think ye died like I did? Is yer love lost to ye forever?"

"Do ye remember Professor Carruthers?"

"Aye." Breanna's eyes widened, and her mouth formed a shocked *o*. "Did he time travel, too?"

"He is now Friar Law, personal healer to the Bruce." Satia frowned as she curled up more comfortably in the chair. It had been a long day, and her adrenaline surges had left her weary. "By studying the data, he determined when the time gateway opens— and where. At least, most of the time." Of course, that didn't explain why this time, he had remained in the past rather than come to the future with her. Apparently, more data and study needed to be done. "That's how I got back."

"So…anyone can do this?"

"As near as he can tell, only certain people have the ability, but he doesna ken why. Whether it's a DNA fluke or something else. All he knows is that the first time he went through, it left behind his three interns."

"I remember reading their interviews!" Breanna bounced to attention on the couch. "They said he disappeared. It was as if he had never been there with them wading in the water."

"Exactly." Satia yawned and pulled the throw off the back of the chair and spread it across her. "But he was supposed to return with me this time and didn't. So, I'm not sure what that's about."

"Maybe he's already gone back and forth as many times as he's allowed." With a studious scowl, Breanna slowly nodded. "I've read texts about such, and so have ye. Remember the Celts' fascination with *three?*"

"Could be. But I thought he said he'd only returned twice so far." At this point, Satia believed in any possibility. She had witnessed too much not to.

"But ye still didna say why ye returned? If ye loved the man enough to marry him, why would ye risk never seeing him again."

"I found the answer." Excitement coursed through Satia. The kind she felt when giving Breanna a Christmas gift she knew she would love.

"The answer to what?"

"It's the secretions from the leeches that provides the elusive strand. Not the water or algae in *An Lochan Uaine.* It's the leeches. And without any dilution from bacteria in the loch water, the secretions should work, Bree. Now, ye dinna have to fear if yer cancer returns."

Breanna stared at her with a look she couldn't quite decipher. No excitement. No joy. Just a frowny sort of quiet contemplation.

"Did ye hear what I said? I completed the research and found the answer." Satia sat straighter in the chair and pushed the coverlet away.

"I dinna ken how to tell ye this, Satia." Breanna shook her head. "But a team of Danes came in a few days after ye disappeared. They disproved the conjectures Cameron faked when he published yer work, then announced the verra same thing ye just said. A pharmaceutical company has already hired a firm to set up sustainable leech farms with water runoff from *An Lochan Uaine* so as not to drive the organism into extinction. They're also doing more testing on leeches from other lochs." Breanna made her *I didn't want to tell you* face. "I am so sorry, pet. But it sounds as though the reason ye came back is already well in the works."

"I was only gone three feckin' months." Satia stood, knocking the throw to the floor. "How could so much happen in three short months?"

"I dinna ken, pet. All I know is that it did."

Satia moved to the window and pressed her forehead against the coolness of the pane. Was this another of Fate's cruel jokes? She had risked the love of her life to help her sister, and it hadn't even been necessary? "I have been such a fool." She closed her eyes, willing herself not to cry.

"No. Never a fool." Breanna rushed to her and hugged an arm around her shoulders. "Ye did as ye've always done. Ye put me first. Above yer own wants." She leaned in and touched her head to Satia's, as they had done so many times as children. "I love ye buckets and gobs, sister of mine, and I canna tell ye how good it is to see ye again."

"I missed ye, too." Satia flattened her palm on the windowpane, idly appreciating the clarity and cool smoothness of twenty-first century glass compared to the flattened animal horn or oiled parchment used to let light into rooms in the fourteenth century. "Ye know most windows dinna have any sort of coverings other than shutters or tapestries. I imagine it'll be wicked cold in the winter."

"Ye're going back to him, aren't ye?" Breanna hugged her tighter, then gave her a gentle shake. "I dinna blame ye, though.

Especially if ye love him."

"I promised him I'd come back." Satia caught her bottom lip between her teeth. "I just hope he'll forgive me."

"Forgive ye?"

"Aye. He didna want me to leave."

"Does he know…" Breanna's voice trailed off as she tugged on Satia's arm and led her back to the chair.

The fond memory of him holding her while she spewed out the loch water on their first meeting made her smile. "Aye. He knows. He doesna understand, but he accepts whatever I tell him as the truth." She shook her head and huffed out a sad laugh. "I thought dogs were the only creatures capable of such unconditional love, but I was wrong. Kane possesses the patience of a saint." She plucked the blanket up from the floor and spread it across her lap. "But I hurt him by coming here." With an embarrassed shrug, she shook her head. "He's not had an easy way of it, and I fear his loving me has turned more into a curse than a blessing for him."

Breanna plopped back down on the couch. "I wish I could meet him. He sounds like a fine man."

"I wonder if ye could come back with me?" With Breanna in the fourteenth century, life would be grand indeed. "We could try it. It doesna hurt a bit. Now that I know all ye have to do is touch the water at the right time." She grinned. "Ye dinna have to drown yerself like I did the first time. Promise!"

Breanna looked away, avoiding the suggestion. She always did that when she didn't wish to share what she really felt.

"Tell me." Satia waited. There had never been any secrets between them, and they weren't about to start now. "Go on now. Ye can tell me anything."

"It's…I have found someone, too."

Satia squelched a selfish pang of jealousy and forced an excited smile. Breanna deserved love as much as she did. "That's wonderful. Have I met him?"

Breanna lifted her chin and blew out a deep breath. "No. But ye have met her. Once or twice, I think."

"Her?"

"Aye, Lara from the library." Breanna fisted her hands on her knees. "She's all set to move in this weekend." She twitched an uncomfortable shrug and offered a smile that begged for understanding. "Surely, ye knew. Or at least suspected?"

Now that Satia thought about it, Breanna's announcement made perfect sense. While her friend had occasionally dated men and even brought them home now and then, she had never seemed very enthused about any of them. Satia had passed it off as a byproduct of their traumatic childhood or the fact that Bree just hadn't found the right guy. Now she understood Breanna's truth and contentment lay elsewhere. "Are ye happy?"

"Happier than I have ever been."

"Then I am happy for ye and wish the both of ye nothing but the best." And she meant it. If Breanna had at last found genuine love, she was happy for her. It occurred to her she might be in the new couple's way. "I canna go back to Kane until at least the next full moon. Will Lara be all right with my staying here 'til I leave? I'm sure neither of ye planned on a third wheel when ye talked of living together."

"Are ye comfortable telling her everything?" Breanna touched the side of the teapot and frowned. "Gone cold as a stone. Let me fetch us some more."

"I dinna mind telling her my story, but do ye mind me telling it? She might think ye friends with a lunatic." Satia settled herself more comfortably in the depths of the overstuffed chair as Breanna made more tea in the small kitchenette.

"She's the head librarian, and I think she's read every book and bit of information in the archives. I'm sure she'll have thoughts about time travel. She might even help ye with the era if ye have questions ye need answered." She plugged in the electric teakettle, pushed down the lever to turn it on, then turned and leaned back against the counter. "I worry about ye going back, though. Illnesses. Disease. The dangers of childbirth." Both her dark brows lifted, and her mouth twitched in dubious reflection. "Will ye be having children? No offense, pet, but I never saw ye as the type."

"Kane wants them."

"Aye, but that doesna answer my question, now does it?"

"I want him happy." She skirted the issue as best she could because she wasn't sure of the answer. "My only fear is that history repeats itself when it comes to neglect and abuse, ye ken? I dinna wish to become my mother."

"Ye could never be yer mother." The teakettle clicked off, and Breanna turned to pour the steaming water into the waiting teapot. "And yer Kane doesna sound the sort to abandon his bairns like yer Da did." She placed the pot on the tray and wrapped a tea towel around it to keep the contents warm. She added a small pitcher of cream and refilled the dish with biscuits. "Ye can break the cycle, Satia. Others have."

Satia accepted a fresh cup of tea and a biscuit. "It might be a moot point anyway, I fear." After dunking the square of shortbread, she nibbled the soaked portion away and dunked it again. "Birth control choices aren't easy to find in the 1300s. And I'm late. Going on three weeks now."

"We should make a trip to the clinic before ye go back." With a worried huff, Breanna glared at her. "Is there no chance of him coming here if ye're pregnant? Delivery would be so much safer."

"He would be more lost here than I ever thought about being in the fourteenth century." Satia finished the shortbread, then sipped the tea sweetened by the buttery flavor of the biscuit. She frowned, watching the tea leaves swirl at the bottom of her cup. "I think women are more adaptable than men. I can't imagine him surviving here."

Breanna grew quiet, sipping her tea and becoming almost thoughtful. "I dinna want ye to leave again," she said quietly. "This is the longest we've been apart since we met all those years ago. It's been terrible without ye, pet."

"I've missed ye more than I can say." Satia joined Breanna on the couch and gave her a fierce hug. "I canna imagine life without ye, but I canna stay here, Bree. I dinna belong here anymore." She took her hand and patted it. "Besides, this time, ye'll know I'm not dead. I've just resettled somewhere else."

"Somewhere I can never visit."

"We could try it, but ye canna leave Lara behind. Not when ye've just found love." It killed Satia to say it, but she wouldn't be selfish and try to coerce Breanna into coming with her alone. "Besides, we dinna ken if it would even work. The professor still hasn't worked that part out."

Breanna squeezed her hand. "I'll see if Lara might be interested in giving it a go. Knowing her, she'll jump at the chance to visit a time she's only read about." She frowned. "How do ye control where ye end up?"

Satia shook her head. "We dinna ken that either. It just happens." Misgivings made her stomach tighten. What if the gateway dropped Breanna and Lara off somewhere else? Could that be what happened to Law this time?

"Sounds dangerously sketchy." Breanna eyed her. "Since when do ye jump into things with so little data?"

"Since I was pushed when that ledge collapsed and tossed me back in time."

"Fair point." Breanna gave her knee a friendly pat. "Lara and I are meeting at the corner pub this afternoon. Ye'll come with, aye?"

"I'll meet ye there after I've had a nice long bath." She sniffed herself, then wrinkled her nose. "I'm a bit gamey by twenty-first century standards."

Breanna grinned. "Well, I wasna going to comment because I love ye, but ye do reek a wee bit."

"Did ye toss my things, or are they boxed up somewhere?" While the thought bothered her, Satia reminded herself that as far as Breanna had been aware, she had died.

Breanna shook her head. "Havena touched them. Didna have the heart. Lara said I should keep yer room as is as long as I need.

Everyone mourns in their own way."

The sentiment touched her and reassured her that Lara was good enough for dear Breanna. She brushed a kiss to Bree's cheek, then headed toward her room. "To the bath, so I dinna repel yer Lara with my stench." She paused inside the doorway. "Ye think she can find some soap or perfumed oil recipes I can take back with me?"

"I'm sure she'd be happy to try."

And some effective birth control methods, she silently added as she rummaged through the drawers and picked out clean clothes. "If it's not too late," she whispered. "Please dinna let it be too late."

IT WAS TOO late. Satia rushed out of the clinic, needing fresh air. Breanna and Lara followed close behind, both loaded down with pamphlets. She didn't slow her panicked stride until she reached a park bench on the other side of the street. Her stomach churned, threatening to expel the tea and scones she'd had for breakfast. What a fool she had been. Counting on blind luck to protect her.

"It's soon enough ye could end it," Lara suggested, offering a pamphlet.

Without hesitation, Satia shook her head. "I canna do that." She blew out a bitter huff. "I've done enough things in my life I regret. That option is not a choice I'm willing to make. It's just not for me."

"He needs to come here," Breanna insisted. "It would be so much safer for both yerself and the baby." She beamed a persuasive smile. "And ye'd have a pair of aunties who could babysit any time ye needed."

Satia lowered herself to the bench and held her head in her hands. "I was always so careful in this century. Condoms, pills, abstinence. But three months in the fourteenth century made me forget every sex ed class I ever sat through."

"Ye said ye werena sure he'd take ye back when ye returned. Will ye tell him even if he doesn't?" Breanna sat beside her and gently combed her fingers through her hair, sweeping it out of her face. "If he doesna take ye back, promise ye'll come back here. The three of us will raise that baby just fine."

"I'm going to fetch ye some water," Lara said, then sprinted across the park.

Satia lifted her head and leaned back. "She's nice. I'm glad ye found her."

"Satia Nicole Josephine, answer the question." Breanna gave her a stern glare.

"I dinna ken what I'm going to do." And she didn't. She had suspected the pregnancy but avoided thinking about it as much as possible. But now, the inevitable had caught up with her. "I have to tell him either way. Trouble is—I dinna want him taking me back just because he thinks it's his duty." She shrugged and blew out a heavy sigh. "He's verra big on duty. It's quite the thing in the fourteenth century."

"If he willna take ye back, or if anything happens to him, promise ye'll come back and raise the baby here." Breanna scooped up her hand and squeezed. "Promise me."

"I promise," Satia said, wishing life didn't always have to be so feckin' complicated.

CHAPTER FIFTEEN

"I STILL CANNA believe the Bruce allowed yer leaving." Albie tugged on the reins, leaning forward to prop his elbows on his knees as he steered the wagon around a mud hole.

"He won Bannockburn and regained Stirling. Our liege is satisfied for now." Kane rode alongside the wagon, keeping close to help watch over their wounded friend. "And he won them at the cost of Toff and Jac. He kens well enough they were like brothers to me." He cast another concerned look down into the wagon. "As is Rob. Our king knows better than to deny me anything right now."

Young Rob, laying on a generous pallet of straw, tolerated the ride in silence, for the most part, occasionally moaning when the wagon hit a rut that Albie couldn't maneuver the team around. His bandaged head attested to the nearly fatal blow that had robbed him of sight in his right eye. An Englishman's ax had also nearly cleaved off his arm just above the elbow. The arm remained attached for now, but it was doubtful he would ever have much use of it again. They were headed to the McBride homeplace, where Kane hoped the sisters could nurse their brother back to health. Or, at the very least, give him some ease for whatever time he remained.

"Full moon tonight." Albie sidled a narrow-eyed glance in his direction. "First one since she left, ye ken?"

"Just because I need ye to drive the wagon, old man, dinna think I willna kill ye once we reach the McBrides'." Kane shifted in the saddle, rolling his shoulders against the constant dull ache that haunted him every waking hour.

"Ye've opened the gash in yer shoulder again." Albie brought the wagon to a creaking halt. "And yer face. Get yerself over here and let me reapply the poultice Friar Law sent along. Ye'll need fresh bandages as well since ye've bled clean through yer léine and surcoat."

Kane pressed his fingers against the wound running from the corner of his left eye down to his jawline and held it to staunch the bleeding. The cloying wetness of his shirt stuck it to his chest. "If Law had stitched them proper, they wouldna bleed so."

"Ye canna blame the man for yer bleeding when ye keep popping the stitches. Get down here and let me see what I can do for ye." Albie grabbed a wooden crate out from under the wagon seat and waved him forward.

"See to Rob first." The lad had been quiet too long. Kane feared him dead.

"He lives, Kane. Just passed out again from the pain." Albie slid the lid off the box, dug inside, and pulled out a handful of white linen strips and a crock sealed with a wax-coated cloth. He dampened a rag with water from the leather bag and cleaned the blood off Kane's face and chest. His squinting glare tightened into a disapproving scowl. "Ye're making a wicked scar for yerself. How do ye keep breaking these stitches?"

"As I said, the man handled the task poorly. Stop yer nattering and get on with it, aye? I would have Rob home within the hour. No longer." Besides, scars on the outside meant little. The gashes across his heart and soul pained him the most. He clenched his teeth as Albie pricked the skin on his face and then his shoulder, pulling new stitches taut to replace those that had failed.

"Kane!"

Kane closed his eyes, dreading Laoiri's reaction when he told her of Jac's death. While the woman might not have really loved the quiet, red-haired hulk, he had no doubt she held a fondness for him.

Cheeks flushed from running to meet them, her smile disappeared when she glanced into the back of the wagon. "No, Kane. Not wee Rob." Her keening sobs filled the air as she bowed her head and clutched at the sideboards to keep from falling to the ground. "Not our sweet Rob."

"He is not dead, woman," Kane said. "But he's in sore need of all the care every one of his sisters can give."

"Praise God Almighty." She crossed herself over and over, but then her movements slowed as she looked from Albie to Kane. "And Toff? My Jac?"

Kane shook his head.

Her face crumpled again, and she pressed a fist to her mouth. "Where did ye lay them to rest?" she whispered. "Why did ye no' bring them back here where we might pray over them every day?"

"The Bruce buried them near Stirling. Their graves are properly marked." Kane blew out a heavy sigh. "We had to get Rob home. Our concern was with the living since there was naught we could do for the dead."

With a quick nod, she sniffed, then dried her face on her sleeve. "I understand. Come. Let us get him where we can take care of him, aye?"

"Aye." Kane hoisted himself back up into the saddle. Laoiri had taken the news better than he had foreseen. But then he remembered the McBrides had endured much loss and suffering. They were anything but weak. "Ride with him in case he wakes. I'll turn the sheep and head them back with *Mèirleach*. He enjoys charging at the wee beasties."

Laoiri clambered up into the wagon and rested a hand on Rob as the wheels lurched into motion.

When the homeplace came into view, Kane spotted Mairi, Anne, and Jennet, sitting on the bench, weaving baskets, while the twins played at the water's edge. Their expressions when they looked up and spotted the men revealed they feared the worst.

"He lives," Kane called out, hoping to ease them as much as possible. While he couldn't predict how much longer Rob might last, at least the lad lived for now.

"Ye're bleeding," Mairi said as she and her sisters hurried to help.

Kane shook his head. "'Tis old blood. See to yer brother. Dinna fash yerself about me."

"She wouldna wish ye dead," Anne said with a defiant lift to her chin.

"She gave up her right to wish about me when she left." Kane hated speaking harshly to Anne, but he would not suffer her defending Satia.

Anne's mouth tightened into a disapproving line, but, thankfully, she said no more. Instead, she quickly assessed Rob's situation and took over. The youngest of the sisters, she led them as if the eldest. "We can move him with that blanket that's beneath him. We must lift him, then hand him down. Step lively now, and dinna jostle him. Jennet, run and turn down the bed in the corner."

Kane helped as much as he could but found himself more or less in the way. The McBride sisters had their baby brother well in hand. They soon had him settled on the cot, cleaning him up and changing his bandages in worried silence. Kane stepped outside, finding the interior of the modest dwelling almost unbearable. He had once thought of the place as a home of his own. But no more. Not since Satia. Too many memories haunted the dwelling now, chasing away all the peace and comfort it once held.

"Full moon tomorrow," said a defiant voice behind him.

"Let it be, Anne," he warned.

"I miss her, too, ye ken? She was my friend." Anne stepped around and took a battle stance in front of him. "I dinna ken all her secrets, nor where she went when she disappeared that day. But she said she told ye she would return, and I dinna take her for a liar."

"Then ye are as big a fool as I was." He tried to step around her, but she sidestepped and blocked his way. "Anne. Step aside." If forced, he would pick her up and set her out of his way.

The thin girl thumped a fist to her chest. "She will return. I feel it in my heart."

He shook his head. "Of all the McBrides, ye have always been the most level-headed. The most solemn. Why do ye waste yer time with such foolish notions?"

"Because Friar Law promised she would return. He wouldna say where she went that day either, but he swore he knew. As a holy man, he wouldna lie."

"Ye possess a much higher opinion of the man than I do." He grabbed hold of her by the shoulders, picked her up, and set her aside.

"And what will ye do when she comes back?" she shouted after him as he stomped away. "Will ye swallow that infernal pride of yers and welcome her like ye should?"

Kane ground his teeth tighter to keep from cursing at the woman. He kept walking, lengthening his stride, until he reached higher ground well away from Anne's endless nattering. What would he do if Satia returned? He scoffed at the idea, snorting out a bitter laugh that echoed across the loch. She would not return. Why would she? He had seen the longing in her eyes whenever she talked about her world.

But she had promised to return in one month, and that meant her time away ended tomorrow night. He daren't allow himself to hope she might be true to her word. If he did, and she didn't show, he couldn't bear it. He had barely borne the loss of her the first time. Never could he stomach the loss of her again.

"THESE CLOTHES ARE so authentic," Lara said while running her fingers across the knitted stockings and ribbons draped across the bed.

"They are authentic," Satia said as she pulled the shift on over her head and shook it down in place. She pointed at the dark blue kirtle. "That's next, and I'll need help with the ties in the back and on the sleeves."

"So many layers." Breanna helped her with the gown, the buttons, and ties. "I know this is Scotland, but do ye not get overheated?"

"I havena yet." Satia held out her arms and nodded at her elbows. "Start lacing at my wrists and end at my elbows, so the strings dinna hang down in the way. Not too tight, or I willna be able to bend my arms."

"The shoes are crude but still show a great deal of craftsman-ship." Lara picked up one of the soft slippers and peered closer at the seams. "Such stitchery. Do ye ken how much these would cost in a shop? With stitching like this?"

"Jac made those for me so I wouldna be stuck walking around in my sock feet." She grinned at them both. "I shed the waders when they filled with water, so I was left with no shoes."

"I told ye those waders were nothing but trouble." Breanna scooped up the hosiery and frowned at the tops. "How do ye keep them up? There's no elastic."

"Ye tie these ribbons above yer knees. Tight enough so ye canna feel yer toes." Satia showed them, struggling to keep the conversation lighthearted, even though she dreaded leaving Breanna again. Her throat ached at the thought of it, and she kept having to turn away to hide tears that refused to be controlled.

"I'm going to miss ye, too, pet," Breanna whispered as she hugged her close. "I canna believe our month went by so fast. Seems like ye just got here."

Satia sniffed. "I know." She flitted a hand through the air. "I guess we had such fun catching up, it just whizzed by." She plopped down on the bed, donned her slippers, and tied them snug. "I'll come back again someday and check on ye both. I promise."

The cheap replica of Big Ben sitting on the dresser chimed its tinny bells, announcing the eleventh hour. Satia jumped up, patted her braided hair, then cast a glance back at her favorite jeans crumpled on the bed. "I dinna guess there's any reason to take anything with me. Nothing I have belongs there, really." She drew in a deep breath and blew it out. "Best get going now, aye?"

"I'm going to stay here," Lara announced with a kindly smile. She combed her fingers back through her wild red curls and shrugged. "The two of ye need the chance to say yer goodbyes in private." Then she sprang toward Satia and gave her a fierce hug. "Be safe, you."

Satia hugged her back. "Take good care of my sister, aye? Keep her happy?"

"I will do my best," she promised.

"Come on, Satia. We must go if we're to make the loch in time." Eyes glistening with the threat of tears, Breanna waved her forward. "And bring the tissues, aye?"

"Good idea." Satia scooped up the box, blew a kiss to Lara, and followed Breanna down the steps to their tiny compact car parked at the curb out front. "I remembered to sign over the title, right?" She settled into the passenger seat and buckled in. They had bought the auto together years ago and licensed it in both their names. To make things legal and easier for Breanna, Satia had tried to clear up everything they co-owned before heading back to the fourteenth century.

Breanna nodded as she pulled out onto the street. "I think everything's all set. The flat. Auto. Bank accounts. The spare storage unit with the equipment the council didna take. I believe ye took care of everything." She glanced at Satia with a pained smile. "Ye're sure about this?"

"Aye. I am." She clasped her hands tightly in her lap, a calm knowing warming her heart, but a nervous edginess about traveling through time once again churning in her gut. "If I say stop, stop quick as ye can so I dinna chunder in the floorboard. I shouldna have eaten all those biscuits."

"I wondered about that when I saw the empty cartons in the bin. Two whole cartons? No wonder ye're feeling sick."

"They dinna have shortbreads in the 1300s." She patted the leather purse tied at her waist. It hadn't come from the fourteenth century, but it looked the part. "I copied a recipe and brought it. Thought I'd try my hand at making them."

"Cook? You?" Breanna laughed, but it sounded forced. She resettled her grip on the steering wheel, leaned forward, and peered up at the sky. "There's yer friend."

"I'm not so sure I'd call it my friend." Satia eyed the moon, both cursing and blessing it for all the pleasure and pain it had brought her. Or should she blame the loch? Or the land? She suddenly wished she'd studied Scotland's myths and legends with a more critical eye. "Ye would like Anne," she said, desperate to break the tense silence that had risen.

"I'm sure I would." Breanna turned into the Glenmore visitor's center car park and brought the vehicle to a stop. "Shall I park here or get closer to the loch?"

"Here's fine. I've been training remember? I'll have almost an eight-kilometer walk to get where I need to be."

"I dinna like ye traipsing across the Highlands what with ye pregnant and all. Why can't I just take ye to Loch Avon, and ye go back there?" Breanna reached into the back seat and retrieved a backpack stuffed with food, a thermos, extra socks, and a woolen wrap that would help repel any inclement weather. "And ye're taking this with ye. I'll not hear another word of it, ye ken?" She hugged the bag and looked ready to cry. "Let me drive ye to Avon, aye?"

While Satia appreciated her friend's intent, it just didn't work that way. "It has to be *An Lochan Uaine*, remember?" She shrugged. "I dinna ken why. All I know is that's the only one known to have this…gateway…or whatever ye want to call it."

Breanna gave a jerking nod, sniffed, and swiped at an escaped tear. "Well, we best be about it then. Ye said the timing starts at midnight, aye?"

"Well, whenever the moon reaches its fullest point and then begins to wane. The professor and I started waiting at midnight just to make sure we wouldna miss it."

"When ye get back, are ye going to look for him?" Breanna swung the pack over her shoulder, smacking Satia's hands away when she tried to take it. "None of that now. I'll carry it 'til we get there. Now, about Professor Carruthers, do ye have any notions about what might have happened to him?"

Satia was too afraid to even think about it. So many things could've happened to the poor man. "I hope when I get back that he's still there and the gateway just didna work for him for whatever reason."

"I hope so, too," Breanna said. "For his sake."

They continued on in silence, arriving at the shimmering loch entirely too soon. Satia turned to Breanna and held her arms open wide. "Give us a hug, then. I have to stay in the shallows, and ye dinna need to touch me or the water, or ye might get pulled back there with me."

With a stifled sob, Breanna hugged her hard, as if she'd never let her go. "I love ye, pet. More than boots or shoes or purses."

"I love ye more, Bree." Satia clung to her friend, turning her face into Breanna's soft dark curls and breathing in her favorite floral scent, and committing it to memory. "Be happy and live large, dear one. Promise me?"

"I will try my best." Breanna tightened her embrace one last time, then stepped back. She swung the pack off her shoulder and held it out. "Here, pet. Yer favorite tea's in the thermos, and I even packed a box so ye can brew yerself a cup now and then."

Satia nodded her thanks, unable to speak because she feared she'd start sobbing and make them both even more miserable. She looped her arms through the straps and settled the pack on her shoulders. Time to step into the shallows and wait. As she stepped into the chilly, ankle-deep water, she forced an understanding smile back at Bree. "Ye can go if it would make it easier for ye. I understand."

"I willna leave here until ye're gone." Breanna's tone echoed with firm finality that brooked no argument.

Satia sloshed back and forth, glancing up at the sky and idly noticing the stars. "Both times before it was around dawn. Maybe a little after, I think."

"There's so many variables," Breanna said as she seated herself on a nearby stump. "Ye said professor thinks DNA has something to do with it?"

"Aye. Remember when he disappeared? Three interns were in the water with him."

"How many times did he say he'd returned?" Breanna leaned forward, propping her arms on her knees as she laced her fingers together.

"I dinna ken for sure. For some reason, I think this time wouldha been his third time back?" Satia wondered how the time gate counted trips. Did it count each time through, no matter the direction? And what made them pass back and forth consistently between the same planes? "I still canna figure out how we target which time we wish to go to."

"Bloody hell. That's not verra reassuring. What if ye hit the wrong era?"

Breanna would speak aloud Satia's greatest fear. "I canna think like that." She gave a determined nod and clutched the straps of the backpack tighter. "I shall concentrate on Kane. That will get me back to him."

"So now we wait? With ye standing in the water?" Breanna rose from the stump and moved as close to the water's edge as she could without actually touching it.

"Aye. Last time, I walked around the loch to stay awake."

"Clockwise or widdershins?"

"Clockwise, and since when do ye use the term widdershins?" Satia turned and eyed her friend as if she didn't know her at all.

"Lara's been studying Wiccan, druidic, and pagan histories

while sorting through them in the archives." Breanna grinned. "Some of it is quite interesting."

"Nothing more on time travel, though?" Unfortunately, all Lara had found other than quantum physics textbooks and a few debunked scientific papers were fiction. Very little helpful data at all.

"Afraid not." Breanna walked beside her along the shoreline, dodging overhanging branches and fallen logs, while Satia walked in the water. She smacked her neck and waved her hands in front of her face.

"Midges?"

"Aye, I hate the wee blood-sucking devils." Breanna smacked her arm and walked faster. "Are they not after ye?"

"Not yet." Which Satia found a little strange. Was that a part of the time travel puzzle, too? "What time is it?"

"We've only been at this an hour," Breanna said, sounding breathless from her bug-fighting workout.

Satia couldn't quite put her finger on it, but something seemed—off. She stopped walking and stared up at the moon. The glowing blue-white orb stared back at her, leaving her with the distinct impression that it knew a secret and wasn't about to share it. It looked full enough, but as she studied it, she wondered if it might not be a little less. "Breanna, do ye have yer phone?"

"Aye. Why?"

"Google the current moon phase, please." A sick feeling settled deep in Satia's gut, a nauseating churn that had nothing to do with pregnancy or too many shortbread biscuits.

"It reached its fullest point at 1307 GMT and is now waning." Breanna tucked her phone back in her pocket. "We checked it several times. Ye didna miscalculate."

"Something isna right." Satia scanned the shimmering waters of the loch and the shadowy pines on either side. An ominous knowing knotted in the center of her chest, making it hard to breathe. "It's not going to work this time," she said. She pressed a trembling hand to the base of her throat and stared upward again.

"Ye said it was closer to dawn last time." Breanna turned toward the east. "We've a few hours yet. Dinna give up hope, pet. See? The sky's still dark as can be."

"I hope ye're right, but I fear ye're wrong. It doesna feel the same." Satia didn't know how to describe it. All she knew for certain was that a sense of terrible loss, a painful emptiness filled her. She gripped her skirts tighter and pressed on, continuing her walk around the loch.

"Tell me more about him," Breanna urged. "That'll keep ye focused."

"He's a braw, rugged alpha male with the patience of a saint, the unconditional love of a dog, and more tenderness and talent at loving than I ever imagined possible." She pressed a hand to her stomach and smiled. "A potent lover, as well."

"And ye love him."

"Aye, I love him." She swallowed hard and blinked at the tears she couldn't stop. "I thought myself broken and unable to love. But he showed me differently."

"Ye will get back to him, sister," Breanna promised. "In another hour or so, ye will be with him again."

"I hope so." She slogged onward, casting glances to the east to gauge the hour.

The longer she walked, the lighter the sky became, shifting to pink, thnn a light blue that chased the night away. Then the sun topped the horizon and rose above the trees. It was full on daybreak, and while she could still see the moon, it had faded to a white shadow of itself disappearing into the field of blue. She stood there. In the water. Still waiting.

Distant chattering of nearby hikers echoed through the trees. The growling motors of autos and tour buses rudely made their presence known. She wanted to scream at them all to be quiet. Wanted to accuse them of frightening the time gate away. But deep down, she knew it wasn't their fault. For whatever reason, *An Lochan Uaine* had refused to answer her knock and allow her to keep her word to the only man she had ever loved.

ARE YE SATISFIED now?" Kane turned to Anne, silently damning her for tempting him with hope, for making him rake open the old wound and refresh and strengthen the unbearable pain that never left him.

"Something must have gone wrong to keep her from coming," Anne defended. "Mayhap, she willna be able to return until the next moon."

"Or mayhap, she will never return because she doesna love me, value our marriage, nor give a damn about her friendship with ye." He didn't care if he sounded cruel. Everyone needed to realize that happiness was nothing more than a fleeting illusion, its sole purpose to make suffering even more painful.

Anne didn't respond, just held tight to his sides from her position behind him on the saddle.

Without another glance back at the loch sparkling beneath the rising sun, he turned his mount and urged the beast into a hard gallop toward Loch Avon. As soon as he'd seen Anne safely home, he would rejoin the Bruce. There was still much to be done to defend Scotland's new independence, and he fully intended to lead the charge in as many of the most dangerous campaigns as it took to remove him from this world. Perhaps, he would even go to Ireland and nurture the Bruce's interests there.

"Ye must not give up hope," Anne called out over the drumming of the horse's gait. "She will return."

"It no longer matters," he tossed back over his shoulder. "I will not be here."

CHAPTER SIXTEEN

THE AUGUST AND September full moons failed her just as miserably as July's. Now, it was October, and at nineteen weeks pregnant, give or take a week or two, her ability to return and safely trek to Loch Avon in unpredictable weather was getting riskier. She crammed more supplies in the already bursting backpack that had grown exponentially in size with each failed attempt at returning to the fourteenth century.

"Did ye pack the pepper spray? And the zapper? I had to call in some serious favors to get hold of that contraband without getting arrested." Breanna popped open the carrying cases and pulled out the charger to the stun gun. "I guess ye dinna need this, though."

Satia grinned. "No. I dinna recall seeing many electrical outlets." She patted an outside pocket of the bag. "Both are right here. And I appreciate ye risking arrest for my safety."

"Promise me this is the last time," Breanna said, her tone suddenly serious. "At least until spring after the baby's born."

"I could still do November if this one fails." Satia refused to give up, and instinct told her that the safest way for the baby to come with her was while he was still in utero.

"Ye'll be twenty-three weeks along then. That's over halfway through yer time." Breanna turned and yanked open the top dresser drawer and selected three more pairs of heavy wool socks. She tossed them on the bed beside the bag. "Take those, too." She assumed a defensive stance. "And not only could ye already encounter a rogue snowstorm, next month would be even worse."

"I canna give up." A nervous sob hiccupped free of her, making her tears start all over again. That's all she did lately was cry. Breanna and Lara blamed hormones. Satia wasn't so sure. "I'm sure he already thinks me a liar. If he survived Bannockburn." She dried her face with the socks, then shoved them in the bag and forced the zipper shut. She turned a panicked look on Bree. "What if he's dead? What if he died thinking I lied to him?"

Breanna took hold of her shoulders and gave a gentle shake. "Stop it. It's the hormones making ye crazy. Ye said yerself he's a fine warrior. He *is* alive. Ye would know it if he wasn't."

"I dinna suppose ye've had any of yer premonitions on the matter, have ye?" It might be silly, but Satia would take any strand of hope she could get.

With a sympathetic smile, Breanna rested her hand on Satia's slightly rounded stomach. "Definitely a boy, and I know he'll meet his Da soon."

"Now, ye're trying to placate me." Satia sniffed back more tears, dried her eyes with a tissue, and pulled on the heavy surcoat she'd rented from the costume shop. "I gave a fake address to the manager, so they shouldna come here looking for the clothes when I dinna return them." Her McBride clothes didn't fit anymore. Too snug around the middle.

"I know. Ye told me already. Remember?" Breanna gave her a gentle hug and held tight. "Please, please promise if this time doesna work, ye will wait 'til after March to try again. November will be too cold to be safe, and ye know it."

"This time will work," Satia said, refusing to make any more promises she couldn't guarantee she would keep. Especially when it came to getting back to Kane. Heaven help her, she missed him so. Dreamed about him every night and cried for him every morning. Damn him straight to hell and back. He had ruined her. She hated the world without him. "Come on. I'm going now."

"It's only ten." Breanna frowned at the miniature Big Ben, then double-checked her watch. "Aye, ten. Why so early when ye know ye're going to have to lap the loch until sunrise?"

"I am refining my data." Satia swung the backpack to her shoulders and headed out the door. "Since midnight to sunrise has failed me three times, time to switch tactics."

"Sound principle." Breanna snatched the car keys out of the dish and followed. "Did ye pack the extra scarf and shawl Lara knitted for ye?"

"Aye. They're in the outer pocket right here." Satia patted the backpack as she settled it in the floorboard between her feet. "I'll put them on once we reach the loch. I'm sure they'll keep me nice and toasty."

"She hated having to work tonight." Breanna gave a cringing shrug. "Ye know she's hoping it doesna work again. She so wants to help with the baby."

"Tonight is going to work." Tamping down any and all misgivings, Satia stared out the window. "It has to."

"Part of me agrees with Lara." Breanna glanced her way again. "Sorry. But I willna lie when I say I'm selfish and want ye to stay."

"I belong there," Satia insisted, feeling it heart and soul more than she ever had before. "This world, this time, is not my home."

"I know," Breanna said softly, then blew out a heavy sigh.

They went silent the rest of the trip. Rather than park at the Glenmore visitor's center, Breanna parked the auto on the side of the road just up from *An Lochan Uaine*, claiming it might bring Satia luck since that's where the car had been the first time she'd fallen back through the centuries.

As Satia closed the car door and slung the pack to her back, she glanced up at the fickle moon. She would take any and every superstition or lucky charm she could get if it meant seeing Kane again.

"Cripes, that wind's bitter cold." Breanna pulled her jacket closed and zipped it shut. She nodded toward the backpack. "On with yer scarf, pet. And yer shawl. Ye'll be thankful for them once ye start wading."

It was easier to comply than argue. Besides, Breanna was right. The wind sliced right through like an icy knife, and it would be worse once she hit the water. Because of the season, she had relented this time and packed an insulated pair of hiking boots. And she wore her wellies. A walk across the Highlands, this time of year, would be difficult enough without compounding the trial by doing it in wet feet.

"Is the moon at an odd angle, or is it me?" Breanna pointed up at the orb. "And look. It's got a halo tonight."

"I'm going to take that as a good omen." Satia studied the sky, willing the alignment of the stars to cooperate. She longed to be back with Kane and couldn't bear the thought of failing again.

"Ye know that means bad weather's coming." With a scowling up and down look, Breanna nodded toward Satia's skirts. "Did ye wear yer thermals? I dinna care if ye're not supposed to have them, ye're going to need them."

Satia hiked up her kirtle, not only displaying her bright red rubber boots, but the white thermal underwear as well. "And my wellies, thank ye verra much. I'll have much to hide when I reach the McBrides."

"At least ye'll be warm and dry." Breanna shook her head as they came to a stop beside the frigid shores of the loch. "Or at least somewhat so."

"I'll be fine." Or she would be as long as she made it back this time. She hated the taste of failure, especially when it came heartily seasoned with unbearable loneliness. "A hug for luck." With a stern shake of her finger, she added, "*Real* luck this time, ye ken?"

Breanna hugged her tight. "I wish ye nothing but happiness

and success, pet." Still holding tight to her shoulders, she held her at arm's length. "Truly, I do."

"To success," Satia repeated with a curt nod, then stepped into the shallows. She stared down at the water, then looked up and locked her glare on the moon. "Send me back to him." She held her gently rounded middle with both hands. "He needs to meet his son, damn ye! Open the gate and send me back!"

Nothing happened.

"I dinna think ye can bully the cosmos," Breanna noted.

"This night isna over yet. The cosmos doesna ken who it's dealing with." Satia slogged forward with slow determination, one slippery step after another. The rising wind made her eyes tear and blurred her vision, so she ducked her head and pushed onward. "Just stay there, and I'll see ye on the next lap 'round. There's no need for ye to fight the trees like last time. I'm sure frost is forming, and I'm afraid ye'll slip and fall."

Breanna didn't answer.

Holding the heavy scarf closer about her face with one hand while keeping her skirts safely above the waterline with the other, Satia glanced back to make sure her friend had heard. The shoreline was empty. She fully turned and scanned the moonlit beach. "Breanna?"

The wind rustling through the pines was all that answered.

Satia retraced her steps, her hopes rising. Either Breanna had gone back to the auto and taken shelter from the cold, which was highly unlikely, or the gateway had finally opened and sent her back in time. Hopefully, to the era she sought.

When she reached the point where she'd stepped into the water, she swallowed hard. The bench was gone. As was the rock-lined path. Wherever, or more aptly, whenever she was, it was no longer the twenty-first century. She clomped out of the water and looked around. There. The burial cairns of the men who had attacked her. Since the cairns existed, at least she knew she hadn't gone back too far.

The wind gusted, howling through the trees and sweeping

down across the loch with an icy bite. Whenever this was, it was colder. She tugged on the gloves that Lara had knitted to match the scarf and shawl, thankful for their warmth. Best get moving. At least while moving, she'd be warmer than if she stood still. She was too excited to build a fire and wait until dawn to set out, even though she had included a plastic zipper bag full of matches in her backpack. Time to head south to Loch Avon. She switched into the hiking boots for easier walking. The red rubber boots wouldn't fit in the overstuffed pack, so she lashed them to it with a creative use of the strapping.

"Onward ho," she said, mildly concerned when her warm breath fogged in the air and stung like icy spikes in her nostrils. It hadn't been this cold in the future. Apparently, timelines were parallel, but weather wasn't. Something delicate and wet plopped against her face. And then again. Snow. Satia hoped it turned out to be nothing more than flurries. She remembered the advice of an intern who had also been an avid hiker and found two sturdy sticks to use as walking poles to help with balance and stamina. With the overstuffed pack on her back, her extra layers of clothing, and her baby bump, she was a bit unwieldy.

"Time to find yer father," she informed her belly, then settled into a steady pace southward. The longer she walked, the heavier the snowfall became. She tried to remember what Lara had said about the weather patterns she had simulated on one of the library computers. Satia rolled her eyes and kept plodding along. It didn't matter what the simulation said, nor that it was only the second of October. Nature often made it a habit of laughing in the face of predictions.

"It's just a little snow." She refused to let it shake her even though the ground was already covered. As long as she didn't let it disorient her, she would be fine. If snow clouds blotted out the stars, she had packed a compass just to be on the safe side. She had survived the streets of London in the dead of winter. An early snowstorm in the Highlands wouldn't stop her either. Although she did need to pee. Badly. And a drink of water sounded heavenly. She did not miss the irony of needing both a drink and a pee.

She glanced all around, then felt foolish. "There is no one here, ye numpty," she said aloud. It made her feel less alone to talk to herself, and she had read somewhere that even in the womb, babies liked the sound of their mother's voice. "We shall have us a fine pee right here. Get a nice drink of water. Then be on our way again."

She stuck her walking poles upright, gathered her skirts out of the way, and wrangled her thermal underwear down around her knees. "Cripes' sake." Already out of breath, she squatted and blew out a sigh of relief, hoping she wasn't urinating on anything she didn't want to get wet. The cold air nipped at her bum as she stood and sorted herself back out. After several sips of water from an insulated body flask Breanna had found online, she recapped the container and adjusted its strap, so it returned to its spot underneath her arm. Satia grinned. She was a walking campsite with everything she needed either strapped to her back or around her neck. "On we go," she announced as she took hold of her walking sticks and resumed her plodding stride.

A glance upward eased her worries about deeper snow. The clouds had drifted away, revealing the moon and a breathtaking starscape. She paused, taking in the beauty. With no other lights, nature's wonder made her feel small and insignificant compared to the grand scheme of things.

A steady thumping sound caught her attention. She lifted her head and listened harder. Maybe it was her heartbeat pounding in her ears. The rhythmic thudding grew louder. That was no heartbeat. It was a rider galloping her way. She pushed her scarf back to determine the direction of the sound, behind her. Her adrenaline spiked, spurring her into motion. She swung the pack off her back, unzipped the side pocket, and armed herself with both the pepper spray and the stunner. Feet planted for steadiness, she waited for the dark, hulking form to reach her. "Dinna fash yerself, my wee one. Mama willna let them hurt ye."

⫸⫷

KANE HALTED HIS mount and squinted at the small, dark form in the distance. With it silhouetted against the moonlit snow, he struggled to identify it. Some sort of animal huddled low to the ground? An injured one, perhaps? He eased toward it, the horse's careful steps muffled by the new-fallen snow. The McBrides would welcome fresh meat.

Then the thing stood upright, revealing itself to be a misshapen man. Probably a beggar or a cripple, since it leaned heavily on two sturdy sticks to walk.

"I mean ye no harm," he called out, urging *Mèirleach* to a faster trot. Silence and stealth no longer mattered since a hunt was off. He clenched his teeth, hating that he had come across yet another soul in need of help. Helping folk had led to his downfall with Satia. That mistake had left him broken and cold. But he couldn't very well ignore whoever this was struggling in the bitter cold. His conscience wouldn't allow it.

The unfortunate soul appeared to be a humpback. Or so he thought until the hump slid off the man's back and fell to the ground. The beggar pawed at it, then set his stance as though ready to defend himself.

"I mean ye no harm," Kane bellowed louder, wondering if the man was deaf.

"Kane? Is it really ye?"

That voice. He yanked back on the reins, coming to a halt so fast the horse turned aside. It couldn't be her. What wicked mischief did the haloed moon play this night?

"Kane?" The beguiling wraith moved toward him, pushing back the cloth covering her head. Her familiar mane of silvery blonde hair blazed with the eerie, blue-white fire of the moonlight. She flashed a dazzling smile. "It's me. It's Satia."

He urged his horse back another step. "Be gone, spirit. Dinna haunt me with such a cruel image."

She advanced closer, pulled off her mitten, and held out her hand. "I promise it's really me. Not a ghostie." Her pale cheeks glistened with wetness that suggested tears, and her voice trembled as if overcome with emotion. It was a lie. She hadn't loved him enough to stay at his side.

"The feckin' gateway wouldna open for me. I tried to come back in July, August, and September. I swear I did." She took another step, still reaching for him. "Finally, it opened this time and brought me back. Please believe me. I didna lie to ye. I just couldna make the damn thing work until now."

"I dinna believe ye." Caution, leeriness, and the raw burning of renewed pain tempted him to gallop away as fast as his mount could fly across the land. "Ye canna be real," he growled, wanting to believe but knowing better. To believe meant trusting, loving her again. To do so would only bring more suffering. "Go back and trouble me no more."

Her hand dropped to her side, and she bowed her head. With a pitiful sniff, she pulled her mitten back on, then dried her eyes with both hands. "I know I hurt ye, and I am sorry. I never shouldha left. Believe me when I say I know that now." She pulled her wrap back over her head and adjusted her shawl. Her bitter laugh fogged the air in front of her face. "They already knew about that cure I was so prideful and pompous to think I had discovered." She shrugged. "Breanna's better than okay and settled just fine without me. No one there needs me. Never has, really." She stared up at him, her face shadowed by her hooded wrap. Pain dripped from her every word. "I dinna belong there, Kane. I belong here with ye. Please—please try and forgive me?"

He didn't answer. Couldn't. He had made the mistake of loving and trusting her once. Never again.

With a heavy sigh, she turned back to the cloth sack he had mistaken for a cripple's hump. She looped her arms through the straps and hefted it onto her back. Taking hold of her staffs, she turned southward and started walking.

"Where are ye headed?" He drew his mount alongside her.

Without slowing or looking his way, she answered. "I thought I would go to the McBrides. Since I didna ken where ye might be, I figured I'd start my search there." She sniffed again, wiped her face on her mitten, then glanced up at him. "Ye came from the north. Inverness, I guess?"

"'Tis none of yer concern." Something about her shape bothered him. Even with the extra layers of a surcoat and shawl, her form was…different. "Halt."

"I am not a bloody horse nor one of yer soldiers." Her tone quivered with a weary hopelessness that she attempted to conceal with snappishness. She kept plodding along at a steady pace, leaning on her wooden poles.

He stopped his mount, dismounted, and stepped in front of her, blocking her way. "Stand straighter," he ordered quietly.

She leaned on the right walking stick, still somewhat hunched over. "Look. I understand ye're hurt. Ye're angry. And ye hate me now. But that doesna mean ye can give me orders or act like an insufferable arse. Understand? Ye're not the only one hurting here. I missed ye. Cried for ye. Dreamt about ye every night. Now, I finally get back here, and ye kick me in the teeth."

"I havena touched ye—yet." He took hold of her shoulders and straightened her while allowing his gaze to travel across her. The belt she wore wasn't fastened at her waist. Instead, she wore it buckled higher. It rested atop the small mound the folds of her clothing failed to hide. "Ye are with child," he whispered. He released her and stepped back.

She blew out another frustrated huff. "Yes. Near as the clinic can calculate, around mid-March, ye will be a father." She gave a dismissive shrug. "Sorry to upset ye even more. Since ye hate me, I'm sure that doesna come as good news."

"I dinna hate ye," he forced through clenched teeth. "But I damn sure dinna like ye right now, nor have I liked ye since ye left me."

"I didna leave ye. I went there to save Breanna. I told ye I'd be back, and now I'm here, and ye dinna want me." She flipped a hand as though shooing him away. Her face crumpled, and her keening sobs became louder than the howling wind. "And that was stupid of me. I made the wrong feckin' choice and lost ye." She stomped a foot and wailed. "And now all I do is cry all the time because I've ruined everything, and I've come back to the fourteenth century, and the McBrides probably hate me, too, and I dinna ken what I'm going to do now." She paused long enough to gasp in a gulping breath, then cried even harder. Her shoulders shook with her misery as she leaned her forehead atop her fist clutching the staff and unleashed another despondent howl.

God's beard. He had never seen her like this. Never had she babbled on and on like a mad woman. "Dinna…dinna cry." He didn't know what else to say. He wanted to hold her, comfort her, but prideful stubbornness wouldn't allow it. A small part of him gloated at her suffering. She deserved it for all the pain she had inflicted upon him. And as he admitted the terrible feelings, he hated himself for them. She carried his child. How had he become so heartless? As heartless as his cruel father. Shame bowed his head and weighed heavily in his chest.

"Well, I am going now, since there's obviously nothing left to say." She stepped around him, then whacked the ground with one of her sticks and unleashed a frustrated shriek. "Shite, shite, shite!"

"What is it?"

"I need to pee again." She pointed one of her canes at his horse. "Go over there and turn yer back. I'm squatting right here. Ye have no idea how difficult it is in all these clothes."

God help him, he ached to hold her. Kiss her. Thank her for carrying his child. But he daren't. Not when at any point, she might decide to destroy him by leaving him again. Without a word, he did as she asked, wrestling with his sense of right, wrong, chivalry, and self-preservation.

"I will take ye to the McBrides," he called out without looking back at her. He would do that. After all, 'twas only right to help her in her condition. He cocked an ear, waiting for an answer.

Nothing came. As he walked back around his horse, he spotted her already several strides ahead, slowly plodding along while holding tight to those ridiculous sticks. He scooped up the reins and tugged for his mount to follow. "Did ye hear me, woman? I said I would take ye to the McBrides."

"Dinna do me any favors." She stared at the ground as she walked. Even in the moonlight, he made out the hard line of her tensed jaw.

"It is too far for ye to walk."

She ignored him, continuing on as if he wasn't even there.

"Satia! Ye must see sense and think of the bairn."

"The bairn's fine. He likes walking. It makes him feel like he's in a nice, sloshy whirlpool."

One word jolted Kane. "*He?*"

She snorted like a bull ready to charge. "Last ultrasound showed a boy, and they're fairly sure it's accurate." She sniffed. "And Breanna confirmed it. She said she knows it's a boy for certain."

"What is an ultrasound?"

"It's like a magical window to yer insides." She paused, pulled in a deep breath, and blew it out.

"Are ye unwell? Is something wrong?"

She pulled off the pack and let it fall to the ground. "If ye could tie that behind yer saddle, it would make my hiking much easier." She stretched, arching her back. "I didna realize I'd packed it so heavy."

Enough of this foolishness. He picked her up and set her in the saddle. When she squirmed to get down, he stabbed the air with his finger. "Sit still lest ye fall." He secured her bag and mounted up behind her, then spurred the horse into a gallop. The scent of her nearly undid him, pummeling his fragile heart with tender memories. He gritted his teeth and sat taller, lifting his nose in a futile attempt at escaping her familiar essence that swirled all around him.

She leaned forward, holding fast to the front of the saddle.

"Slow down! I'm slipping!"

He snaked an arm around her and pulled her back against him. When putting her atop the horse, he'd settled her sideways because of her delicate condition.

She twisted and wrapped her arms around him, burying her face in his chest. God help him. The feel of her clutching him tight came close to killing him. He had waited so long to have her like this again.

"Dinna let me fall." She pushed a foot against his knee in a panicked attempt at climbing higher.

He slowed *Mèirleach*'s gait and resettled her in the saddle. "Ye're safe, lass. I swear it."

"I am so verra sorry," she said so quietly he almost missed it. "I promise I didna stay away on purpose, and I will never go near *An Lochan Uaine* again. Not ever."

He so badly wanted to believe her, but it was too soon. The pain still too fresh. He halted the beast. "We are here, lass. Ye will feel better once ye've warmed by the fire."

She sat straighter and faced him, resting her mittened hands on his cheeks. The moonlight made the vivid green of her eyes look almost blue. She searched his face, her fair brows puckered in an unhappy frown. "I willna feel better until ye forgive me. Until we are back like we were before."

Even though he saw the truth of it in her eyes, he forced himself to shake his head. "We will never be as we were before. Too much has changed."

The delicate fullness of her bottom lip twitched as renewed tears welled, then overflowed. "Then I am sorry I ruined what we had," she whispered. "Help me down, and I will trouble ye no more."

Her words dug into him like the jagged edge of a rusty blade, then twisted deep into his heart. With an arm looped under both of hers, he carefully lowered her to the ground, then dismounted. He walked closer to the door and called out, "Hello to the house. Might a weary traveler enter?"

"'Tis as much yer house as ours," Mairi answered as she swung the door open wide. As soon as her gaze lit upon Satia, she peeled out a joyful cry. "M'lady! Ye have finally returned." She waved them forward, shooing and flitting like an excited bird with nestlings newly hatched. "Here by the fire. Let me take yer fine scarf and shawl. And mittens, too! Such wonderful knitting." She eyed the things, admiration filling her face. "Ye did a fine job, m'lady. I see Anne taught ye well."

"I didna make them." Satia lowered herself to a stool beside the fire and stared into the flames. With her arms hugged around her middle, silent tears streamed down her face and dripped onto her kirtle.

Mairi whirled about and glared at Kane. "Is she unwell? Where did ye find her?"

"She is with child, and I found her walking here from *An Lochan Uaine*." He stood taller. "Of course, I didna let her walk any farther."

Anne appeared from behind the curtained-off sleeping area, yawning as she patted and straightened her hair. When she spotted Satia, her face lit up with a rare smile. "M'lady! I knew ye would return." She rushed across the room and gave her a fierce hug. "And a bairn. Bless my soul! Ye've got a bairn on the way."

"It's good to see ye, Anne. I missed ye." Satia attempted a smile and failed.

"Tears?" Anne turned and shook a finger at Kane. "What have ye done to her?"

"I have done nothing." Clearly outnumbered, he stepped to the ladder leading up to the loft. "Rob, would ye leave me defenseless down here?"

"Can a man no' find any rest in his own house?" Rob slowly inched down the ladder, working his way by holding tight with one hand. When he stepped off onto the floor, he steadied himself before attempting to walk across the room. A cloth sling kept his useless right arm lashed to his body, and a dark patch covered his blind eye. He grinned at Kane. "Ye look like shite, man. What ails ye?"

Kane shifted his gaze to Satia and nodded.

"Lady Satia!" Still unsteady, Rob lowered himself into a chair and gave her a welcoming smile. "I knew ye would come back. Dreamed it often whilst I was healing. Ye brought me good fortune, m'lady."

Satia rose and went to him, making his face flush red when she gave him a gentle hug. "I missed ye, too, Rob. It's so good to see ye."

Kane could tell by her expression that Rob's gaunt appearance coupled with his infirmities shook her. "Toff and Jac died at Bannockburn," he said with a cold bluntness as if it were her fault. "Rob almost did."

All color left her, and her mouth went ajar. "Died?" she whispered, swaying sideways.

"Catch her, Kane," Rob called out, twisting to reach for her.

He lunged forward and scooped her up before she hit the floor. Limp in his arms, he turned to Anne, but before he could speak, she charged toward him.

"To the cot with her, ye insensitive bastard. What the devil is wrong with ye? Are ye trying to kill her and the bairn?" She ripped back the curtain to the sleeping area and ushered him inside.

The twins sat up, blinking and rubbing their eyes. "What is it, Mama?"

"Nothing, my wee ones," Mairi reassured as she shoved around Kane and helped Anne turn down the bed. "Auntie Satia has returned but isna feeling well." She shot a fierce look at Kane. "Lay her down, then get yerself outside until ye can behave, ye ken?"

As soon as he settled Satia on the cot, he turned to inform the women they would not speak to him in such a manner. "I willna—"

"Aye, ye will." Anne stormed toward him with a wooden rug beater. "Out of here! Now!"

"Rob?" Kane looked to him for help.

Rob pointed at the door. "I am not about to cross them. Ye best sleep outside tonight."

"Of all the—"

Anne caught him with the rug beater, landing a stinging swat across his arse. "Out, I said. If ye behave, we *might* let ye inside come morning."

An enraged growl escaped him as he barreled outside and slammed the door behind him. He'd sleep with his feckin' horse. At least he could trust *Mèirleach*.

CHAPTER SEVENTEEN

"WHERE DID YE say Laoiri and Jennet had gone?" Satia poked at her parritch with a wooden spoon, wishing the McBrides had a dog so she might feed it the breakfast that reminded her of Kane's tender caring when she had been sick.

"Aberdeen. Jennet's Thomas, God rest his soul, had kin there, and they invited her to stay with them through the winter." Anne set a platter of steaming bannocks on the table. "Last letter we received hinted they both may have found husbands." She tapped on the table in front of Satia's bowl. "If ye dinna feel able to eat the parritch, try the bannocks. Mairi suffered with a terrible unsettled stomach the entire time she carried the twins."

"Ye're a true gem, Anne." Satia managed a smile as she slid the bowl aside and picked up a bannock. "I'm sorry I left ye so long, too," she added quietly, unable to look the kind lass in the eyes. "I tried to come back sooner but just couldn't." She had no idea what Anne knew or believed about her absence, but it didn't matter. She didn't want the dear woman thinking she had purposely abandoned her, too.

Anne perched on the end of the bench, leaned forward, and peered up into Satia's face. "Ye're back now. That's all that matters. And I'm more than a little glad to see ye." She gave

Satia's arm a gentle pat. "He will come around. Give him time." Mischief and a dash of wickedness flashed in her soft gray eyes. "Mairi and I will help ye win him back. Dinna fash yerself."

Raised voices from the loft made them both glance upward.

Anne shook her head. "The twins like to play in the loft when the weather's dreich, which means they bedevil poor Rob when he's resting."

Satia blinked hard and fast, fighting another onslaught of tears. She pressed a cloth to her mouth and concentrated on breathing and getting a handle on her hormone-infused emotions. She couldn't believe Jac and Toff were gone. Both so young. So full of themselves and yet kind to a fault. "Is Rob getting stronger?"

"He is alive." Anne's smile didn't reach her eyes as she pushed the small plate of butter closer to Satia. "For the bannock. 'Tis fresh and will help the bread go down easier." She rose and rested a hand on Satia's shoulder. "Ye're still too thin. Especially to be carrying a wee one. Ye must try and eat more, ye ken?"

"I will." She slathered the creamy butter across the toasty brown ridges of the bannock's crust, then stared at it. Almost hypnotized as it melted and soaked into the bread.

"Eat," Anne ordered as she went to the wash bucket and poured a steaming kettle of hot water over the soiled dishes.

Mairi blew inside, the fringe on her shawl flapping in the wind as she hurried to close the door with a firm kick and a bump of her butt. She scuttled across the room and added more wood to the dwindling pile stacked beside the hearth. Cheeks rosy and eyes sparkling, she brushed her hands clean as she joined Satia at the table. "Ye've no' touched yer parritch," she gently scolded, craning her neck to peer into the bowl.

"I'm not that hungry." While Satia appreciated their concern, what she needed right now was time alone to think and plan. What would she do if Kane couldn't forgive her? The thought of raising a child alone in the fourteenth century terrified her. But could she get back to the twenty-first century? Should she? Or should she stay here and hope that her child might someday get to know his father? She tossed the bread back onto the plate and pushed up from the chair. "I think a walk might help. Clear my head and settle my stomach, ye ken?"

"It's wicked cold out, lass." Mairi grabbed hold of her hand. "Feel how cold."

"Ye shouldha worn my mittens." Satia cupped Mairi's icy, calloused hands between hers, trying to warm them. "Ye're welcome to wear them anytime ye wish. Yes?"

"I wouldna wish to ruin them, m'lady." Mairi gave her a reassuring smile as she rose and stood beside her. "They're fine things. Yer friend must care about ye verra much."

Satia nodded but couldn't comment for fear of sounding ready to cry. Which she was. Again. She hurried to the pegs beside the door, donned her wrap and scarf, and pulled her mittens out of the ingenious pockets Lara had knitted into the oversized shawl. "I willna be gone long," she said without turning. She needed out of here. Time alone. Her *everything will be fine* act had grown too burdensome. Swaddled in yards of wool and still wearing her insulated hiking boots, she charged out the door without another look back.

"Walk and breathe," she chanted to herself as she turned into the wind. "Bollocks, it's cold." She hugged the wrap tighter around her and ducked her head.

"Ye should be inside. Out of the wind. 'Tis too cold."

She clenched her teeth, determined not to rise to the bait but knowing she would fail. It was not her nature to back down. "Good morning to ye, too, Kane. Sleep well?" She couldn't resist a dig about his banishment outdoors. Served him right for being so freaking stubborn.

"I slept well, thank ye." He swaggered along beside her, looking like a great woolly beast with his furry black mantle draped across his shoulders. "I have endured worse."

While she wouldn't take any crap, she wasn't in the mood to fight or argue. She had come outside to be alone and think. "Is that a shot?"

"A what?"

"A shot. A dig." She couldn't resist rolling her eyes. "Are ye saying that being with me was worse than a frosty night with yer horse?"

"Being without ye was."

She ground her teeth harder and walked faster. "I apologized. Remember?"

"All I remember is ye refused to stay at my side and then didna return as ye promised." His boots crunched harder across the frost-covered rocks, as if stomping helped drive his point home.

"I told ye I tried, but the time gate, or whatever ye want to call it, wouldn't cooperate. There are so many unknowns about why it works and why it doesn't." She shook her head. "I've decided it's blind luck." She came to a stop, turned, and glared up at him. "But I kept trying. And would've kept trying all winter long just to make sure the baby made it through with me. I couldna be sure it would be safe for him after he was born."

"At least ye love the child," he said with a cruel jut of his chin.

"I loved ye, too," she retorted, matching his defiant stance. "I still do. But since ye've made it quite clear that I am not to be forgiven, I have to figure out what to do."

His defiance became muted, settling into an angry scowl. "What is that supposed to mean?"

"A place to live. A safe place to raise my child. *Alone.*" She stressed the word, hoping it might make it through the icy fortifications he'd built around his heart. "I may have to go back. I canna imagine surviving here and willna burden the McBrides with taking care of me and the baby."

His hands closed into fists. The wind whipped strands of his black hair across his dark eyes, but he ignored them. "Ye said ye would never go near *An Lochan Uaine* ever again."

God help her, she loved this wild Highlander, but how in Heaven's name could she make him forgive her and love her back? "I said that when I hoped ye could find it in yer heart to forgive me and give us another chance." She returned to her charging stroll along the shoreline of the loch, clutching her shawl tighter. "Ye've made it quite clear ye canna do that. So, why should I stay here?"

"So I might know my son, and he might know me." Pain and so much more echoed in the richness of his deep voice, giving her a wee bit of hope that she might be getting through to him. "I will provide for ye both. Ye willna be a burden to anyone."

She rested a hand on her stomach, rubbing it like a wishing stone. *Make yer father love me again,* she silently begged. "Ye will protect him and be a good father to him? Even though ye hate me?"

"I told ye I dinna hate ye." His nostrils flared and his snorting huff fogged in the cold air. "I am angry with ye. That is all."

A small improvement over last night's vow that he didn't like her, but she would take it. "Then I will stay here so ye can know yer son."

"Will ye come inside now?" His earlier order had softened into a request.

"Aye. It is cold." She turned and walked beside him, noting that his crunching stomp had also softened. "I am sorry about Jac and Toff," she said. "Is Albie still alive?"

"Aye. He is with the king and Friar Law."

She halted and turned to him. "So, he stayed here?"

"Nay. He is with the king and Friar Law at Cardross." He gave her a befuddled frown as if worried about her hearing.

"I meant Friar Law. He was supposed to travel to the future with me, but when I arrived, I was alone. I didna ken what happened to him. If he'd gone somewhere else in time or stayed here." She felt better knowing the man was alive and well and in the time he preferred more than the future.

"He said he didna ken why the thing didna send him with ye." Kane pushed open the door and held it for her. "He feels the thing has a mind of its own."

"It does at that." She knocked the frostiness and dirt from her boots as best she could, then entered and peeled off the layers of wool and hung them on the pegs.

"Will ye eat now?" Anne asked before she'd even had a chance to turn around. Then she arched a stern brow at Kane. "She's had naught to eat this morning. If ye upset her, then it's back outside with ye, ye ken?"

"Anne, I can fight my own battles." Satia went to the table, retrieved her bannock from earlier, and took a bite.

"He made ye faint dead away last night," the girl argued.

Kane shook his head and shrugged off his mantle, and hung it on a peg. "Where is Rob? Still resting?"

"I'm over here," the lad called out from his seat, partially hidden by the cloth wall concealing the sleeping area. "The wee demons wouldna leave me be, so I came down here for some peace." He glared at his sisters. "There's no such thing as quiet around here, but I hoped to at least find some peace."

"Ye must eat more than one bite," Anne said. Eyes narrowing, she fixed a stern, motherly look on Satia. "The bairn needs food and will take what it needs from the mother. Ye must eat enough to maintain yer own strength."

"She should eat the parritch," Kane said as he lowered himself to a stool beside Rob. "Buttered bread is nay enough."

Satia gave a hard, sharp clap of her hands. "Enough! I will eat what I want when I want. Understand? I'm a grazer."

"A what?" Mairi turned from the wash bucket, a plate and a rag in her hands.

"I nibble and eat small amounts throughout the day. If I gorge myself too much at any one time, it comes back out." She'd learned that lesson the hard way. Several times, in fact.

"Then we'll keep food on the table at all times," Mairi said with a decisive nod. She turned back to the wash bucket, humming under her breath as she cleaned the dishes.

"Ye could sit over here," Kane said with a glance at the chair between himself and the hearth. "Bring yer wee bit of bread, if ye wish. 'Tis warmer by the fire."

Both Anne's brows arched to her hairline as she turned toward Satia and hid her knowing look from Kane. She gave Satia's arm an encouraging squeeze, then handed her another roll. "A fine idea. Do ye not think so?"

Even though she didn't want it, Satia accepted it with a grateful smile and seated herself beside Kane. "Where are ye headed?" He wouldn't tell her where he'd come from last night, but maybe today, he would.

"Headed?" He leaned forward, propping his elbows on his knees, and stared down at his clasped hands.

"Are ye going to Cardross to winter with the Bruce?" That would make the most sense. After all, the king had seemed to favor Kane as a trusted advisor.

Kane kept his gaze on his hands. "I see yer perception is sharp as ever." With the barest tilt of his head, he shrugged. "I was headed for Cardross after business in Inverness." He glanced at Rob. "But I wished to check on this brave man and his sisters." His eyes flinched to narrow slits as though he felt a sharp pain. "Come spring, I go to Ireland with the Bruce's brother."

Satia vaguely remembered reading where Robert the Bruce had sent his brother, Edward, to invade Ulster and eventually become the king of Ireland. She picked at the bread in her lap, wishing she could remember the exact date. She thought it to be sometime in May but wasn't sure. "So, ye'll winter in Cardross. Ye'll miss the birth of yer son in March. Will ye come back to meet him before ye leave for Ireland?"

Kane's jaw flexed, and his short beard twitched. Still staring at his hands, he pulled in a deep breath, then blew it out. "I will miss nothing," he said with a slow shake of his head. He looked up at Rob again. "I should winter here. And help with the homeplace." He clapped a hand to Rob's shoulder. "'Tis the least I can do to express my thanks and the thanks of our king to this brave man for all he's sacrificed."

Anne snorted out a short, disbelieving laugh, and Mairi echoed it with a shake of her head. Satia held her breath to keep from telling Kane if he was going to make up a lie, he needed to try harder. No. She would not call him on the lie. Not when it gave her hope that he might be letting down his guard and wanted to be around her. "I think that very valiant," she managed to say with a straight face.

Rob looked away while coughing as though about to choke. "Aye," he agreed after clearing his throat again. "We thank ye for yer kindness, Kane."

"Well, then." Kane clapped his hands atop his knees, then stood. "I best check on the sheep and goats. No time like the present to start my chores." He grabbed his mantle off the peg and was out the door before anyone could comment.

Rob shook his head. "God help that man. He's not got a chance against ye three."

Satia hoped and prayed that Rob was right.

SHE HAD SAID she would stay so he might know his son. Even though she believed he might never forgive her, she'd said she would stay for the good of the child. And for him. The smoldering embers warming his heart erupted with a hesitant flame because of her meaningful vow. It meant more to him than she would ever know. But could he believe her? He remembered the look in her eyes. The sorrow. The regret. Everything he had witnessed so far did much to convince him he could.

Kane scooped up the soiled hay with the pitchfork, then tossed it into the cart. The backbreaking work helped him sort through the highs and lows crashing inside him.

Satia also said she had tried to get back for months, but the magic of the loch refused to cooperate until now. Friar Law had also spoken of the same temperamental nature of the place, making her excuse seem as though it might be true.

One goat sheltering in the stable grumbled out a warning *bah*, then head-butted his knee. "Away wi' ye now, wicked beast. Back to yer feed in the corner." Kane shooed the creature aside and continued cleaning. And thinking.

Could he risk forgiving her? God help him. He loved her more now than he ever thought possible. Even more than before she left. But was he brave enough to let her know that? To become vulnerable to her once again?

A rustling on the other side of the stable broke through his inner turmoil. He straightened and peered over the stalls. In the far corner, where he and Rob had built cubbyholes and boxed nests for the chickens and geese, Satia stood with a basket on her arm. He leaned against the handle of the pitchfork, losing himself in the beauty of the woman he had never thought to see again.

"Dinna peck at me, or ye'll be tonight's supper." She shook a finger at a plump hen who looked ready to fight. "I need to check for eggs. So...be nice, ye ken?"

Kane grinned, remembering her initial fear of the horses. Apparently, she wasn't on good terms with chickens either. "'Twill go better if ye go in fast and let her know right off that ye're the one in charge," he said. "If they smell yer fear, they'll use it against ye."

Satia glared at the chicken, who glared back at her with an indignant cluck. "Eggs or chicken soup? Which is it going to be?" Flinching with the expectation of a hard pecking, she shoved her hand under the bird, then jerked it back out and smiled at the three eggs she held. She proudly showed Kane. "Look! I did it!"

"Well done, m'love." Then he clenched his teeth, wondering if she noticed the endearment.

She did.

She moved closer. "Ye used to call me that all the time."

"Aye. I did." It came to him that with the stall at his back, he had no easy exit. "Are ye certain ye're not too cold out here? I can finish gathering the eggs for ye."

She set the egg basket in an empty manger and continued her

approach. "I would be much warmer if ye would hold me."

He swallowed hard and gripped the wooden handle of the pitchfork so tightly it crackled.

"Please forgive me." She kept moving toward him. "I love ye so much, and if ye had known me in the future, ye would realize how improbable that sounds. I never thought I could love anyone. Didna think I was capable of it. But with ye…" She shook her head. "I need ye, Kane. Please try to find it in yer heart to understand. I never meant to hurt ye, and I am so verra sorry."

"I can bear this no longer." A low rasping growl escaped him as he tossed the pitchfork aside and lunged to pull her into his arms. He clutched her to him, fearing she would disappear and leave him once again. Burying his face in her hair, he whispered, "Ye destroyed me, lass." He breathed in, rubbing his face in the silkiness of her curls. "I beg ye—never leave. Not ever. I would rather die than face such pain again."

Her muffled sobs vibrated against him. She fisted her hands in his tunic, then pounded against his chest with every gasping word. "I willna leave again. I swear it, ye understand?" She keened out another high-pitched cry, hiccupping and gulping for air as she lifted her face to his. "I love ye, damn ye. God help me, I love ye more than a heart should love anyone."

He silenced her with the kiss he had longed for ever since she left. Her soft, supple lips tasted even sweeter than he remembered. She clung to him with an urgency that filled his emptiness and made him forget every pain.

"I need ye," she rasped across his mouth, wrapping a leg around his.

"But the bairn…"

"It will be all right. I promise." She arched tighter against him, rubbing his aching hardness with a delicious wiggling that promised so much more.

He swept her up into his arms, strode across the aisle to a stall filled with fresh, clean hay, and laid her down. As she slid her hands up inside his shirt, he did the same to her skirts. Instead of finding the silkiness of her skin, a linen-like cloth bunched beneath his fingertips. He paused and stared down at her. "Ye're wearing those feckin' trews again?"

"Thermals," she corrected, shoving the frustrating barrier downward and forcing a leg of the things off over one of her boots. "Ye canna blame me. I didna ken how far I'd have to walk in the cold."

He didn't hear a word she said. Her nakedness demanded the full attention of every sense he possessed. He kissed her stomach with its small, precious bulge, then moved lower, reveling in her taste, her scent, the way her skin brushed like warm velvet across his mouth and tongue. "I have missed ye, my precious one," he whispered.

"Not nearly as much as I've missed ye." She laced her fingers in his hair and pulled him up for another kiss while she wrapped her legs around him. "I canna go slowly this time. Please—I beg ye. Take me now."

"With pleasure, dear one." He joined with her. Gently. Fully. Heaven help him. He feared he'd spill before finishing the first stroke, so he slowed even more.

"Ye're killing me, Kane." She squeezed her legs tighter and arched to meet him as she raked her fingers down his back and clutched his buttocks. "Faster. Please."

"I willna last," he forced through clenched teeth as he fulfilled her request.

"Neither will I," she gasped, closing her eyes and biting her bottom lip.

"Good enough." He cast aside everything but the ecstasy of having her beneath him, rocking into her until they both cried out and startled the livestock within the small shelter. Elbows locked, he hovered above her until fully spent, then rolled and curled her into the curve of his arm. "Next time will be longer," he promised.

Cuddling tighter against him, she patted a hand atop his chest. "Do ye hear me complaining?"

"Ye're certain we willna hurt the bairn with our loving?" He had heard…stories. Old wives' tales. He would do nothing that would injure his son.

"I'm positive." She nestled her head more comfortably in the dip of his shoulder. "The clinic said baby and I are verra healthy and right on course for a fine delivery." She stretched and kissed his throat. "And she even said when the time grows near that sex can help put me into labor and get things moving along."

"I feel it best to let the bairn decide when he wishes to come out." He didn't like the sound of *getting things moving along*.

Her weary but satisfied chuckle shifted her in his embrace.

"And what do ye find so amusing?"

"Yerself."

"Why?"

"Because ye're already protective of yer son, even though he's barely the size of a large bell pepper." She hugged him tighter. "I like it." She sniffed. "And I'm grateful that ye've found the strength to forgive me."

"I love ye, Satia," he said. "So verra much that it scares the hell out of me." He released a deep sigh, and with it, finally let go of the last of his worries and fears. "I think I always have loved ye. Since that first day I pulled ye from the water." He snorted a soft laugh, then kissed her forehead. "There is no helping me. I am a doomed man for certain."

"I'm flattered." She cocked a brow. "Maybe."

"Ye should be." He adopted a teasing tone. "Ye're the only woman able to claim she has such control over Kane McPherson."

She raised up and smiled down at him. "Then we both should be flattered, because not only did I win my Highland warrior, but ye won yer stubborn woman from the future."

"Amen to that," he agreed, then pulled her down for a kiss. The chickens, goats, and horses had already settled back down. Time to disrupt them again with some more satisfied shouts.

EPILOGUE

Loch Avon
Scottish Highlands
March 16, 1315

KANE PACED BACK and forth in front of the hearth, at war with himself. He wanted to rush to Satia and hold her tight as she fought to bring their bairn into the world, but the MacBride sisters forbade it. The sounds of Satia's suffering tore at him, making him wish he could bear the pain for her. His dear sweet lass had been at it since the wee hours of early morning when her waters broke and soaked their pallet. He clenched his fists as she filled the house with a long, low groan.

"Why is this taking so long?" he demanded.

Rob looked at him as if he had taken leave of his senses. "How should I know? I'm not a midwife." He hurried to the counter in front of the window, filled a tankard, then carried it back to Kane. "Good thing the two of ye stayed here rather than move before the bairn came." He nodded toward the curtain separating the makeshift birthing area from the rest of the dwelling. "Ye wouldha been sore pressed to find two as good as Anne and Mairi to help yer lady wife with this chore."

Kane raked a hand back through the wildness of his thick hair he'd not bothered to tie out of the way. "She'll need help once we move. Anne wants to come but doesna wish to abandon either yerself or Mairi. There's much to keep up here."

"We should all go with ye," Rob said before tossing back his own drink, then squinting his good eye from the stoutness of the freshly brewed ale's burn. "This place was nothing but hard times for our parents, and it's nay been all that kind to my sisters." He shrugged, then poured them both another. "Jennet and Laoiri will never return. Not with them married to seafaring men with fine warehouses based in Aberdeen."

"Enough!" Satia shouted from behind the curtain. "Bollocks! Bollocks! Bollocks! Get this baby out of me!"

"I wonder if that means the bairn's almost here?" Rob asked in a low voice as he handed Kane his refill.

Kane put a finger to his lips and shook his head. With her advanced pregnancy, his beloved wife had developed exceptional hearing. He headed toward the door and waved for Rob to follow. Even though it was pissing rain, outside was a safer place to have any conversations that Satia might overhear.

"All of ye come with us," he said as they sidled their way under the eave to stay out of the rain as much as possible. "I had no idea there was a huge keep on the land until the Bruce took me there a few weeks ago. Workers are still there following his orders regarding repairs to the place." The disbelief he had felt that day rushed back across him in full force. "Our king's generosity is both kind and worrisome." Kane wasn't a fool. He was well aware the king relished it when people owed him rather than the other way around.

"I shall have to ask Mairi if she's willing to leave here. She should agree. She herself said that living here grows more difficult every year."

"Ask her, then." Kane felt certain Satia would welcome them with open arms.

The wailing of a newborn filled the air. Loud, strong, and

clear as could be even with the windows shuttered.

"He's here," Kane whispered, a sense of awe and pride making his chest swell.

Rob laughed and smacked him on the shoulder. "Listen to that bellowing. What a fine lad."

The door jerked open, and Anne appeared. "Yer son is here, Kane Macpherson. Braw, healthy, and full of fire about leaving his mother's cozy womb. He's a tad on the wee side but strong as can be."

"And Satia?" He almost feared asking, even though the happy weariness on Anne's face eased his heart some. But he needed to hear the words of reassurance that his dear one thrived.

"She is well." Anne smiled and waved them both inside. "Exhausted. But good as can be." She stepped closer, took hold of his arm, and prevented him from going to Satia. "She'll be needing help with that large manor and a new bairn. So, I shall come with ye, after all." With an arched brow, she added, "We might should take some goats as well. Their milk will help the wee one grow strong once he's big enough to drink it."

He nodded, willing to agree with anything if she would just let him by so he could see his Satia.

She released his arm and stepped back but lifted a finger in warning. "Not too long, aye? She needs her rest."

Before she could stop him again, he slipped behind the curtain just as Mairi was nestling the squirming bundle in Satia's arms. With no words but a broad smile, she slipped out. Kane appreciated her giving them their privacy.

Propped among the pillows and blankets, Satia gave him a weary smile. "Finally."

He eased down onto the side of the bed, careful not to shake or disturb his precious family. "Such a wee thing," he whispered.

"But hungry," she said, smiling down at the newborn tugging on her breast. When she lifted her gaze, her brow creased with worry. "I've never been all that big to begin with. I hope I've got enough milk for him."

In awe, he cupped the velvety softness of his son's downy head. "I'm sure ye do, m'love, but if need be, we'll find a wet nurse. Whatever ye need, anything ye need, ye shall have it. The both of ye." The tiny fingers amazed him. When they closed around his little finger, his heart nearly stopped beating. "My son." He brushed a kiss to the child's silvery pate. "He has yer hair, m'love."

"That could change." With the corner of her bottom lip caught between her teeth, her worried frown creased deeper. "How will I ever take care of that monstrosity of a house and this precious mite?"

"Ye will have plenty of help." He leaned forward, kissed her troubled brow, then pressed his forehead to hers. "I have asked the McBrides to come with us to our new home. It's plenty big for all. Dinna ye think so?"

"That would be—" She exhaled a relieved sigh and smiled down at the little one. With a sheepish shrug, she finished, "Fantastic. Absolutely fantastic." She shook her head. "I'm afraid ye married a very inept woman when it comes to knowing how to keep house, keep a husband happy, and raise little ones."

"Ye made me happier than I ever thought possible when ye returned to me." Once again, he cupped his son's tiny head. "And happier still by giving me such a braw healthy lad." He swallowed hard, his heart so full it risked cutting off his wind. "I love ye, my own. More than ye will ever know."

"I love ye more," she whispered. "More than I ever thought possible."

"And what shall we name him?" Satia had refused to talk about names, saying she couldn't possibly choose until she met the babe. Kane smiled as the wee one flexed his fingers on his mother's full breast as he nursed. "We should call him Lochlann," he said before she could answer. "Since it was a loch that brought ye to me."

Satia brushed a fingertip along her son's rounded cheek, then nodded. "Aye. Lochlann. Perfect." She smiled as the child's suckling slowed, and he drifted off to sleep. "I think he's finished for now. Would ye like to hold him?"

"More than anything." Breath held, he accepted the precious bundle and cradled him close. "Wee Lochlann," he whispered. "My fine son." He lifted his gaze to the wondrous woman who had seen fit to give him such a gift. "Thank ye, my dear one." He slid his fingers along her jawline, laced them into her hair, and cupped her cheek. "Thank ye for my son, for returning to me, but most of all, thank ye for making me whole with yer love."

She pressed her hand atop his as tears overflowed and rolled down her cheeks. "Thank ye for yer love—the kind of love I never thought existed anywhere but in books." She kissed his palm, then sank deeper into the pillows. With a weary smile, she added, "I'll love ye even more if ye'll keep Lochlann safe while I sleep. I'm a little tired."

"I will always keep both of ye safe, m'love. I swear it." He leaned forward, brushed a tender kiss across her mouth, then rose with his son held close. "Come, m'wee one. Ye've worn yer mother out." When he reached the curtain, he glanced back and smiled. "I love ye, Satia. Heart and soul, I love ye."

"I love ye more, my Highland warrior," she said in a sleepy voice. "More than ye will ever know."

He had a fair idea, but he never tired of hearing her say it.

About the Author

If you enjoyed WINNING HER HIGHLAND WARRIOR, please consider leaving a review on the site where you purchased your copy, or a reader site such as Goodreads, or BookBub.

If you'd like to receive my newsletter, here's the link to sign up:
maevegreyson.com/contact.html#newsletter

I love to hear from readers! Drop me a line at
maevegreyson@gmail.com

Or visit me on Facebook:
facebook.com/AuthorMaeveGreyson

Join my Facebook Group – Maeve's Corner:
facebook.com/groups/MaevesCorner

I'm also on Instagram:
maevegreyson

My website:
https://maevegreyson.com

Feel free to ask questions or leave some Reader Buzz on
bingebooks.com/author/maeve-greyson

Goodreads:
goodreads.com/maevegreyson

Follow me on these sites to get notifications about new releases, sales, and special deals:

Amazon:
amazon.com/Maeve-Greyson/e/B004PE9T9U

BookBub:
bookbub.com/authors/maeve-greyson

Many thanks and may your life always be filled with good books!
Maeve

www.ingramcontent.com/pod-product-compliance
Lightning Source LLC
Chambersburg PA
CBHW070921190726
48292CB00004B/1046